PRAISE FOR *THE WALL*

"Fans of tense speculative novels of fallen near-future Americas will find themselves caught up in Penn's debut, a dystopian Romeo-and-Juliet story.... Penn has crafted a fast-paced story that doesn't scrimp on character, romance, and a revolutionary impulse.... Danger, heartbreak, and mystery are around every corner."

—Publisher's Weekly BookLife Review

"Brian Penn has created a masterpiece with his incredible debut novel, *The Wall*—the best book in the dystopian genre since *The Hunger Games*.... It is so rare to see a thrilling story with tight morals in both story and characters, but this work is indeed a rarity. It is full of unique and thrilling elements, including a character so hell-bent on bringing a dead character back to life that they'll sacrifice their own grandchild to achieve their twisted goal. The book is also expertly written and is diverse—it will appeal to both youths and adults.

"A war story, a love story, and a tale of rebirth all in one, *The Wall* is a one-of-a-kind dystopian thriller that will have readers on the edge of their seats. Highly recommended by Chick Lit Book Café."

—Micah Giordonela for Chick Lit Café

"*The Wall* by Brian Penn is a heart-racing, action-packed, and nail-biting dystopian story you don't want to miss. It follows two lovers whose journey is rife with secrets, love, and a daunting battle for survival. Fans of George Orwell and Margaret Atwood will find this book fascinating."

—Foluso Falaye, San Francisco Book Review

"Packed with heart-pounding action, deadly danger, puzzling mysteries, and even a poignant romance, *The Wall* is a thrilling young adult dystopian novel that will leave readers anxious for more."

—Erin Britton, Los Angeles Book Review

"For readers of dystopian and science fiction tales, this novel is a must-read. Penn's adept storytelling, combined with the riveting character dynamics, make *The Wall* an absorbing read—one that challenges you to reflect upon the depths of love and the indomitable nature of the human spirit."

—Literary Titan

"Grim, gripping, and entertaining. . . . A young man gets caught up in a terrifying rebellion in Penn's engrossing dystopian tale. . . . Penn's dark vision of the future is well crafted. . . . [T]here is always an interesting plot point or exciting action around the corner, which keeps readers engaged. . . . A thorough page-turner."

—The Prairies Book Review

"I don't like to fly. So when I have to fly, I look for a good book that will hopefully hold my interest so I can ignore the fact that I am 35,000 feet above the earth in a thin aluminum tube. If you have to fly in the near future, then grab a copy of Brian Penn's *The Wall*. It's an easy read that you will fall right into, with engaging characters and a strong plot. I did not even notice we were landing until I was forced to put my tray table in the upright position. I spent most of the night trying to finish it but couldn't. I woke up and started reading again with breakfast, finally putting it down sometime after lunch, feeling thoroughly satisfied. Thank you, Brian Penn, for inviting this reader into your wonderful, captivating world. I look forward to the next one."

—Endy Wright, Author of *The Omicron Six*, *Blood for the Fisher King*, and *The Garden Plot Diaries*

THE
WALL

BOOK 1

The Wall
by Brian Penn

© Copyright 2023 Brian Penn

ISBN 979-8-88824-135-6

All rights reserved. No part of this publication may be reproduced, stored in a retrieval system, or transmitted in any form or by any means—electronic, mechanical, photocopy, recording, or any other—except for brief quotations in printed reviews, without the prior written permission of the author.

This is a work of fiction. All the characters in this book are fictitious, and any resemblance to actual persons, living or dead, is purely coincidental. The names, incidents, dialogue, and opinions expressed are products of the author's imagination and are not to be construed as real.

Published by

Ink Penn
Ink Penn LLC

THE WALL

A NOVEL

BRIAN PENN

Ink Penn

For my wife.

"Death is terrifying, but it would be even more terrifying to find out that you are going to live forever and never die."

–Anton Chekhov

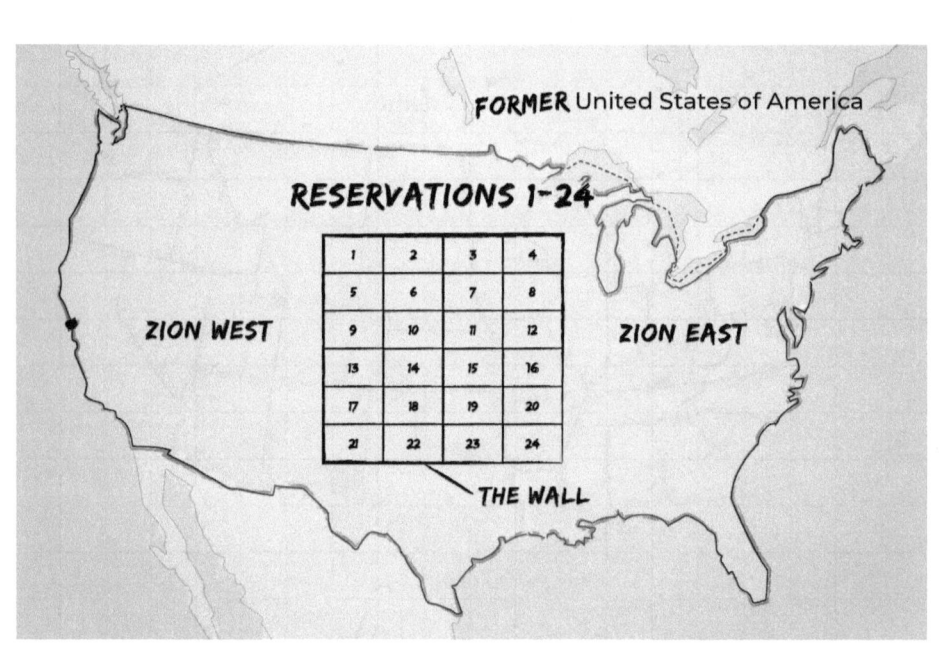

CHAPTER ONE

The Wall went up virtually overnight. We should have seen it coming, but we were too busy with life directly in front of us. Too distracted by the moment. Who wouldn't be? After all, we were first-lifers. Once we figured out what was happening, it was too late.

The revocation of second-life rights was unfair. If we had known, we would have lived our lives differently. Some will say our anger isn't justified. Just because we have a second chance, is that merit enough to waste the first one?

I stand beneath the massive weeping willow tree. For me it's a salve. On the other side of the hundred-foot-high, near-translucent wall rests another weeping willow of almost identical proportions. This is where Sarai and I first kissed; this is where we were to be married. She used to say we were soulmates. I prefer eternity mate.

I inch closer to The Wall, careful not to touch it. Once it was erected, many first-lifers flung themselves towards it, thinking they could scale the massive structure, only to be hurled backwards and killed by 100,000 volts of blue electrical current. Our new cage, consisting of Middle America, reeked of seared flesh for weeks.

I can't see through it, but I picture her there on the other side. The sorrowful strands of the weeping willow whip ferociously in the wind. They remind me of Sarai's thick, braided obsidian hair.

It's the year 2099, and at twenty-five, my dark hair is preemptively birthing flecks of gray, betraying the burden and responsibility I'm yet to bear. When she was here, she took my breath away. Now that she is on the other side, I labor to breathe, like she has pilfered one of my lungs. My heart has been ransacked. It has been five long years since I last gazed into her vast, deeply set copper eyes, touched her silky oblong cheeks. Her elongated eyelashes remind me of the flowers that grow atop mosquito grass in the damp meadows of spring. Five years since they snatched her from my arms.

I was seventeen and in high school the first time I saw her. If you can call it a school; it was more of a dilapidated building where parents send their children to learn basic reading and arithmetic from volunteers. In The Middle, there is no publicly funded education or government to speak of. It's more of a controlled chaos. Some kids didn't attend school. My parents made sure I went and did well. In fact, my mother was one of those volunteers.

The story of how I met Sarai differs, depending on who you ask. I say it was an accident-at least that's how I recall it. I close my eyes and reminisce. I had arrived at Sarai's aunt's farm in my rusted, barely oscillating 2040 black Mustang. Almost sixty years old and the last gasoline engine built in the former United States. I would climb her apple trees and trim them before next year's harvest. The pay was awful, but it gave me a chance to see Sarai outside of school.

It was a particularly windy day, and I had to hang on extra tight while perching twenty feet up in the tree. Typically, when she sauntered by she would ignore me. It would change that day. I was mesmerized by her beauty as she slipped inside. I wasn't ready for the potent gust that made me lose my footing, causing me to fall out of the tree and hit my head on a rock. Blood was streaming from my forehead.

Moments later I was on her couch while she tended to my head. The pain was worth her touch. She asked me what happened, but I couldn't find the words, raptured by her proximity.

"Maybe you have a concussion?" she asked.

I did, but not from the fall; I was hypnotized by her angelic beauty. Speak, you fool.

I said, "I'm . . . I'm . . . I'm Asher."

After that we would spend our lunches together. After school she would monkey around in the trees with me and help with the trimming. Seeing as I was adept with tools, I would repair farm machines and work on her aunt's car, free of charge. It didn't take long until we were inseparable.

Until they separated us.

Now she is on her second life on the other side of the seemingly decorative wall. It is even garnished with digital images depicting Zion's affluence, reminding us we have nothing. Boats. Beaches. Fancy cars. An abundance of different foods I have only read about. None of that matters to me; the only thing I want or need from Zion is her. I wonder if she still feels the same way or if her soul has been festooned with Zion's prosperity. I must reboot my mind daily to keep such thoughts from festering; this is how they want me to think. I still say we were meant to be, even if we can't be together.

Whoosh. I duck down as a swift helidrone flies overhead on patrol. Its rotors emit a barely audible whine. It surveys the area like a nimble dragonfly searching for its prey. I wonder if it's running surveillance for some security reason or on a kill mission.

I peer over at The Wall, which consists of tall steel towers every twenty feet that radiate the semi-opaque barrier of electricity. This way they can open and close portions of The Wall with efficient expediency. Each section is labeled with a number. Five hundred yards to my right, a section opens. A platoon of Lazurite soldiers marches out of Zion West and into MiddleLand. I scurry behind a tree, not wanting to be seen. The wilted leaves of autumn crunch under my worn, fraying boots. Ants detour around my foot, their work unaffected. The soldiers don gray and black exoarmor and carry plasma guns. Sunlight reflects from the visors of the soldiers' oversized helmets. From afar they look like two-legged garden beetles.

My face absorbs autumn's windy chill. Ahead, a group of a hundred MidLanders, or Drecks as they like to call us, don mismatched shoes and tattered clothes from the turn of the century. They are escorted to an open section of The Wall by Lazurite soldiers. It's the first Wednesday of the month; Lottery Day. That explains the helidrone. I thought maybe it was here for me. Every month a lotto is held for a *lucky* few to be allowed to emigrate from MiddleLand into Zion. Out of the decay and into paradise. Out of the fire and into the frying pan is a more apt description. The elated smiles on their dirty faces will be short-lived. Don't they find it strange they're not allowed to bring their belongings?

I have since stopped trying to warn them that they are marching into ruination. Into the hands of the cell-pirates as we call them. They scoff at me and call it mere rumors. They are blinded by the decadence and abundance they believe awaits them on the other side. Like a get-rich-quick scheme or a compulsive gambler who always returns to the table, the truth becomes veiled when you believe the promises of a better future that isn't earned. To them, perhaps something is better than nothing, even when you are unsure of what that something is. Besides, to them I'm just a Dreck from Reservation 9. They don't know I'm Asher, the last son of The Great Defiance.

That is why I hide.

Sarai stands under the identical weeping willow on the other side of The Wall. Her father, Renatus, ruler of Zion, would be less than merry if he knew she was here. Her armed escorts act like sentinels, following her every move. It took some convincing for her security detail to take her to the edge of Zion, right to The Wall, considering what she had done in the past. They fear Renatus's wrath if he ever finds out. Or if she is ever hurt.

Today is the anniversary of Sarai's secret engagement to Asher. She doesn't know that he is on the other side at this very moment, but she can feel him. The wind pelts her face as she edges closer to The Wall, but it doesn't bother her. The Lazurite guards make sure she doesn't get too close, as they keep a wary eye out for anything out of the norm. The willow's tress thrashes against its branches making it come alive. In its powerful beauty Sarai sees Asher.

Her father built The Wall fourteen years ago. It's a modern engineering marvel that both connects societies and separates them. Its design is almost a perfect square located in the middle of the former United States of America. Its northern border starts in what used to be Northern Wyoming and stretches to Wisconsin; the eastern side goes from Wisconsin through the former states of Iowa, Missouri, and Arkansas; the southern border goes from Arkansas to New Mexico; the western side from New Mexico back up to Wyoming. No ocean access, no way out. The former states that now encompass MiddleLand have been divided into twenty-four equally sized reservations. Reservation 9, which sits on the Utah-Colorado border, was where she first met Asher.

Sarai was tired of being a sultana and the constant primping, prepping, and schooling at the Lazurite private schools. At seventeen she sneaked out of Zion to live with her Aunt Esther on Reservation 9. It was only supposed to be for a season, an adventure, a distraction before her forced marriage at the Canonization.

Then she met Asher. She smiles and recollects that day. There was a knock on the door, and she opened it, wondering why this handsome boy in front of her had blood dripping from his forehead.

"What happened?"

"I . . . I fell."

She dragged him to the couch and told him to lie down. She then grabbed a wet rag, cleaning the wound before bandaging it.

"How'd you fall?" she asked.

He just stared at her.

"Perhaps you have a concussion?"

Still nothing.

"What's your name?"

"I'm . . . I'm . . . I'm Asher."

"Sarai."

"I know."

"You stalking me?" she asked.

"No, I . . . I heard your aunt call your name."

It was Sarai's aunt who told her that she saw Asher purposely use a branch to make a small cut on his forehead, so he could pretend to be hurt. Then, he accidentally fell out of the tree while gawking at Sarai. Asher had hurt himself on purpose just so they could meet and spend time together. It was a daring and partially stupid gambit, Sarai thought, but one she now cherished. Asher's head wasn't the only thing cut that day. Her perception of what love meant was shattered. He had wrecked her notion of love.

Asher was different than any of the Lazurite boys Sarai was used to. And he was different than most Drecks. He didn't live recklessly like so many first-lifers—except when trying to impress a girl he was enamored with. Part of it had to do with his family lineage. He was being groomed to be a leader, a warrior, but all he wanted was his own quiet corner, a garden, a few boisterous children to take to the playground, and, now, for Sarai to be his eternity mate.

But Sarai's father had other plans. When she died in a car accident six months after her engagement to Asher, she was imported back to Zion where she was secretly given second-life protocol. The brakes on her car had failed. Ironically, the same brakes Asher had replaced weeks before. But in her heart she knew Asher was not to blame, that he hadn't made a mistake. And even if he had, she would have loved him no less. It was an accident that brought them together and another one that separated them. At least, that is what she believes.

"Sultana, it's getting late," one of the guards informs her.

Sarai ignores him and slowly stretches out her hand towards The Wall. She imagines Asher's strong hands clasped with hers. His hands teemed with callouses from the countless holes his uncle forced him to dig as they unsuccessfully tried to tunnel under The Wall. The first time she gawked into his buoyant sapphire blue eyes she felt like she was staring into a vast ocean. She adored the way his bulbous nose curled upward and how his chin would jut when he smiled. His short, spiky hair flouted the presumptuous elongated locks of the Lazurite boys she grew up with.

Since being separated from Asher, Sarai's numerous attempts to contact him had been in vain. There had been multiple rumors of his death. She wondered if he was still alive. And if so, why hadn't he done more to contact her? Maybe he has moved on? The willow shakes, balking at such thoughts.

"Sultana, I must insist." The now unsettled guard shakes her from her remembrance.

"My father won't be sultan forever," she says, reminding him that she is next in line and that he should mind his tone. "Let's go."

"We're clearing out!" the guard orders the others.

They create a perimeter around the armored helidrone and escort her into the back. Her drone is wedged between the protective custody of two more. She grabs a book and settles in for the long flight home to the Pacific Ocean she has grown to hate.

Sarai turns the frayed pages of a Hemingway novel. She prefers paperback to autoreaders or heads-up displays. Something about reading and turning the pages makes the reading experience more intimate. The paper comes alive when she touches it. The simulated voice that attempts to duplicate what the great authors might have sounded like annoys her greatly. Most of them sound like a computer-generated version of an uptight snob just having poured his second bourbon.

She peers back at the diminishing Wall as they travel west over the rugged expanse of former Utah. She can see a person on the other side but doesn't know it is Asher. If she did she would have her escort land immediately on the other side, despite the danger.

She may be going home, but as far as she is concerned, she is leaving home. As she turns and re-immerses herself in the poetry that is Hemingway her ears suddenly ring. She doesn't hear the concussive blast that pushes her entire body into the steel roof of the drone. She spins in circles until the drone crashes into the side of a hill.

Her confusion mounts as she cranes her neck towards the window and witnesses the sky flip end over end at least a dozen times. The aging drone's frame groans as the metal slowly twists with each somersault. Then her vision leaves her as acrid inky smoke saturates the flying beast. She doesn't hear her guards squawk her name as her senses vacate her.

This wasn't an accident.

I wrap my knuckles against the decaying door of the ramshackle house that sits on twenty acres of former farmland. The soil's now sterile from years of neglect. A microcosm of our once productive society. Before second-life rights, before The Wall. It's early as the sun still hasn't scaled the mountains, but if I recall correctly, Sarai's Aunt Esther is an early riser. I knock again, softly, as it feels that the door might rip from its hinges.

"It's five in the morning; who is it?"

"It's Asher."

Esther quickly opens the squeaking door. Her gaunt frame has seen more bountiful days, her silver hair wispy. She was once a stunner, but the hardships that have befallen The Middle have slowly chiseled away her beauty. More Zion's doing than the years, she liked to say. "Get in here before somebody sees you," Esther squawks.

She drags me in by the arm and then checks that I'm alone. Her grip is like a vice from years of farming. When Sarai lived with her aunt I used to give Esther a hand with plowing, planting, and anything else that she asked. Her husband died of cancer years before I met her. Now things are falling apart. Her carpet is frayed and worn to dirty nubs. I smell coffee brewing, which is a welcome change to the otherwise musty aroma wafting up from the carpet.

Since her *death*, I have seen Sarai a few times on the holotube while watching a pirated signal coming out of Zion West. I know she has been taken to The Mountain and that her father and the Lazurites have resurrected her.

"What folly is this? I told you not to come here anymore. Sure you weren't followed?"

"I'm sure," I reply. I can't blame her for being miffed. She could be executed if the Lazurites knew I was here. Besides, she blames me for Sarai's accident. That is why I'm here. I sit on the rickety wooden chair and place my hands on the dusty table. She sits across from me. She throws me a vexing stare. I notice a small hole in the ceiling where the morning sun leaks through.

"I can fix that for you if you like."

She ignores my offer.

"You're lucky I was up; what is it you want?"

"The wreckage. You sure they didn't mention where they were taking it?" I refer to her Toyota pickup that Sarai had died in.

She uses the sharp nail on her index finger to scratch her yellow front teeth, almost as if she can scrape them white again. "I know I look older than the trees, but I'm not senile yet; we have been over this, Asher. Like I said before, they didn't say."

"And they took it east, correct? The wreckage?"

"Yes." She leans in, her bony hands shake. Her cracked fingernails look like yellow shards of bone. "You're obsessed with this. You need to let it go."

But I need to know what really happened. Was it actually me? The hydraulic system on the brakes was something I had never seen before, but I'm certain I put them together correctly.

I think.

She senses my guilt and despair; her enmity for me temporarily abates. "I'm petered out, you want coffee?"

I nod.

"Black, right?"

"Yes, thank you."

Her bones creak as she pushes herself up from the table and trudges to the coffee pot. Her quivering hands pour me a cup, with a few drops splatting onto the carpet. She places it on the table and slides it in my direction like a bartender would a pint of ale.

I sip the searing two-day-old coffee and stifle a grimace. I eye the muffins in the corner, and my stomach bellows. I haven't eaten in over a day. "Have you . . . have you talked to her?" I ask, wondering if she has a way to communicate with Sarai, being family and all.

"No," she replies simply. "Pretty sure they got her under lock and key after what she pulled. Sand that girl's got! But I don't need to tell you that boy."

"If you ever do get the chance to talk to her, tell her."

She softens, "I know Asher. I will."

I stand, "And if you ever need anything."

She cackles. "You trying to peddle contraband to an eighty-year-old woman?"

"You would get the family discount, of course."

"How about a Ruger 9mm?" she blurts out, only half joking.

"I'll see what I can do," I lie. All weapons are reserved for The Defiance.

I head towards the door, "Take care, Esther."

She yells, "You would think that you are the one senile!"

"What do you mean?"

"You come here every month asking me the same questions."

"I need to know," I say quietly.

"Maybe it's best you don't, boy. Why do this to yourself?"

"I have to know."

She shakes her head and then swiftly stands, buoyed by the caffeine. "Asher. Mark's wrecking yard. East of here."

I nod my gratitude. She throws me a muffin. It's hard as a rock, but I'll take it.

"And Asher, don't come back here. Got it?"

After all these years, why tell me now? Perhaps she wanted me to live, thinking there was a chance it wasn't my fault. But I have to know. I close my eyes and reminisce about that fateful day:

Inky tire marks guided me to where a hole had been punched through the median, below it a rocky ravine. Grimy soot still exhausted into the air. I sprinted towards the fractured guard rail. My legs moved so fast that I almost did not stop in time when I reached the edge of the cliff. I tried to balance myself; my knees shook, and my heart throttled. A hundred yards below me was Sarai's red Toyota pickup lying upside down.

I scrambled down the hill, falling multiple times until I reached the truck, which was still belching smoke.

"Sarai!" I screamed.

I peeled open the passenger side door, only to see the cab empty. There was a gaping hole in the windshield with her blood dripping from the jagged edges. My entire body was shaking as I exited the truck and followed the blood trail further down the hill shouting her name.

Then I found her.

She lay lifeless behind a rock, blood spots like freckles on her face and arms.

"Sarai!" I bawled, enveloping her in my arms.

She had no pulse; she was not breathing.

"Wake up, Sarai! Wake up." I rocked her back and forth, tears plummeted from my cheeks, splashing onto hers, mixing with her blood, causing tiny crimson pools to form that then splashed to the ground.

"No! No!" I shrieked, wondering if it was her brakes, the very ones I had repaired the week before.

"C'mon Sarai, wake up. Wake up!"

Thirty minutes later I was still holding her, still crying. That's when they showed up. Ten Lazurite elites shouldering their plasma rifles. *They ripped her from my arms.*

"What are you doing?" I barked, my legs unable to move, my body and soul numb. I crawled towards them as they carried her up the hill and then disappeared. Not long after, a giant magnet descended from a helidrone above me and took away her truck. The cleanup happened so fast, almost as if she or her truck never existed.

I shake off the memory and approach Mark's Wrecking Yard, donning a hooded sweatshirt, sunglasses, and a Star Wars hat. This is my usual guise. Most of us in Reservation 9 don clothing from the 80's. Not 2080 mind you, 1980. You see, inside an abandoned textile warehouse a massive amount of clothing was discovered in plastic crates. Most contained nostalgic replicas of a time we will never see again; the 1980's. I have seen some of the movies and heard a bit of the music from that time. I think I would have fit in nicely. Although I'm not sure who MC Hammer is, but his pants are sure comfortable.

Two addicts, fresh from smoking helldust, loiter out front. Their rotten teeth are the color of an aging banana peel. Their dilated eyes make them look inhuman, possessed. I grip my electric ricochet strapped to my side in case they try to make a move on me. They eye it, then go about their business. Before second thoughts seep in, I wander into the office. Mark is friendly enough. His rotundness tells me business is good. Car parts are hard to come by these days. The front desk is laminated with grease as is his faded Knight Rider T-shirt. He rubs his thin slick-stash and peers over his inventory worksheet.

"A 2052 Toyota pickup, eh?"

"Yeah, hydrogen. Red."

"Got a couple by the east fence; feel free to have a gander."

I sift through the maze of wrecked cars and junk metal stacked like pancakes. Something about the smell of auto grease and gasoline comforts me. It reminds me of my father and how he taught me how to fix anything mechanical. That was before his death. Before *The Defiance*. To my right, I spy a silver Mustang, similar to my year. I make a mental note in case I need parts for mine–if I can ever afford the fuel, that is. My uncle thinks it's frivolous. I'm not a dragger by any means, but I relish speed, the thundering snarl of an American-made V-8. Sure, it doesn't have the instant torque of an electric engine, but it beats the vexatious whine its engine makes.

I step over electric motors and hydrogen fuel cells. Much of this technology is contraband, but I assume Mark hasn't been discovered or is paying off Lazurite enforcement patrols. Probably the latter. Zion had most electric and hydrogen vehicles in The Middle destroyed or confiscated so The Defiance couldn't utilize them. Petrol is so hard to come by that they didn't bother with vehicles equipped with combustible gasoline engines. Speaking of gas, Mark secretly sells that as well, but I can find it cheaper elsewhere.

I finally reach the east fence. There it is. Esther's red Toyota. Or what's left of it. It instantly brings back memories of Sarai. But what doesn't? Her aunt told her to steer clear of me on account of who my father and uncle were. That I would bring them trouble. She was correct. Because of me, she is back in Zion, and her Aunt Esther's apple farm was torched. If I close my eyes, I can smell the sweet fragrance of charred apple wood. I take a deep breath and approach with trepidation. I ask myself, *Do I really wanna know?*

Yes.

Bit by bit, a consciousness of being in limbo grates at my soul. From guilt to anger. The anger comes from not knowing. Without the truth, there can be no acceptance.

I crawl under the truck, my stomach moans with hunger, wishing the flashlight in my hand was an oat bar. Yes, I'm that hungry that I'm thinking about a freeze-dried MRE made with oatmeal and soy. Esther's hardened muffin is long gone. The stale coffee rumbles with my bladder. I shine the light and inspect the hydraulic system. Then the brake pads and rotors. Then I see it, a severed brake fluid line. A clean cut. Relief washes over me, now knowing I wasn't at fault. She was murdered. I know who did it.

And why.

CHAPTER TWO

Sarai's head feels as if it were inside a vise. Her hazel eyes throb. After recovering in bed for less than a day, she suffers from cabin fever. She is lucky to have escaped the attack with a minor concussion and a paltry array of scrapes and bruises. She eases out of the massive foam bed and slips on a pair of onyx training pants and a loose-fitting Van Halen T-shirt. She slowly opens the blinds and peeks at the magnificent view. Two hundred feet below her, the sublime blue-green ocean bruises the rocky shore. Fog is beginning to dissipate. She wishes her headache would, too.

Renatus's heavily fortified palatial compound sits atop Point Reyes of former California. The views are astonishing, but the wind is horrendous. Loathing the ocean, she swiftly shuts the blinds.

Sarai fetches pain medication from her nightstand. Her head hasn't hurt this much since her second-life protocol, a protocol now deemed illegal by her own father, unless, of course, you are a sultan or wealthy. She doesn't remember being at The Mountain. Inside is where they keep the dead bodies, the building blocks required for second-life. Or if you believe The Defiance, the *living* bodies. Either way, one short life with Asher in The Middle is worth more to her than numerous lives in Zion opulence.

Sarai saunters down the hallway. Her thin training shoes glide across the bone-colored marble floors. The hallway leads to at least two dozen guest rooms, three ballrooms, five formal dining rooms, and two indoor pools. All this, just in the east wing. Wanting to avoid her father, she heads downstairs to the basement, where she finds her trainer, Hagar.

"Feeling better, Sarai?" he asks in his deep baritone voice. His hair is golden blond and stretches to the middle of his back.

"A few bumps and bruises, nothing to fret over. I thought we would have a session."

"Scourge's today?"

She nods, "See you down there."

Minutes later, Sarai and Hagar make their way down to the beach. The fine, silky sand massages her bare feet. They each don a *scourge*—a long whip with a pulsating electrical current. The steel handle is two feet long, with a rounded knob on one end to double as a club. The electric pulse is turned off for obvious reasons.

She strikes at his legs, and Hagar leaps into the air, snapping his scourge towards her head. She dives into the sand and does a tuck and roll, then, like a cat, she flops back onto her feet.

"How are the guards?" she asks, whipping at his side.

Hagar sidesteps the attack, his face grim, "Two dead."

"And the escorts?"

Hagar gives her a knowing look. *Renatus*. She is certain in his fury they were either executed or imprisoned. She feels guilty. Sarai tried to visit The Wall on her own, but her security detail insisted they go with her. She grimaces at the thought. One of them had a family.

WHACK! Hagar's whip wraps around her left leg. He pulls and she topples to the ground. She cracks her scourge before he can pull her in, and the tail end of her whip swaddles Hagar's handle. She snaps it back, sending his scourge flying out of his hand.

He chuckles, "Very good, Sultana."

"C'mon Hagar, you know I hate that."

"Sorry, my baroness," he jokes.

She holds up her scourge and smiles. "Don't make me turn this thing on."

Suddenly, his smile fades as he peers behind her.

"What the bloody hell is this palaver?" Renatus bellows through his teeth. His square face is flush with anger. He is bald, with a hawk nose and perfectly straight teeth. His tranquilizing blue eyes fail to mask his ire. His gait is bouncy and light, as if he's walking on his toes. This makes him look more imposing.

"Good morning, Father," Sarai responds coldly.

"Are you daft, my daughter? What are you doing out of bed? The doctors said—"

"I'm feeling better," she interrupts.

Renatus glances at Hagar. "Could you excuse us for a minute mate?"

"Yes, my sultan." Hagar trudges back towards the palace.

"Why? Why did you go The Wall? For him?" Renatus asks, implying she tried to see Asher.

Sarai doesn't respond, turns her back to him, and faces the ocean.

"He's part of The Defiance Sarai. These are the same people that just tried to assassinate you."

"Does it really matter? Won't you just take me to The Mountain again?"

"The only reason you are standing here is because of me and The Mountain you speak so disdainful of!"

"I didn't ask to be here. I never asked for protocol."

"Come Sarai, why be so difficult? Everything you could ever need is right here. Besides, rumor has it that Asher is dead."

Those words demolish her. She steadies herself to keep from crying, looking at her father with a stubborn resolve.

"And you can release my security detail, I forced them to take me. They are not to blame."

"Impossible. Disobedience breeds chaos and recklessness. Zion cannot be Zion without order. That is what led to The Middle's downfall."

Sarai cringes at this hypocrisy. Renatus is a thrill seeker, an audacious and reckless daredevil. But he can afford to be. He has been to The Mountain more times than she can count. *What is sacred when time is not limited?* she thinks.

"Anything else, my sultan?" she asks bitterly.

Renatus glances at her grubby shirt.

"Must you insist on wearing this bloody garb? You look like a Dreck. And smell like one. You are driving your mother batty."

It vexed Sarai that the Lazurites spoke in a British vernacular because it sounded regal, further distinguishing themselves from the bourgeois and riffraff. American English and Old-World English had been tossed into a melting pot, and out came a bouillabaisse of tepid idioms. Sarai openly rejected such pomposity. She still saw herself as a Dreck, hence her attire and speech.

"Your mother wants you to start picking out dresses."

Sarai goes numb at the thought of it. Without even realizing it, she wanders into the ocean, wading up to her ankles. She doesn't feel the cold.

"Perhaps you have forgotten, but the Canonization is just weeks away."

The sliced brake line proves Sarai was murdered. I suspect Renatus had her killed just so she could be imported back to Zion. He very well wasn't going to let his only daughter marry me, a son of The Defiance. And what better way than to make it look like an accident. I wonder if Sarai knows her father's dirty secret. That the life of another was taken to bring her back from the dead. A Dreck's life, no doubt. Someone like me.

After draining my last two gallons of petrol into my thirsty black Mustang, I figure it's time to make more money. Work has been scarce lately, but Boaz, The King of Contraband, had informed me of another drop between sectors 258 and 260 near The Wall. I'm headed there now. I slam on my brakes as two draggers race through the intersection. To my left, a mother and her two toddlers beg for food. To my right is a former Denny's restaurant converted into a casino. A brothel above it.

This is why second-life rights were revoked. The first-lifers had become lavish in their recklessness. Bank accounts drained, indulging in a multitude of free sins, like gambling and prostitution, living dangerously knowing that if they perished, they could be resurrected as second-lifers. Rulers emerged, concluding that this morally bankrupt society was no longer sustainable. To give some a second life meant taking that of another.

That's why Renatus created The Middle and herded all first-lifers into it. Once The Wall went up, second-life rights were revoked. But by looking around, you wouldn't know it. I guess old habits die hard.

This is why my father, Silas, a former senator, opposed the implementation of second-life protocol. He knew human nature; he predicted it would come to this. He used to say, "No life is worth wasting, no matter how many you have. When life isn't precious, no day is treasured." It wasn't until he discovered The Grand Lie that he finally accepted my uncle's pleas to become the leader of The Defiance. A position that cost him and my mother their lives.

I have to stop again as a walking skeleton trudges in front of me. Helldust now has jurisdiction over his vacant, black, demon-like eyes. He's a walking zombie, a phantom of a man. Seems a strong wind would rattle his bones.

I drive past the remnants of a park. The children have tied a thick stick to a rope where a swing set used to be. The chains long since stolen for weapons or locks. The oxidizing tilt-a-whirl no longer spins. Needles litter the sandbox. The parents watch, their eyes muddled with despair and regret. They have spent the winnings of a promised lottery whose check never came. Now the innocent children are left with the debt of this generation's improvidence. What chance do they have?

I leave town and edge closer towards The Wall. My gas needle quivers towards empty. My stomach is not far behind. My hostel rent is overdue. I finally arrive at Sector 258 about four hundred yards from The Wall; beaming florid images of wealthy, fat, contented Lazurites. Then I see it, a massive, compacted heap of trash freshly parachuted in compliments of Zion, which has been dumping its trash in The Middle for years. There are mountains of waste as far as the eye can see. But we Drecks are proficient at finding utility in what has been discarded by the privileged.

I park my pony and remove a pair of bolt cutters from my trunk. I snap the aluminum banding that holds the trash together, careful not to let them snap and whip me in the face. It has only happened twice before. I put on my face mask and rubber gloves, plug in my earbuds, and like a stray dog, I start digging. A young couple trudges past and shakes their heads. They think I'm a refuse rat, which is fine by me; it covers the fact that I'm actually a contraband mule. Boaz has people on the other side of The Wall who pack contraband into red, sealed plastic canisters and place them in the middle of the trash piles right before they are compressed. Once I procure the items, I deliver them, take a cut, and give the rest to Boaz.

Before working for Boaz, I was a customer. That is how I came to own the rare ricochet that hangs on my belt. My contraband weapon of choice. It is similar to what the Aborigines of Australia called a boomerang but with a broader angle. Its electric current is not enough to kill a Lazurite wearing exoarmor, but it will knock them to the ground, if not unconscious. The small receiver on my wrist sends a signal that the ricochet always returns to. It's more elegant than a gun. And I don't have to buy bullets, which cost more than gas, if you can find them.

I dredge through the muck, filth, and unmentionables for about an hour. From dirty diapers to rotting meat. As we starve here in The Middle, the Lazurites throw away surplus food. I finally find what I'm looking for. It begins to rain. *Wonderful.* I thought I smelled bad five minutes ago. I gag as the rain leeches the abhorrent stench from my skin and the odor now permeates through my mask. This won't be the first or last time I vomit standing knee deep in Zion's sediment. Maybe this is why those on the other side call us *Drecks*? Meant to be a derogatory term, we in The Middle now have affectionately embraced it.

I'm so consumed with the pungent aroma that I don't see the unmanned helidrone release a small green pallet three hundred yards above me. A narcdrop. Its parachute opens, and it's floating right towards my car. I trudge through the trash heap and gallop to my Mustang. Seconds before the large pallet crushes it, I fire up the engine and floor it. The thick tires spew rocks and dirt before jolting me back, and the pallet barely misses as it hits the ground.

I know the addicts will be swarming within the hour. Refuse isn't the only thing deposited into The Middle. The green pallet contains the usual—helldust, speedrush, and The Devil's Syrup. It's a form of control, along with the revocation of arms. Renatus keeps us hooked on substances, quelling our desire to resist or rebel.

Such demonic control started before The Wall went up. The first step in what was then an emerging dictatorship was to take away means to defend yourself, then force the population to become dependent on your provisions, then mollify them with drugs and booze. Soon they no longer care that The Wall even exists, perhaps they don't even notice it anymore. Like living next to a noisy freeway. Over time, the cacophony of cars is no a longer a nuisance, and its familiarity might even become soothing. It reminds me of a quote by the Russian novelist Fyodor Dostoyevsky. "The best way to keep a prisoner from escaping is to make sure he never knows he's in prison."

Other than the plasma and pulse weapons of the Lazurites, all other firearms have been banned. At least attempted so.

At the beginning of The Defiance, my father would send out patrols to find as many narcdrops as possible. The opiates would be rounded up, then destroyed. My mother started clinics to help the addicts overcome their addiction. But it soon became too much; the frequency of drug and booze drops was overwhelming. When my Uncle Cephas took over as leader of The Defiance after my parents' deaths, he deemed The Defiance no longer had the resources to destroy narcdrops or run rehabilitation programs. In his defense, he is probably correct. So flooded are we with addictive substances that half of The Middle is now hooked on Renatus's Demon Tonic. What is free has cost my people everything.

Certain no one is watching, I drag one of the red plastic containers from the smelting heap into the trunk of my car. I put two more in the back seat, and a smaller one sits shotgun. I need a truck. And air fresheners. I fire up the throaty V-8 and stare at the green pallet. I exit my car, cut the banding from the pallet, reach in, and grab a bottle of Renatus's finest. It's not for me as I rarely touch the stuff. Just as I'm leaving the helldusters, and tonic swillers begin to arrive. They go from a mindless stumble to an awkward jog as they get closer to the drug pallet. You can see the avarice in their insatiable eyes; each one wants to be the first to arrive to pick their vice of choice.

I have three stops to make; the last delivery is for my uncle Cephas. I do a quick scan for any Lazurite patrols, then turn on the radio and tune to a pirated signal of Zion's central news: *"We have been informed the sultana wasn't seriously injured when her convoy of drones was bombed from what was yet another terrorist attack by The Defiance. Renatus has promised to ramp up his patrols in The Middle to eradicate the terror group."*

My heart pauses as the oxygen is sucked from my lungs. Shades of crimson sheathe my vision. I turn a hard and screeching left. Uncle Cephas will be my first stop.

The rain has fizzled. My pockets are drained, but my gas tank is no longer impoverished as I pull away from the black-market mini refinery hidden within a steel warehouse. Since Renatus has elevated his patrols, the price of gasoline has tripled in the past nine months, vastly hurting my bottom line. Boaz has not kept up with inflation. I could complain, but as he reminds me, I'm easily replaceable.

I wind my way through the long and dusty road until the asphalt ends and a dirt road begins. Rain batters my windshield, and my wipers can barely keep up. Sentries hide within the trees and the bushes. I can't see them, but I know they are there. A rickety barn rests in the dirt field just up ahead. The red paint has faded into the wood. It looks like a building made of rust. I flash my lights four times, count to two, then twice more. Three Defiance guards armed with double-barreled shotguns approach my Mustang. Most of the turn-of-the-century firearms that remain have been procured by The Defiance. Which isn't a lot. They don't ask for any identification or pass codes; they know who I am. They wave me through. One of them opens the creaky barn door and I park inside.

Two more armed Drecks help me carry the red containers down an earthen stairwell underneath the barn. This is one of many underground compounds Cephas has built throughout the twenty-four reservations. It's dank and muggy, adding to my repugnant aroma. The dull lighting of the fire lamps instantly depresses my soul as I trudge down the dirt stairs. I helped dig this tunnel as a teenager, but not by choice. We continue down the vestibule until we reach a wide opening. A ragged Dreck careens past me, singing "The Dreck's Dirge." His voice is raspy and dysphoric.

> *"They took our freedom, and with that our soul*
> *With Zion's Tonic, we are no longer whole*
> *One day it will finally fall*
> *The oppression that is The Wall*
> *As Drecks we have no more hope*
> *We hung ourselves with Zion's rope*
> *Second-life used to be for all*

That was before The Wall
Now we live in a giant cage
Where no one can hear our rage
There was a day we used to stand tall
That was before The Wall
We are now deemed a lower class
Forced to live with Zion's trash
Happier times I can recall
That was before The Wall"

Some say my father wrote it. Others say my mother; the latter is more likely.

"Wait here," a guard orders me.

I watch as the guard approaches Cephas. He is fifty-seven, burly, stout, and barrel-chested. He has three massive scars wedged into the left side of his face. Some say it is from a scourge. Others say he fought off a grizzly bear with his bare hands. I can believe both. His cleft chin and crooked nose peer down at his frayed Bible. He and his leadership are in a circle around a small fire. The irony is not lost on me that most of them attending this Bible study don Iron Maiden and Black Sabbath T-shirts, both heavy-metal 80's bands. To them it's free clothing, and they probably have never heard their music. Cephas's smile is like a mouthful of pebbles; his yellow teeth have been ground down to almost nothing. Surely from the stress of being the leader of The Defiance.

Cephas is concluding an anemic attempt at a rousing speech. "We all know that second-life protocol was an abomination," he bellows in the raspy voice of an ex-smoker. "Yes, we all miss our loved ones, our fathers and mothers, our sons and daughters. But God had called them home; who are we to snatch them out of His hands?"

Speeches weren't his thing. He has a way with words, but his delivery is stale and languid. A deathly skinny man with overgrown eyebrows that have grown together spots me and sniffs, "Is that the sweet stench of the prodigal son?" His name is Jude, Cephas's right-hand man.

They all stop and stare at me with acrimonious eyes. I don't blame them, nor do I resent them. These people are the salt of the earth. The last remaining remnant of a people who used to be free. People unaffected by the narcdrops. Undeterred by The Wall. People who still have hope. Even if it's that of a mustard seed.

Cephas lumbers towards me, "Bearing gifts, Nephew? Or do you need something?"

"Was it you? The drone bombing?" I ask accusingly.

A pelican is tattooed on his right arm—the symbol of The Defiance.

"The attempt on Sarai's life? You know that isn't our modus operandi."

"Then who was it?"

"You know who it was."

"It was The Sons of Levi," Jude shouts.

The Sons of Levi is a rogue offshoot of The Defiance. Their methods are radical, bordering on terror. They will do anything to stop Renatus and his army, even if that means the killing of innocent civilians.

Cephas places a stumpy, dirty hand on my shoulder, "You need to forgive yourself, Son."

But I can't, nor him.

"Let's see what you got."

His men bring him the red contraband containers. He opens them. Inside are a stack of tattered Bibles, a few pistols, and ammunition. Inside the other one is the crown jewel.

"You found one?" Cephas asks jubilantly.

To the exuberance of his men, he holds up a black and gray exoarmor suit.

"That one will cost you," I say plainly.

"Excellent," he says and hands it off to one of his technicians.

Exoarmor suits were designed to absorb the energy of Zion's plasma weapons. With traditional weapons outlawed, they make Renatus's army near invincible. They are light and ambulatory. What they won't stop is a bullet, making conventional firearms worth more than gold. The rub is that each one is manufactured to the DNA of the specific Lazurite soldier it was created for, rendering them useless to us—unless Cephas can find a way to hack into the suit's operating system and activate the protection mechanism to make them universal. If he can accomplish that, he can then find a way to procure more of them, leveling the playing field.

Cephas's placid eyes cannot mask the pity bordering on disdain he feels for me. He disagrees with my day job. Unless, of course, when it behooves him as it does now.

"Come back to us, Asher, stop wasting your God-given talents and join us. You have a chance to do something meaningful."

"I thought I just did."

"Boaz has plenty of contraband mules I can contract with. You have a different purpose, Son."

"Is digging through trash not noble enough for the son of Silas?" I say bitingly.

"You know that's not what I meant."

"Your brother used to say that every job mattered, none more important than the other."

"True, but we also all have our callings."

"And you think you know what mine is?" I say flippantly.

Cephas claims he is a changed man, and maybe he is. But I still remember the man who tried to raise me after my parents died. The inebriated man who would slurp the devil's syrup and beat me for the slightest infraction. The polluted man who had me bore tunnels day and night until my callouses bled and my spirit withered. The man with the indurated soul who forced me to clean his muddy boots with my own spit. *"I want to be able to eat off of them!"* The man who would stumble home and pull me from my slumber to fix him whatever slop our barren cupboards might have held while butchering old-world songs at a pitch much too loud for that ungodly hour. The sloven man who convinced my parents to join The Defiance. He is the reason they are gone.

"Can you get more of them?" Cephas asks, referring to the exoarmor suits.

"Maybe."

"You wanna stay for dinner?"

I'm hungry, but I don't.

"I almost forgot I have something else for you." I reach into my faded acid-wash jean jacket, pull out the bottle of DemonTonic, and place it next to his sullied boots. "Your boots are dirty."

He sighs, then gapes at me in disappointment, at my pettiness, as I know he hasn't touched the stuff in almost three years.

"Goodbye, Asher."

Cephas regards the bottle of DemonTonic. "Buckethead," he says to himself. He can't blame Asher, considering their past. It's true he was an addict, and a vicious one at that. It started soon after he lost his wife at the hands of Zion. A drink here or there turned into a bottle here *and* there. They didn't have children, and she was as barren as the stomachs of half of his people. He didn't know how to raise Asher, or any teenager for that matter. What he did know was that Asher was a born leader and a skilled warrior. Cephas had set up a training camp for young new recruits. Asher was always at the top. He was grooming him to eventually lead as his father had.

But when Renatus siphoned Sarai away from Asher, everything changed. Asher lost interest in their cause. He disengaged and withdrew into isolation. Receded into his own little world of sifting through trash for money. Cephas was angry at himself for not reaching out, for not doing more to bring Asher back into the fold. Truth of the matter was that Asher hadn't forgiven him for being abusive, and he hadn't forgiven himself for abandoning his father's cause.

Cephas grabs the bottle and clutches it. He closes his eyes, and it speaks to him. *One drink never hurt anybody.* Before he falls for its seductive snare he smashes it against the rock wall. Glass shatters at his feet. He watches the dirt swiftly guzzle the bronze liquid like a zealous addict. He takes his long boot and stomps on the broken glass, as if tamping down temptation. He made a promise to himself, God, and the people he now leads to never again touch the stuff.

"We're ready," Jude informs him staring at the shards of broken glass.

Cephas turns, surprised that he isn't alone. "How long have you been standing there?"

"Long enough to know you weren't thirsty."

Cephas nods at the shattered bottle. "I wanted to."

"I know. But I wasn't about to let you."

"You think you can take me now, huh, Ace?" Cephas says with a grin.

"Dang skippy!"

"Thanks for having my back."

"A shaggy one at that!"

Cephas shakes his head and rubs the dimple in his chin as he stares at his gaunt second-in-command. "Why do I feel this is a desperation play?"

"Definitely a Hail Mary pass, sir."

"For the love of Pete, stop calling me sir."

"Of course, sir." Jude smiles; he loves to rip on his friends, especially Cephas, who is an easy target.

"Can this really work? Or do you think it's wishful thinking from an old man ill equipped to lead?"

"Yes to the second part."

"What? That I'm not qualified?"

"No, that you're old."

Cephas won't admit it, but he quite enjoys the banter.

"Ha! Let's get going, buckethead, before I change my mind."

"Forgot to tell you, Mark is out, broke his leg yesterday."

"Who has our six in case things go south?"

"Sam."

"Sam? He's about as fast as an asthmatic ant."

"True, but he also volunteered to take point on this; maybe you should let him, sir. Or let me."

Cephas rises; his knees creak like rusty door hinges. "It won't be the first stupid thing I've done, let's hope it's not the last."

Snow frosts the tip of the Rockies. Cephas plods in the middle of the street. His boots scratch against the decaying asphalt, kicking up tiny pebbles that scatter like mice eluding a stray cat. His hood covers half of his face. It's dark except for the nineteenth-century gas lights that line the seedy establishments. Electricity is at a premium—when the grid is actually working. Zion routinely drops electromagnetic pulse (EMP) bombs to scramble their communications. Wireless cell towers and email servers are constantly being destroyed. It is an effective way to kill the messenger. The Defiance has had to resort to Paul Revere type tactics to communicate. Handwritten notes on horseback aren't uncommon.

Rambunctious squawking comes from the casino to his left, where two demondusters loiter out front. It's dangerous to be out after dark, but he is probably the only one around carrying a COLT 45. Cephas hears a husband and wife quarreling. Through the open windows come the cries of children from the other room. He spots narcdrops in the distance floating to the ground like a dying helium balloon. The family squabble and what is being dropped in on those pallets are surely related, Cephas muses. As a child, Cephas remembered this street being safe. Families visiting ice cream parlors.

Children laughing on the swings at the local park while their parents discussed the weather. Dogs barking and playing fetch—before they became food. *One day again.* He shakes his head and takes captive his attention to the task at hand.

"Here goes nothing," Cephas mumbles as he pulls out the handgun and fires it twice into the air.

The addicts in front of the gambling hall hit the ground. The noise from the casino dissipates as patrons peek outside, wondering who the man with the death wish is. Cephas waits another minute and then fires more precious lead into the air. His scouting crew had spotted a five-man Lazurite patrol two miles east about an hour ago. Once they hear the gunfire, they will surely come to investigate the person who dares to defy Zion and its contraband laws. Cephas doesn't like being bait, but he refused to let anyone else do it. Besides, once the patrol recognizes who he is, they'll be more apt to bring him in for the reward than kill him on the spot. This kind of self-sacrifice and courage has endeared him to his men.

Cephas steels himself as the patrol races towards him on their electric speedcycles. They quickly make a perimeter around Cephas, aiming their plasma guns. Cephas holds up both hands, one of them holding the gun. The leader of the patrol hops off his cycle and wearily approaches Cephas, knowing full well his exoarmor will not stop a bullet. "Put it down."

Cephas obeys and rests the gun on the asphalt. One of the guards swiftly scoops it up.

"Where did you get this?" the leader asks.

Cephas doesn't answer.

"Give me one reason I shouldn't kill you right now for your insolence!"

Cephas smiles. "Surely Renatus would want the leader of The Defiance brought in alive for questioning. Keen?"

"Ha! You claim to be Cephas? Surely you've drank your dinner, Dreck," the patrol leader snickers, pointing his plasma gun at

Cephas's head.

Cephas shakes his head, and his hood slides off, fully revealing the scars ingrained in his face like three indiscriminate rivers weaving their way down a mountain.

"It is him! It really is him!" one of the Lazurite guards shouts.

The leader smiles through his large, bone-white teeth. "You boys ready to retire on the coast?" His men hoot and holler; they have hit the jackpot. "Cuff him."

A guard sidles up behind Cephas and wraps thick metal handcuffs around his burly wrists. They barely fit.

"Cephas, leader of The Great Defiance, for crimes against Zion, you are officially under arrest." The leader is so overjoyed he can barely get the words out of his smirking mouth. "Amos, he rides with you."

Amos, a muscular Lazurite guard with long platinum hair and large dimples, escorts Cephas to his speedcycle. Cephas climbs on, and the guard cuffs him to the second seat on the back. Another pair of metal restraints latches onto his legs.

"To The Wall, Sector 319!" the leader roars in triumph.

They fire up their speeders and race down the deteriorating street. The electric engines whine as they reach the edge of town. None see the thick braided rope lying on the ground tied to a concrete pillar on one side. On the other side of the street is Jude and four other Drecks holding the other side of the rope, which is already wrapped around a pole of a broken streetlight. Cephas says a little prayer as Jude and company pull the rope tight, creating a clothesline about four feet off the ground. By the time the three lead speeders spot it, it is too late. The rope hits them in the chest, and they fly off their bikes like bugs being flicked by a giant. Their speeders are ghost-ridden until they finally wobble to a stop and clunk to the ground.

Amos and the leader skid to a stop inches away from the rope. Before they find their bearings, Jude and his Drecks storm the street swinging stunclubs. The leader is hit first. Amos aims his plasma rifle at Jude and readies to shoot. Cephas, still perched on the speeder behind Amos, hands and feet cuffed, can do nothing but bite the back of Amos's neck. He squeals in pain, distracting him just long enough for Jude to swat him with the stunclub, which delivers a burst of voltage that renders them temporarily paralyzed, then unconscious. Cephas watches as Amos's body convulses. His limbs fling about like a ragdoll being thrown from a building. His eyes flutter, and then he collapses. Cephas needs them alive and is hopeful that the initial shock doesn't kill them. They quickly do the same to the other three guards as they try to pull themselves from the ground, aiming their plasma guns. Cephas snorts at the aroma of singed hair.

Jude grabs the unlocking card from Amos's belt and uncuffs Cephas. "You alright?"

Cephas ignores him, swipes his gun from the leader's satchel, and carefully inspects the five unconscious Lazurites. He points to Amos and another patrolman who is about the same build. "These two, check them."

Jude stabs a small needle connected to a digital readout into the guard next to Amos. "A-positive."

"And him?" Cephas points to Amos.

Jude repeats the process. "AB-positive."

Cephas rubs the scars on his face and grins. "We have a winner."

CHAPTER THREE

It's seven in the morning when I come out of a light drizzle and stroll into Timothy's Vintage Books. The room is dark and drab. The dusty shelves are lined with dank-smelling books written by J. K. Rowling, Stephen King, C. S. Lewis, J. R. R Tolkien, to name a few. Every year more and more books are deemed contraband by Zion. I'm quite certain some of these will soon join the Bible as one of them.

I spot a Tom Clancy book that I have not yet read. I gingerly pull it off the shelf and examine it, still in decent shape. I carry the book to the front desk, where Timothy is nose-deep in a Danielle Steele novel. His frayed, bushy hair and scraggly, wispy beard don't peg him as the romantic type. Although he does don a *Flashdance* T-shirt that is at least a size too small. The odor that wafts from the hamster nest growing on top of his head tells me he hasn't washed in at least a week. But there is nothing unusual about that, as water is expensive here in The Middle. I place the book in front of him.

"Timothy."

He ignores me, still buried in his book.

"Timothy," I say again.

He puts his finger up, and I wait until he finishes the page. He closes his book, somewhat annoyed.

"Is that all for today?" he mutters.

I lean in and whisper, "And five minutes."

He peers over to my right towards the door. "You sure you weren't followed?"

"Sure."

"Fifty."

"Fifty? Inflation? Last time I was here it cost me twenty bucks for ten minutes."

"Risk. There have been raids all over town in the last week. In fact, a patrolman was sniffing around here yesterday."

I hand him a fifty and follow him to the back supply closet full of janitor's supplies. He opens a wardrobe and removes a shelf on the back panel, which reveals a keyboard. He makes sure I'm not looking and then types in a code. The entire back wall opens, revealing a bank of computers on rows of tables reminiscent of an early 90's internet cafe. Computers and email are illegal in The Middle. Timothy could be executed if Zion ever found out about his little operation.

"Terminal six, five minutes," Timothy tells me before handing me a green slip of paper and disappearing back into the closet.

I perch myself in front of terminal six and turn on the monitor. I wait for Timothy to unlock the computer remotely from his office. Once done, I see the five-minute countdown in the lower left corner just below the background picture of Kevin Bacon in *Footloose*. There are four other people, all wearing hats and sunglasses. They are most likely communicating with loved ones on the other side of The Wall, or perhaps they are Sons of Levi, or even Defiance members scheming against Zion.

I open the green piece of paper he handed me. On it is a URL managed by Timothy that changes daily. I type it into a web browser and go to his private email server, where I have set up an account. I know of two email addresses once used by Sarai. Recently, she hasn't responded to either, perhaps because they have been deleted or her access is restricted. Either way, I still have to try. I type her a quick email pretending to be an old friend, but with obvious references about our past where she would certainly know it was me. I essentially want her to know I'm still alive.

I also desperately want a response. If I can't hear her voice, reading her written words is a close second. I still have three minutes left. Before I hit send, I search to get the latest news from Zoogle, Zion's regulated version of what used to be Google. Corny? Yes. I search for news on the bombing of Sarai's drone and her condition. Most of what comes up has been redacted, of course. Only that she is alive and well and that the terrorists responsible will pay dearly. Most of what I find is Zion propaganda; there are some black sites I could visit that sometimes speak the truth, but my minutes are dissolving. Then, in one of the articles I find a picture of her. She is more beautiful than I remember. But her eyes are different. Once full of spunk and moxie, they are now morose and wistful. Her spirit is held captive. While everyone else wants into Zion, she wants out. With twenty seconds left, I get ready to hit send, and the entire room vibrates. Then the lights go off, and the computer dies.

A Zion drone has dropped an EMP. Whether it was random or targeted, I do not know; the Lazurites have been known to drop EMP's at rumored communication hotspots. EMPs and computer smashing: the new book burning. Like the Nazis before them, it has the same effect—withholding information and education. But I'm not sticking around to find out if this was random or not. I pop up and hear the familiar whine of a plasma rifle discharging, followed by a scream I recognize to be Timothy. Two of the other four men in the room duck under the desk, the other two pull out 9mm handguns. Only The Defiance or Sons of Levi have access to that type of contraband, most likely courtesy of yours truly. I grip my ricochet with my right hand and stare at the closet door, which is the only way in or out of this room. I hope it's a minor patrol and not a platoon. Me and my two new friends take cover behind old concrete pillars in the middle of the room. I think this used to be the ground floor of an old parking garage. Not a word is spoken. Even though we are technically on the same side, secrecy is still paramount.

The closet door explodes open, and wooden shards fly like projectiles, bouncing off the concrete pillars. Lazurite soldiers file in blasting their plasma rifles and filing in one at a time, which makes our job easier. I fling my ricochet as my cohorts fire their pistols. A blast knocks off a chuck of concrete from the pillar inches from my head. I dive towards a table and fire off my ricochet once again. The two men beside me eye my odd weapon as they reload. As soon as it returns to me, I hurl it again, taking out the last of the Lazurite patrol. Still, no words are said between the three of us, neither knowing who is what, as there is a big rift between The Defiance and The Sons of Levi. Besides, with the amount of Lazurite spies, trust is something rarely found in these parts.

My email is now particles floating somewhere in cyberspace, zapped away by Zion. Like my parents, like Sarai, they have taken everything from me.

There is another internet cafe across town; I'll try my luck there.

The internet cafe across town was also hit. Seems Zion is ramping up their patrols as my uncle's Defiance is becoming more than just a thorn in Renatus's side. I decide to go old school and write Sarai a letter. Surely one of Boaz's couriers can deliver it to Zion. I have a last known address for Sarai's second cousin; maybe she will deliver it to her. Again, my letter is coded in case her cousin decides to become nosy.

Dusk is creeping in. I shuffle through the filthy streets of my Reservation. Two drunks fight on the sidewalk. Demondusters watch from a distance, hoping one of them might drop money or anything of value during their melee. On the horizon, trash and narcdrops rain down, littering the otherwise beautiful skyline. If I squint, their red transponder lights make them appear as if they are giant fireflies slowly falling from the sky, or red roses being dropped from a bridge, lazily fluttering to the ground. The acrid smell of burned rubber assaults my nostrils as I pass an array of homeless camps burning tires to stay warm. Sadness creeps in as filthy children kick around a tattered volleyball in a makeshift game of soccer. More and more orphans end up in these camps every day. Their parents stolen from them by the snare of Zion's drugs or killed by Lazurite thugs. What's worse is when you find these camps empty, swept into Zion as part of Renatus's harvest. And the children, why does he take so many children? A Lazurite patrol bullies a street vendor, stealing his roasted peanuts. And his coat. I pull my baseball cap over my eyes and flip up my hood, not wanting to be recognized.

"Hey!" one of them hollers at me. "Where you bloody going?"

I grip my ricochet and hurry down an alley. It seems they are too lazy to take chase; they would rather rob that poor man of his livelihood. And his warmth. I make a mental note to bring him a jacket next time I come this way. You won't believe the clothes Zion throws away. Famished and parched, I make my way to Rick's, a broken-down shack of a diner, but the food is terrific. I really can't afford it right now, but I also can't stand to eat one more oatbar. Out front is a skeletal woman with bloodshot eyes that look like streaks of crimson lightning. Her emaciated child grips her ragged coat.

"Food please," she barely manages to whisper.

She definitely is or was on helldust. But that doesn't mean her child should suffer. I kneel and look into the young boy's eyes.

"You like hamburgers?"

He simply nods, staring at the dusty ground. I pull out a matchbox car from my pocket, it is a black Mustang like mine and hand it to him. He quickly snatches it as if I might change my mind.

"And you?" I ask the mom.

"Hamburger is good."

Incurring this extra expense is going to hurt, but seeing the boy crack a smile as I enter the diner makes it all worth it. The creaky door squeals as I push it open. Three of the six tables are taken. Rick, a man with massive arms and unusually skinny legs, rings up a customer. He mans the cash register with his left hand and holds a baseball bat in his right. That is typical in The Middle whenever cash is involved. I settle in a corner and order fried eggs, toast, and one of my favorite indulgences—Newer Coke. Ironically, for the second time in their history, Coca-Cola changed their recipe, which was an utter disaster again. Now they are selling their leftover inventory at a bargain basement price. I pop the top and listen to the carbonation slowly fizzle. Never tried the original Coke, but this tastes just fine to me.

I overhear the conversation of a middle-aged couple with three younger kids to my right.

"Order anything you like; we're celebrating!" the dad says.

I see in his pocket the familiar red and black envelope. Seems they have been chosen for this month's lottery.

"Once in Zion, kids, we will be eating like this every day! And the ocean! Wait until you see the ocean!"

"And the showers? I heard the showers have warm water?" one of the kids adds innocently.

"Piping hot!" the father exclaims.

I am screaming inside. I want to tell them the truth, but they won't believe me. All that would happen is that I might ruin their dinner and frighten their children. Once the allure of Zion's abundance has set its hook, it's hard to convince anyone that it is a red herring. I can hardly blame them, wanting a better life for their children. It won't be me that wipes the smiles from their dirty faces with the coarse towel of truth.

At least not tonight.

I only agreed to return to the compound because Cephas promised me gasoline. Two Drecks lead me through a dark tunnel of the underground fortress and deposit me into a room at the end of the dingy hall. The musty smell brings back memories of digging this tunnel. Memories I would rather not relive. As I turn the corner, I overhear two people arguing. I peek around the next corner and see

Cephas. His voice is gruff and angered; he is pointing at someone.

"This alliance is over!" I hear Cephas say.

I grit my teeth in anger. He is speaking to the leader of The Sons of Levi, who goes by Dagger. No one knows his real name. To be certain, I spy the Liberty Bell that he has been branded with, the symbol of freedom for old America. He is in his forties, but his inked, wrinkled skin makes him look a decade older.

Dagger shakes his large fist. "Listen to me, Cephas; our methods may be different, but our endgame is the same. Don't you understand? This is what Renatus wants. To separates us, to divide and conquer."

Cephas shakes his head. "First the bombing at the bazaar, then Sarai. I can no longer condone your actions."

Dagger paces around Cephas's wide frame. "Sarai is a daughter of Zion; she is no friend to us or our cause. LifeCells have been used on her! I understand your nephew—"

I charge into the room and slam Dagger up against the wall. "What about me!"

My hands at his throat, he grabs my arms and tries to pull them away. "Let go of me, kid!"

"Let him go, Asher!" Cephas barks.

I turn to Cephas. "I knew you were chummy with the likes of him. He tried to kill my fiancée!"

Cephas explains, "I was just ending our arrangement, now let him go, Asher."

As I squeeze harder, Dagger pleads with me, "Listen to your uncle."

I am now nose to nose with him, can smell his breath, almost taste his sweat. "Sarai is off limits, you got that?"

"She is not who you think she is."

My hands clamp harder on his throat. "Do you got that?"

He finally relents. "Yes."

I let him go as he gasps for breath, his hands on his knees. Cephas grabs the back of his shirt. "It's time for you to leave."

Dagger looks at us both. "You won't win this war. You lack resolve. Our enemy will do anything to defeat us, so we must do the same."

Dagger is escorted out by two of Cephas's men.

"What was he doing here?" I ask Cephas.

"He was looking for weapons. Look, I don't agree with his methods either. You heard me; our partnership with them is over."

My blood pressure has finally abated as Cephas stares at me with weary eyes. "And Son, the bombing at the bazaar, that wasn't your fault."

I ignore him and ask, "Where's my petrol?"

"Hear me out, and I promise you a full tank."

I peer around and see the room is divided by a stained yellow and green cloth curtain. "No food?" I say with a dash of sass.

"Dinner after."

"Who's cooking? It's not Jude, is it?"

"Could you stop being a buckethead for just one moment? I want to show you something."

Cephas pulls the curtain open to reveal a Lazurite guard lying on a bed, unconscious, his vitals are being monitored by various machines.

"So, you captured a Lazurite. Is this what I missed two deliveries for?"

"According to his data card, his name is Amos, and we nabbed him last night."

"He a patrolman or a soldier?"

"Patrol."

"Just patrol? Not even a soldier? Zion won't even pay ransom for their elites. You won't get anything for a menial patrolman."

"He's not for ransom."

"You going to turn him? A spy for The Defiance?"

Cephas smiles, "Sort of."

I know what he is thinking, but I'm not sure why he is telling me about it. "Who's the brave fool that volunteered to be sculpted?"

"Nobody yet."

He wants me to do it, "You're out of your gourd, Uncle."

"He's about your same size, your blood type."

"You want to perform plastic surgery on me to look like a Lazurite patrol guard just so I can get inside Zion and spy for you?"

"No. What I'm asking is much bigger."

"Bigger?"

"You're a natural-born leader like your father and a cunning warrior like your uncle used to be."

I cringed at the comparisons.

He leans into me, his eyes grow as big as apples, his tiny teeth peek over his dry, cracked lips. "The Canonization."

"You must be on the tonic again speaking such folly."

The Canonization is a yearly event held in Zion, where the top Lazurite soldiers are chosen to square off in a set of trials and challenges where the one winner is given command of an entire brigade of Lazurite soldiers.

"If any Dreck can pull it off, it's you, Asher."

"No. I'm not a part of your Defiance anymore. And you must be going senile." I turn to leave.

Cephas is beginning to lose his composure. "That's right, you're a simple refuse rat."

"And Boaz pays me for my work."

Cephas knows I'm referring to all the tunnels I dug for him and the boots I cleaned, which was tantamount to slave labor.

"You think you're free now, Son? It's not just Zion that has enslaved all of us. It's not even about the mounds of trash, or the pallets of drugs, or the filth; it's about what has polluted our souls. We have been willing participants. Renatus didn't force us to drink the tonic. He didn't coerce anybody to throw away a perfectly good life just because we had the promise of another. There is only one way to freedom. The way, the life, and the truth—"

I cut him off. "Save your sermons for your followers."

"Wait. There is something else."

I stop and sigh. "Make it quick."

"Our spies inside Zion have informed us that this being the last Canonization of the century, and that the sultana is turning twenty-five and is to be married off to the winner."

The wind is extracted from my lungs, the room suddenly turns dark. *Sarai.* Just the mere mention of her breaks me. The schism in my heart widens. I suddenly see her. Her halcyon eyes are like rhinestones made from bronze. The small freckles on her nose look like flecks of scattered cinnamon. Her fragile smile levels me. I reach for her hand. Cephas's meaty fingers swaddle my shoulder, snapping me back into the moment.

"This is how you help The Defiance. This is how you return to Sarai. Keen?"

I'm sucked in for a moment, I nod towards Amos. "As him?"

"Don't be daft, boy; she doesn't love you for what you look like. We need you. *She* needs you. Point of life is to die empty, Son, don't hoard your God-given talents."

"You should see me dig through trash," I say facetiously.

"Could you be serious for just a minute, boy, and leave your hatred for me out of this! Tell me what you think your mother and father are thinking right now?"

"Nothing, they're dead."

But I do know what my parents would say, that we were meant to serve others, that all actions should be for the greater good. That everyone has a legacy. That's what got them killed. I peer over at Amos and wonder if he's just another bully menace or if he's a conscript, a slave of Zion.

"This is bigger than you and me, Asher."

His gruff manner can be surprisingly persuasive. But once again, he asks the impossible.

"I'll take my gas now."

"We can't fight this war forever, Asher. At the rate we're going, we'll eventually lose. Or starve to death. We must do something bold, something audacious. We're running out of time."

"What you're proposing is lunacy. Just the gas, keen?"

Cephas rolls up his sleeve and points to the pelican tattooed on his dirt-infused forearm. "You know, when food is scarce, a pelican mother will wound her own chest to the point of bleeding so her offspring can drink her blood instead of starving to death."

"Good for the pelican."

Cephas has always believed the insurmountable is possible. The fact that the only way to see Sarai again would be to serve my uncle's grand and futile aspirations annoys me greatly. Does he really expect me to be sculpted and bloodletted? Even if I survived the process, the chance of me passing as Amos and getting into Zion is slim. Even slimmer is getting selected for the Canonization itself. Those are reserved for the elite, proven soldiers or sons of the rich and powerful. Amos is a simple Lazurite patrol guard. I doubt he checks any of those boxes. Then there is the Canonization itself. Is Cephas really delusional enough to believe that my meager training by his own hand is enough to not only compete but survive such trials against men who were born and bred for this sort of thing?

I drop it into second and hang a sharp corner, then redline it before shifting into third. Can't help myself; I have a full tank. I arrive at what looks like a mechanic's shop, my last delivery of the day. I park in front, flash my lights four times, and hop out of my Mustang. I open the trunk and retrieve a circuit board for what I'm guessing is for an electric engine. I've delivered thousands of these; this piece of contraband looks like it's for a Toyota. I walk towards the open garage roll-up door and spot a Greaser tinkering with something in the corner. I'm about to announce myself when he glances at me sideways and ever so subtly shakes his head. It's a setup. A contraband patrol. I turn on my heel and walk casually back to my car, gripping my ricochet. I quickly check the rooftops on each side of me. Nothing. I'm about to open my car door when I hear it.

"Stop right there, Dreck," a Lazurite guard commands. I gradually slide my ricochet from my belt.

"Hands up and on your knees. Now! Or are you a pillock Midlander who doesn't understand English?"

I drop to one knee, and what I do next is all in one fluid motion. As I turn my hips towards him, I stretch out my right arm and fling my wrist, sending the ricochet towards his head. He ducks, and it misses, as I figured it would.

"You twit," he says with a smile and raises his plasma rifle at me. He obviously isn't familiar with a ricochet. If he were, he would know by its definition that it is on its way back. Before his long finger pulls the trigger, the ricochet swipes the back of his neck. His exoarmor saves him from being decapitated by the razor-sharp blade, but the voltage of electricity forces him to jerk his spine backward, and he drops his rifle, collapsing to the ground. After my weapon returns to me, I barrel into my pony, fire up its five hundred horses, drop the clutch, and watch the tires smoke just as four Lazurites on speedcycles pull up behind me. This is why I don't have a truck. I rocket down the city street, careful to avoid potholes as the cycles inch closer. They shoot at my tires in vain, as last year I spent a month's pay on airless Graphene no-flats. Even their razortack strips won't stop me.

The Lazurite closest to me fires his plasma gun, shattering my rear window. Shards of glass tumble into my back seat. From my rearview mirror it looks like it is hailing inside my car. There goes five hundred bucks. I sink it into third and veer hard left into an alley. My vehicle caroms across the battered asphalt, compelling the beads of glass to dance on the torn, faded black leather seats. Two pursuers follow me; the other two must have gone ahead to cut me off. I'm banking on the hope that I know these streets better than they do. This industrial section is a grid of one lane, one-way streets. Two of the next five left turns will get me out. In front of me, the other two speedcycles appear. I need to make it to the second left before they reach me, as the other two are close behind. The patrol guard in front of me fires his plasma gun just as I jerk left, pulling up the e-brake. The pulse just misses me as I drift into the alley. If they weren't trying to kill me, I would say this is fun.

To my dismay, blocking the alley is a wayward garbage drop. There is no way I can bust through the giant heap of metal, trash, and debris. In my rearview mirror I spot the four speedcycles whisking towards me. I have no other choice but to leave my magnificent stallion behind. I dive out of the driver's seat and into the alley among an array of plasma blasts. I dart into a six-story abandoned office building. Desks, business cards, and wrecked computers are scattered about, remnants of a once prosperous life. It still smells of moldy ink, old paper, and putrid coffee. A knocked-over water cooler in the corner. I picture suits milling around, talking about whatever businesspeople talk about.

I push my way into the stairwell and scamper up them, taking four at a time, careful not to step on the cat-sized rats sniffing for crumbs. I reach the fifth floor when a plasma blast takes out the step directly in front of me. I peer down and spot a Lazurite scurrying up the steps behind me. I snap my wrist, sending my ricochet flying down at him. It smacks him on the left shoulder, the violent burst of electricity causing him to keel over the railing and fall to the first floor. I wait for my flying voltaic crescent-disc to spin its way back to my hand before my burning quadriceps conquer the last set of stairs.

Busting through the final door, I find myself on the roof. Gravel crunches under my Air Jordans. (Not a shrewd purchase I know, but I had to have them). My sweaty face is pelted by a heavy wind. Below me, a Lazurite lobs a pulse-grenade through the smashed window of my Mustang. I watch my livelihood implode in flames. There is no time to mourn or consider the ramifications of what just occurred as the last Lazurite enters the building. A helidrone is probably minutes away. If they knew who I was, I'm certain they would send a flock of helidrones, as well as a platoon.

My only way out is to jump. The building to my right is about ten feet away but only four stories high. I have done jumps likes this before in my uncle's training camps. Emboldened, my legs move with sinew and grace. At the ledge they catapult me into the air. Maybe I'm not as strong as I used to be. Maybe it's the excess lactic acid in my legs from running up the stairs. Or maybe I was overconfident donning a pair of Jordan's. C'mon, Michael, don't let me down. No matter the case, I'm not going to fully make it. I stretch out my arms and nudge my head forward, bringing my body into the diving position. This gives me just enough distance for my outstretched fingers to clasp onto the ledge of the building I had hoped to land on. My massive callouses act like glue.

Then I hear a whizzing. Seems when I slammed against the building, my ricochet was knocked loose from my belt. The whiz I hear is it falling to the ground. But now it is making its way back up to the transponder on my wrist. I have to catch it, or it will hit me. That means freeing one of my hands. It's spinning its way back up towards me at a pretty good clip. When it's ten feet away from reaching me, I slide one of my hands from the ledge and ready to catch it. I'm silently thanking my uncle for the callouses and strong fingers that allow me to hang one-handed in this precarious position. I finally snatch it out of the air and clip it to my belt just as my fingers are about to give out. After pulling myself up, I canter to the door leading to the stairwell, hand on my ricochet, praying the building is empty.

I'm returning empty handed. Boaz will be less than thrilled. But what does that matter now? Without wheels, I'm out of a job.

And gone is my beloved pony.

My dream weaver is a sadist. It's the same dream every night. I watch from afar as a Lazurite patrol parades through the outdoor market. The kind that used to be so prevalent only in Third World countries. The Middle is fifth world. There are no grocery stores to speak of, just outdoor markets and shops run by moms and pops selling their homegrown crops or self-made ceramics just so their families won't starve. A Lazurite swipes a bag of apples from a leather-skinned farmer without paying. It's not uncommon for patrolmen to plunder. Besides, they don't carry cash. Zion uses BitTender. Here in The Middle, we still use good old-fashioned US greenbacks. The Lazurite shoves a gaggle of children playing soccer out of his way before appropriating a handmade sweater from a boutique run by an elderly woman whose gnarled fingers show the wear and tear of knitting thousands of them. She shakes her bony fist and curses at them. I hear him mention something about a present for his wife. Patrolmen are underpaid, even by Zion standards.

Then it happens. Just as the patrol finishes pilfering and reaches the edge of the bazaar, an explosion. Although the blast is small and compact, it wipes out the entire ten-man patrol. Along with them, five children playing soccer. My ears are concussed, not from the blast, but from the soul-crushing sound of wailing mothers. My stomach turns at the cadence of their weeping jowls. A grisly melody that could only be produced by one losing their offspring. Fragments of blood-stained clothing are littered about like confetti. I wretch at the acrid smell of burned flesh. All that survived is the molten soccer ball that rolls to a smoky stop. One of the shocked mothers picks up the still flaming ball and runs off with it as if it were her child. The Sons of Levi may have been responsible, but it was me who sold them the materials to build the bomb. I know I didn't detonate it, but I greased the rails. Their slogan is victory at all costs. But if this is victory, I don't want it. If this is justice, leave me in Zion's shackles. I'm only glad my father isn't alive to witness it.

I wake in a lagoon of sweat. My living quarters in Hostel 322 are not much bigger than a prison cell. Which is maybe where I belong.

It's comprised of four claustrophobic concrete walls, a toilet, and an empty mini fridge. A communal shower down the hall. Wondering if it will work, I flick the light switch. It does. The entire hostel runs off solar power with intermittent rolling brownouts. The cracked mirror reflects my puffy, desolate eyes. It's 2:34 a.m. Not wanting to relive this nightmare, I throw on sweats, a wool coat, a *Goonies* hat, and exit into the narrow hall. The walls are too thick to think. But not thick enough to keep out the pain.

Ten minutes before sunrise, I make it to the top of Mount Caan. Sitting on top of a snowy rock, I watch the sun climb above the mountains. The virgin snow sterilizes my soul. For a moment I feel wiped clean. The moment is fleeting. Cephas tells me I have to stop blaming myself, that if it weren't me, some other contraband mules would have delivered the bomb components. Even so, I told Boaz I would no longer deliver to The Sons of Levi. With my car gone, it's a moot point. What am I going to do? Procure a bike and run smaller items? I can't pay my rent as it is. I have nothing. I could lease a car from Boaz, but my profit margins are already slim. I'd be his slave. Unless of course I start running weapons again to The Sons of Levi who pay top dollar. The higher the risk, the greater the pay, Boaz would say. Like muling guns for The Defiance isn't risky.

My stomach rumbles as I stare west. From here I can see over The Wall and into Zion. Its laundered landscape sparkles. The streets are clean, the potholes have been repaired. My Mustang would have enjoyed its motorways. Somewhere over that wall is my Sarai. My eyes close, my ears hear her say, *Come to me.* Her hands are outstretched, ready to receive me. Her heart as wide as the open expanses before me. My spirit chained without her touch. *Come to me.* Am I to let Sarai be married off to someone else? I stand, the unadulterated snowflakes can't help but melt on my impure flesh. Do I still deserve her? Am I who my uncle believes me to be? A selfish coward with unrealized potential? Or am I my father's son?

I am not sure I can bring myself to fight my uncle's war. Every time I consider it, all I see is more bloodshed, all I hear are the sobs of the now childless mothers at the bazaar.

I cannot fight a war like that.

Sarai watches in revulsion as her father and his roundtable of advisors slurp the raw oysters into their unquenchable gullets. Six imported chandeliers hang over the elongated Victorian dining-room table made from burr walnut. The food is rich and the conversation stale. Her mother, Joanna, a dainty thing ensconced in diamonds and pearls, twirls her curly red hair and scrutinizes Sarai's full plate of oysters.

"Are you not hungry, dear?"

Sarai ignores her and motions to the waiting butler standing at the ready. "Hey Jake, can I get a cheeseburger?"

"Sure thing, my lady."

Joanna is aghast. "A cheeseburger? And his name is Jacob dear, not Jake. It's not toff sounding."

Sarai rolls her eyes, sips her expensive red wine. Her mother frowns at Sarai's faded Def Leppard T-shirt and ripped acid-wash jeans.

"And please wear proper evening attire as opposed to this rubbish. You look like a Dreck, for queen's sake."

Sarai ignores her, listening in on her father's conversation.

"My patrols tell me The Defiance grows by the day," reports Omar, one of Renatus's cronies.

"Tosh," Renatus waves off the statement as if it were a fly.

"As well as their stockpiles of contraband weapons. New black markets are spawning everywhere."

"It's not just weapons I'm concerned with, my learned friend. It's the Bibles and other banned literature. Arm an indifferent man to the teeth and he is worthless, but a man with a cause and a knife is dangerous," Renatus states sagely, clasping his hands as if he was teaching philosophy at a prestigious university.

Omar pours himself another glass, his teeth perfect, his face freckled and pudgy. "What about reassimilation?"

Sarai suppresses a smile as Renatus looks like he's going to fall over. "You want me to turn off The Wall and invite an invasion? Are you bloody mad?"

"Our men grow tired of war."

"War? Our armies are safe, fat, and happy on this side of The Wall."

"Not my patrolmen. Fewer and fewer return. They have not been trained for the type of guerrilla warfare Cephas is waging. And The Sons of Levi are terrorizing our people. Even your own daughter is not immune."

Sarai relishes in the fact that her attempted murder at The Wall is causing turmoil in her father's inner circle.

"The Defiance is a virus," Renatus bellows. "And how do you defeat a virus? You kill it, or you wait it out." He turns to a long-haired Lazurite sitting to his left with a pointy goatee. "Double the narcdrops. Step up the patrols and send in more elites. And find out how their contraband is being procured."

"Yes, my sultan," he responds obediently.

"And their bookstores. Burn them to the ground."

"Of course, my sultan."

"Just as the Nazis did?" Sarai interjects with disgust.

Renatus is losing his patience. "We are dealing with terrorists, my daughter. I'm gob smacked you can't bloody see that."

Uncomfortable by this father-daughter spat, Omar inhales another oyster. "Cephas has spies within our ranks. I fear a manufactured uprising. The Canonization can only distract for so long."

Renatus stares at his daughter. "It's not a distraction, chaps. This year is going to be extra special. My only daughter is going to marry the winner, and the winner is going to lead my armies to victory and annihilate The Defiance once and for all."

"Legion? Is this the year you're going to unleash him?"

"Yes," Renatus states with glee.

Sarai chimes in. "And if I refuse?"

"You're twenty-five and ambling through life. This will no longer be a point of discussion."

A courier enters the room pushing a rolling closet with twenty of the finest dresses money can buy.

"And what timing!" Sarai's mother exclaims. "After dinner, we shall have a smashing good time while you try them on."

"Shall we?" Sarai responds with an icy inflection. She stands, "Pardon my reach," stretches across the table, grabs a bottle of red wine, and saunters over to the dresses. "I do say, red is more my color." With that she pours the entire bottle over the throng of wedding dresses.

A horrified yip escapes Joanna's refined lips as she watches the expensive fabric imbibe what was once delicate grapes grown with great care in what used to be named the Napa Valley. The multitude of white dresses are now stained crimson red. The same color of Renatus's furious cheeks. Omar suppresses a smile.

Sarai's walk turns into a waltz and, once out of sight, turns into a run. By the time she exits the palace, tears slalom down her slim cheeks. She hurries down a rocky hillside until she reaches the beach. She throws off her heels and lets her bare feet settle into the velvety sand. Large whitecaps slam against the rocky shores to her right. She trudges to the edge of the sand where the foamy breakers start to recede. The cold ocean numbs her feet. She wishes it would also numb her heart. The aroma of salt, fish, and decaying seaweed returns her to that fateful day. She slumps to her knees and a vigorous wind mists salt water onto her face, adding to the brine that is her tears. This is where it happened.

She was fourteen; her younger brother Eleazar was nine. He was born with a rare chromosomal cellular disorder. He had a large mouth with wide gaps between his teeth. His eyes and skin were hypopigmented. She used to tell him the white blotches on his skin were the clouds, and he was the radiating sun. His weekly seizures were fierce.

"Why do I shake so much?" he would ask his sister.

"Because you are so full of love, your body cannot contain it," she would answer.

His speech impediments and other developmental delays would keep him from inheriting his father's place at the Seat of Sultans, but that didn't stop Renatus's absolute and unconditional love for him. It was always about Eleazar, his only son, his *wounded prince* he would call him. At first Sarai was jealous, but she too adored Eleazar, his strength, his bravery, his sense of humor, his child-like innocence that was oblivious to this cruel world. He had overcome his deficiencies because he didn't realize he had any. Before Sarai had met Asher, he was her one bright spot.

While her father was off on one of his many conquests and her mother was busy drinking, Sarai would spend most of her time with Eleazar. She didn't want him raised strictly by servants. You could say it was she who raised him. Then her father would come home and dote over him while shunning her. For a long time, Sarai wondered why her brother was so favored until she accepted it.

Sarai remembered how much Eleazar loved the ocean. He wanted to be a dolphin diving through the air, cleaving the waters with its pointy snout.

Frigid and wet to the marrow, Sarai closed her eyes, remembering that fair spring morning when the seas were deceitful. She was tasked with watching Eleazar that day. From the surface, the waters looked relatively calm. But lurking underneath was a dangerous riptide. Before she realized what had happened, Eleazar was being dragged out to sea. She raced out towards him, her hands chopping the water, her feet kicking manically. By the time she had reached his location, it was too late. Eleazar had succumbed to exhaustion, and the ocean yanked him down into its hungry belly.

She screamed his name hysterically, refusing to get into the patrol boat that came to fetch her. Finally, when her arms gave out, a Lazurite guard pulled her to safety. Even then, she had tried to jump back into the cutting ocean. Divers discovered the boy's pale, frozen body hours later. He was instantly taken to The Mountain, where initial attempts to resurrect him failed due to the uniqueness of his medical condition.

Her father's face was a blur when he heard the news. The stinging feeling on her face where he slapped her wasn't. She still bore the tiny indentation left from the backside of his gold rings striking against her high cheekbone. Renatus didn't speak to her for three months, nor did he allow her to go to the funeral. His wounded prince was gone; all that was left was an insubordinate daughter.

Her mother had said nothing.

CHAPTER FOUR

I don't like being back here so soon. The dingy smell, the dreary faces on the Drecks that pass me in the narrow hallway. Cephas's army has outgrown his compound. I turn the corner and stop at the edge of the war room. Cephas, Jude, and other top brass are scrutinizing maps. They are analyzing where and how often The Wall opens for the so-called lucky lottery winners. Digging under it didn't work, and any attempts of flying over The Wall were squashed by anti-aircraft guns and helidrones.

Jude sees me first. "Look who's back? Tired of trash wrangling?"

I smile. "No, still looking for that razor so you can shave those bird nests you refer to as eyebrows."

A loud cackle from Jude's small mouth. "Still have your acid tongue, I see."

Cephas squints his dark eyes, the scars on his face shift as he knows why I'm here.

"Excuse me, gentlemen."

"Don't see any gentleman here," Jude squawks.

Cephas and I trudge down the hall. "You change your mind?" he asks. "Or you out of petrol?"

"I no longer have wheels."

"The 'stang?"

"Long story."

"That's a shame; she was a sweet machine," Cephas says softly, trying to keep it cordial.

"You said she was frivolous," I remind him.

"Maybe so, but that didn't make her any less sweet. How do I miss the sound of American muscle."

Sweet. I chuckle inside at my uncle's attempt at using my vernacular. But at least he is trying.

"You?" I ask, surprised.

"I had 2050 Corvette Stingray when I was your age. It was junk when I found it, but my uncle helped me rebuild it. Sixteen cylinder. Got about a meter a gallon."

"Wouldn't have figured they were still making gas engines then."

"Not many . . . anyway, why are you here?"

I stare at his pelican tattoo. "You want my blood? You can have it."

"I knew you'd come."

"Liar," I say, still not believing I'm here.

"I sure as heck couldn't send Jude."

"If I agree to this folly, and become Amos, how do I get into the Canonization? He's a simple patrolman. Only the warrior elites, sons of senators, and the wealthy get in."

Cephas rubs the deep chasm in his chin. "You mean Amos the Great? The man who killed the last remaining son of The Defiance? Zion will welcome that Amos with open arms as a hero. The slayer of Silas's offspring."

I am starting to see the merit in a plan I originally deemed ludicrous. But why me? I'm not qualified to survive such trials, to defeat the elite warriors of Zion. Cephas surely believes the training I received in his makeshift camps will suffice. But Jude is right; I am a simple trash dredger. Cephas senses my trepidation.

"He doesn't call the equipped, son. He equips the called."

His good book tells him I have been called by God. And maybe I have been, but my motives are less than pure. I'm doing this for Sarai, not for him or his Defiance. Besides, I don't expect to survive the Canonization. But it is worth it if I can see Sarai just once more. Cephas folds his meaty arms, waiting for my confirmation.

"I guess I'm a pelican now."

An hour later I pose in a pool of fake blood. Cephas takes numerous photos. They draw a vial of my blood for further proof. I stare at the photos of my dead self and wonder if this is a harbinger of things to come.

Bloodletting is acutely painful. Two transfusion tubes are hooked up to both Asher and Amos. Cephas watches as Amos writhes in agony, while Asher remains stoic. *Boy always did have a high tolerance for pain*, Cephas thinks. For Asher to pass as Amos, he will need his blood and DNA. He will be heavily scrutinized by Zion upon his return. Not only that, but he will need Amos's DNA to sync to his exoarmor suit.

"Zion will hunt you down and exterminate you for the bloody rats that you are!" Amos grits through his teeth.

"Shut him up," Asher growls.

"Almost finished," one of Cephas's physicians announces.

Amos is horrified as he watches Asher's blood snake its way through the tube and into his bloodstream, "I'd rather die than carry the inferior blood of a feck-witted Dreck."

"That can be arranged," Asher replies, the pain grating at his composure.

The physician checks one of his monitors. "And done."

Asher exhales as the tubes are being pulled out of him. He now has Lazurite blood coursing through his veins.

"You will pay dearly for this!" Amos shrieks.

"Get this cell pirate out of my sight," Cephas orders.

Two Drecks grab Amos.

"Take him to the prison at site four."

"Yes sir," they respond.

As they march Amos out, the Sculptor strides in carrying a black bag. A gangly man with coarse silver hair, spaghetti noodle arms, and a bulky nose.

"Just in time," Cephas utters. "I trust you weren't followed?"

"Of course not."

Asher eyes the Sculptor's jittery hands.

"You're the Sculptor? Your hands are shakier than a hell duster."

Before he can answer, Cephas interjects. "Not to worry. Call it pregame jitters. Once he begins, he's as steady as a brick house."

"You've used him before?" asks Asher.

Cephas can't lie. "No. But Jude says he comes highly recommended."

"One of Jude's finds. Wonderful."

"Relax, Asher, everything is going to be fine." Cephas feigns confidence.

"Easy for you to say, Uncle, you're not about to be carved up by Doctor Jitterbug."

"At least he's a handsome fella, could've been worse, he could've looked like Jude." Cephas is referring to Amos, the man Asher is about to be sculpted to resemble.

"Or my uncle."

Cephas relishes in the fact that even as he is about to go under the knife, then sent into the lion's den, Asher hasn't lost his sense of humor, dry and sometimes biting as it is.

Asher regards the Sculptor's *Doctor Who* T-shirt. "You know, wearing that shirt doesn't make you a doctor."

The Sculptor ignores him and preps his array of tools. Laser scalpels for minimal scarring, a bone file, faux bone fragments for shaping. And bone glue.

"How long will this take?"

"Depends how stubborn your bone is," the Sculptor replies with a gleeful smile.

"We know his skull is thick," Cephas says in jest, tapping his fingers on Asher's head.

"Runs in the family."

Cephas leads Asher to the operating table. "It's time, Son." Cephas can see the acrimony in his eyes, the unforgiveness. He wants to say something inspiring, something loving and comforting, but speeches aren't his thing. One of the physicians injects an anesthetic into Asher's IV tube.

"In twenty seconds you'll be out."

"And a Dreck no more," Asher whispers as his eyes flutter, then finally close.

Cephas watches the Sculptor go to work, steady hands and all. A massive photo of Amos's face hangs on the wall. The Sculptor continually references the photo, then makes adjustments. Shaves some bone here, adjusts the nose a bit there.

"You know it would be so much simpler if I just had his skull," the Sculptor announces referring to Amos.

"I'm not sure what you have heard, but we are not The Sons of Levi. I won't murder that man." Cephas replies, irritated by the suggestion. "The photo will do."

"Pity."

Cephas wonders how it has come to this. This great country was once a beacon of light, a haven for freedom. Now it has slipped backwards into despotism and slavery fueled by greed, negligence, and the want to be immortal. *We closed our eyes and let it happen.*

Cephas shakes his head and trudges towards Asher's sleeping body, his face contorted and lacerated. Skin cut, stretched, and hanging. No more can he look upon his nephew and see his brother's face. He grasps his Bible and prays Asher makes it through the sculpting alive. It aches him to know that he is potentially bringing more hurt to his nephew. There is no going back now. His crazy plan has been set in motion. *Bold plan*, he tells himself.

He closes his eyes and remembers his old self, a wicked man possessed by the DemonTonic. Stumbling home in a stupor, whipping Asher with his belt until his serrated skin bled. All for forgetting to take out the trash. Waking him in the middle of the night so he could clean his boots. The welts he left were more than skin deep. Contusions on his soul. God has changed him, and he has told Asher many times that he is sorry. *Have I truly shown repentance?* A lone tear battles its way through the crags and crevices of Cephas's face.

"I am truly sorry, boy," he says with a whisper as he approaches Asher's feet. He gently removes Asher's muddy boots, careful not to disturb the Sculptor lost in his art.

Cephas slides down against the wall in the corner until he is on his knees. He removes a red handkerchief from his back pocket and begins to spit-shine Asher's grimy boots.

It has been three weeks since my transformation. I peer into the mirror and see the Lazurite staring back at me. It's a surreal feeling donning the pelt of my enemy. It knots my stomach. Unless I'm re-sculpted, this is my new face, the one I'll live with the rest of my life. Which will probably be short anyway. At least he's a handsome chap. The swelling is gone, and the scarring is essentially nonexistent. Apparently, Dr. Who does good work.

I have spent most of my recovery watching video of interviews and interrogations of Amos. I need to master his speech patterns, his cadence, his mannerisms, who his family is. How he annoyingly taps his chin with his left index finger when nervous. His pompous gait. How he pulls on his right earlobe when he's deep in thought, assuming there is an intellect rolling around in there somewhere. From my experience, there isn't much depth to these patrol types. Or for Lazurite soldiers in general. Elitism breeds ignorance. Our eyes are a similar hue, so colored contacts won't be necessary. Certainly, his family thinks he is dead. In true Lazurite fashion I will return alive, and a hero. I only hope it is enough to get me into the Canonization.

Returning as Amos, the murderer of her beloved, Sarai will

surely loathe the sight of me. At least I will be able to look upon her with unfettered eyes. My eyes. And who knows? If I'm not chosen, maybe one day I can work at the palace as a servant and reveal who I really am to her. That would surely piss Cephas off. But I'm getting ahead of myself.

Today is the day I don Amos's exoarmor suit. I snap my ricochet to my belt; I will show it to Zion as a trophy taken from Asher, along with a vial of my blood and pictures of my death. The plan is to give Zion information on one of our older base camps to enhance my credibility. We have made it look like it was recently evacuated. Cephas trots into my recovery room with Jude next to him.

Cephas asks, "Ready?"

"I think so."

Cephas taps my exoarmor suit. "Our techs haven't yet been able to hack into the exoarmor suit you brought us. Seems that won't be an option for The Defiance. You, my boy, are our last hope."

Talk about no pressure.

Jude pipes in. "What about the Fort Worth Armory?"

Cephas waves him off. "The armory is a myth, a legend. Let's not pin our hopes on a fable. We shall be victorious with what God has provided us."

The legend of the Fort Worth Armory has been talked about since The Wall went up. Lore has it that somewhere in Fort Worth, of the former state of Texas, is an underground bunker from the Civil War era, and inside its belly is an entire horde of nineteenth-century arms. Guns, rifles, muskets, ammunition. A windfall for The Defiance as Zion's exoarmor wasn't designed to stop such weaponry. Rumor has it there is even a map pinpointing its location. The area has been searched and probed without a trace of any such weapons cache. Even if it were found, the odds of its contents being viable would be less than favorable.

"I'll walk you to the first marker. From there, you should run into a patrol by the time you reach The Wall." Cephas informs me.

Jude hands me a day's ration, which I stuff into a bag hooked to my utility belt. These Lazurite outfits are nifty. I feel like Batman. Jude pats my shoulder, "Godspeed, son of Silas."

I consider a sarcastic reply, but then I think better of it as he is making a rare but genuine attempt at sincerity. I think of my father and manage a smile in return.

"It's time." Cephas leads me out of the room through the various tunnels of his underground compound until we finally march up the stairs and into the red barn. From there we exit into the crisp morning air. It's an hour of awkward silence until we reach marker one. I speak first.

"If by some miracle I survive the Canonization, then what?"

Cephas clears his throat. "I have many spies inside Zion. Your contact is named Darius, a logistics and communications officer inside Zion's first army. He will be our go-between for updates."

"And if I win and I'm given my own battalion?" I say with a healthy dose of skepticism.

"You must earn the soldiers' trust. Show them the truth about Renatus. But most importantly, you must lead them. If you can do that successfully, they will follow you anywhere."

"I have never led men before."

"It's not difficult, really. The best leaders are servants. Remember that and you'll do just fine."

I don't remember Cephas being much of a servant, at least not in his early years. I look out to The Wall just a few miles west and exhale through my teeth. "I still can't believe you talked me into this cockeyed plan."

Cephas glares at me sideways.

"Oh, did I say that out loud?" I smile.

"I have faith in you. Just remember, you're now a Lazurite through and through. You need to talk like them, act like them."

"Fight like them."

Cephas grabs my shoulder, "No, Son. Fight like a man whose

freedom has been stolen. Whose belly is barren, whose lips thirst for justice, whose spirit has been wrongly enslaved, whose loved ones have been ripped from their arms. Fight like a Dreck."

The poignant moment is drowned out by the whooshing sound of a helidrone in the distance. We scamper to the cover of trees and wait until it passes overhead. I peer down at my boots and can see my reflection. Odd I didn't notice them earlier. They shimmer in the sunlight. They have been shined cleaned. I peer up at my uncle and smile. And with that, no more words are spoken between us. By myself I trudge towards The Wall and wonder if this is the last time I will see my uncle or my birthplace. It's a strange feeling carrying pictures of my death and a vial of my own blood. I only hope it's enough to punch my ticket into the Canonization.

Either way, I'm marching blindly into the lion's den.

CHAPTER FIVE

Renatus's lifeless body lies impacted in the soft soil. Every bone is shattered. His lungs and heart have been crushed. His organs disintegrated. The parachute strapped to his back sits unopened. Renatus loves skydiving, to fly next to the clouds, the wind in his face, watching the world rush towards him at such a ferocious velocity. He likes to have a God's-eye view. It's one of the few places he doesn't think of his precious Eleazar, his wounded prince. He is a perpetual thrill seeker, a daredevil, and why wouldn't he be? If there's a mishap as there was today, they would just take him up to The Mountain.

Two of Renatus's elite commandos cringe as they pull his broken body from the three-foot hole his impact has made. It is like ripping melted rubber off hot asphalt. His cold skin depresses in their strong grip, his bones like crumbled chalk.

"Feels like clay," one of the commandos states.

"Think he did it on purpose?" the other asks.

"What?"

"Not open the parachute."

"I wouldn't be surprised. Remember the motorcycle jump?"

"How could I forget? I had to retrieve his head."

They load his corpse into the back of a military truck. His body bounces in the back as the truck climbs up The Mountain. Armed sentinels and helidrones patrol the perimeter. The truck crawls to a stop in front of a massive five-foot-thick steel door. It slides open, and the truck treks inside the belly of The Mountain. Renatus is loaded onto a gurney and taken to an elevator where a coterie of doctors and scientists bring him twelve stories underground.

They wheel him past the myriad of bodies frozen in cryogenic chambers. Thousands of them. These are the lucky lottery winners. The Drecks Renatus has been harvesting. This is the dirty little secret most of Zion and The Middle do not know. A secret reserved for the powerful, the wealthy, Zion's elite. That second-life protocol is alive and well. What is also veiled from most of society is the process. To give life, life must be taken. And according to Renatus, Drecks are expendable. Secrecy is paramount. Divulging what really happens here is a capital offense.

Renatus's rubbery body is carefully slid into a sealed glass chamber. One of the doctors pecks at his computer. The chamber is then filled with a translucent, pink, gel-like substance. He looks as if he's entombed in Jell-O. Cold robotic arms insert wires and tubes throughout his body. A large tube is inserted into his mouth and is snaked down his throat. Next to him, encased in a cryogenic chamber, is a Dreck who three short months ago thought he had been chosen to live an aristocratic life of opulence in shiny Zion. Now he is about to be reaped for his LifeCell. Doctors insert a massive needle into his heart and inject nano-bots into his bloodstream. These near-microscopic, rapacious, life-stealing robots find the Dreck's LifeCell and pluck it from his body, instantly killing him. These nano goblins will then deliver the plundered LifeCell to Renatus's waiting corpse.

Forty years ago, a scientist specializing in cloning accidentally discovered a hidden cell that activated and enhanced stem cell regeneration technology. It was deemed the Lazurite cell and became known as simply The LifeCell. It is the basis of second-life protocol, what is used to regenerate and resurrect the dead. The cost of leaving God out of the equation.

For two weeks, Renatus will lie in the eerie luminous sediment while the pilfered LifeCell, combined with other cloning activators, rebuilds his heart, lungs, bones, and skin. An expensive process costing others who can afford it up to five million BitTender. More when the supply is low. Omar and a select few generals will run Zion while he's out, with the stipulation that no new laws are created or major decisions made. Just day-to-day affairs.

Now the only thing Renatus fears is running out of Drecks, he likes to say jokingly. This is the main reason he hasn't used any nuclear weapons against The Middle. He would be destroying his future supply of LifeCells. A society that no longer feared death did not fear God. The spawning grounds of noxious corruption and evil. Renatus sees himself as the deity of Zion, the giver of life. He has skirted mortality, made creation his own. A power man wasn't meant to wield. Consequences unforeseen by man's limited scope of eternal operations. For in our world, time is linear.

But for all this power, he is still unable to bring his beloved Eleazar back to life. After a dozen unsuccessful attempts, his scientists informed him they would need another child with Eleazar's same chromosomal cellular disorder to duplicate the boy. Since then he had ordered his men to increase the harvest numbers, each and every child to be tested until they find a match. His prince couldn't be the only wounded one.

And if The Middle doesn't provide him with one, maybe Zion will?

Sarai was a distance caster. Something Asher had taught her. She enjoyed the whine of the fishing reel as she swung the pole back and launched her bait. She watches the herring land into the smooth ocean three hundred feet from Renatus's swanky yacht. The skies are a hazy blue as the sun flounders against the fog. In the distance, a gray whale breaches the icy waters like a missile leaving its silo, then lands on its back, creating a voluminous splash. She loved the fact that the largest animal in the ocean was as harmless as a crustacean. That it didn't use its size and might in a predatory fashion. If it so pleased, it could crush her father's colossal vessel filled with champagne and caviar as if it were made of toothpicks. Her hatred of the ocean stemmed from the death of Eleazar. But she loved to fish. To blindly sink your line into the deep, never knowing what you might pull up. In a small way it scratched her itch for adventure. It gave her a sense of freedom and self-reliance. She could catch it, clean it, and cook it herself; she didn't have to depend on her father's colony of worker-ant servants. It also reminded her of Asher's proposal.

Twice a week they would fish on a small mountain lake in the foothills of the mighty Rockies. Asher would drag his paltry metal boat, built from scraps found in the refuse dumps, from a hidden enclave a hundred yards east of the lake. They affectionately called it the SS *Salvage*. They would spend the day reeling in perch and largemouth bass. The still, quiet mornings would numb the lake, and the only ripples in the water were their bait being dropped or a fish flopping on its belly. Breezy afternoons would deliver the seductive fragrance of jasmine and lavender. It was like God had whittled them a small portion of paradise. A friendly competition emerged in respect to size and fish count. It was Sarai who would normally come out on top.

Asher's proposal had almost gone awry on an early morning in mid-May while drifting on his seaworthy scrap metal. Normally he would bait Sarai's hook as well as his own. Not that Sarai needed him to, but she knew he enjoyed the chivalrous act and was happy to oblige. Besides, it gave him something to do while he was being out fished. She was mesmerized by the sun shimmering on the lake that looked like diamonds dancing on the water. She hadn't noticed the scant diamond ring Asher had tied to her line. She dropped her line in the water and leaned back against his chest; she could feel his pounding heart. His hands clammy with sweat. She wondered why he was so nervous. Without bait and a hook, he hadn't counted on her catching something, but the glint of the ring had attracted a fifteen-pound largemouth bass that swallowed it whole. Asher almost fainted when he saw her line go rigid and her pole bend as if it were going to snap in half. She remembered how he nervously yelled for her to reel it in. "DON'T LOSE IT!" She couldn't understand why he was preparing to jump in and catch the fish with his bare hands. Again he yelled for her to reel it in. After a few minutes and to Asher's relief, she safely landed the magnificent beast.

"For the love of Pete, look at the size of that thing! What did you bait me with? A magic worm?" Sarai had asked.

Asher smiled. "Let me show you." He took out his knife and cut open the belly of the large fish and carefully pulled out the engagement ring.

"What is that?" Sarai couldn't make it out as it was covered in blood and fish guts.

Asher quickly cleaned it in the lake and held it up. "Will you marry me? Will you be my eternity mate?"

She couldn't help but laugh at the proposal that had almost gone terribly wrong.

Asher also giggled. "This idea was so much better in my head. I was thinking it would be a metaphor . . . for you're the only fish in the sea for me and—"

"Shut up, of course I will," she said through tears and laughter. "Besides, it will make a great fishing lure if you ever piss me off." She slid on the fetid-smelling ring, and they kissed for what seemed like a lifetime.

"What would have you done if the line broke or the fish got off?" she asked.

Asher pulled out a Ring Pop—a plastic ring with a candy on top. "No worries; I had a backup plan."

"An engagement ring and sugar! I like this even better."

"Then I can return the diamond?"

"Funny guy. Now will you dance with me? Now that I'm your fiancée?" Sarai asked with an alluring smile.

"Not a chance," Asher answered through a smile.

She remembered how he hated to dance and how it was a running joke between them. She would always ask, sometimes even try to trick him into doing the tango or the Texas two-step by grabbing his hand and shuffling her feet a certain way. That day couldn't have been more perfect, even if that fish had made off with the ring that now hangs on a necklace around her neck. Besides, she was a firm believer that every proposal should have a good story behind it.

Sarai is roused back in time by the mumbling and excited chatter from the staff as they gather around the holotube. They go silent as she approaches. On the monitor is video footage of Amos being paraded through the streets. She listens to the front man for Zion West News, or ZWN.

"Amos, who was believed to be dead just days ago, is now being celebrated in the streets of Zion as the slayer of the Son of Silas. He didn't have the body, but along with pictures, he carried with him a vial of Asher's blood."

Sarai's knees buckle. Her heart ruptures. Her soul contorts.

"SHUT IT OFF!" Sarai wails.

The staff is too shocked to move as they have never seen her lose her composure. She is always so friendly with them.

"Shut it off!"

One of the staff flicks off the holotube as the rest scatter. Sarai falls to her knees and pounds the deck of the boat with clenched fists. Her fingernails dig into her palms until they weep blood. *First Eleazar, now Asher. Zion, the land of plenty, has taken everything from me.* The winds spawn heavy rollers as the boat begins to rock. Even the ocean is angry. That, or it is mocking Sarai's loss once again. Her bereavement quickly transforms into revulsion as the realization hits her. If this man Amos wins the Canonization, she would be forced to marry the butcher of her beloved. She retches.

Again and again.

I'm awed at how clean the streets are, how manicured the landscape. Then again, trash isn't airdropped into their cities. Drug needles aren't strewed about. I could be barefoot if I wanted to. The crowds cheer my name—or the name of the man I'm pretending to be. "Amos! Amos! Slayer of the Son of Silas!"

Even the elite guards laud me. "Death to The Defiance," yells another. It's an eerie feeling watching the crowd celebrate my death. Blood lust swirls in their eyes like leaves in a tornado as they pump their fists into the air. A man dressed in a dapper suit and a ridiculously tall top hat shakes my hand, "Brilliant work, mate, well done!" I'm a stranger in a strange land. The air is dead and the branches on the birch trees droop as if bowing to me.

"Do you think you can win?" a man to my left screeches. I assume he is talking about the Canonization. I ignore the question, but a plump fellow near him answers, "Don't be daft! No one can defeat Legion!"

I pan the crowd, unrealistically hoping to spot Sarai. Folly. Why would she be here? To slay Amos maybe. But it doesn't stop me from looking.

"How was he vanquished?" another asks.

I unsnap my ricochet from my belt and hold it up. This riles them further. My armed escorts take me to the center of town until we reach the part I have been dreading. Waiting there is Amos's family. You can tell by their dress that they are Zion's lowest class but still three classes above anything in The Middle. Amos's mother embraces me, and tears flow. Her hair wiry and curly, her eyes bronze.

"We thought you were dead."

His father is short, and so is his hair, which tells me he might be a tad anti-establishment. Most Lazurite men proudly flaunt their locks. He approaches me and holds out his hand proudly. "Welcome home, Son."

"Thank you, sir."

"Sir?" He looks perplexed.

I screwed up already.

"Since when do you call me sir?" he responds, sounding offended.

I try to replicate Amos's mannerisms. I tap my chin with my left index finger. "Military habit, Father." He shrugs it off, but Amos's brother, not so much. He examines me up and down, my soul. I tug on my earlobe as Amos would, but I'm pretty sure I look awkward as I think I'm overdoing it. *Just settle down.*

"Brother," he says coldly.

"Daniel," I say with a smile and shake his hand. Did I see him twitch? His grip is harder than it needs to be for such an occasion.

"You really going to try your hand at the Canonization?" he asks like I'm a fool.

"Yes," I reply simply, trying not to say too much.

"Never knew you had a death wish."

"I think I have a fair chance."

He guffaws. "Everyone here may be gobsmacked by your latest accomplishments, but you're still the little brat whose nose I used to bloody."

"I remember," I lie.

"She's not that pretty." He rolls his eyes, referring to the prize, Sarai.

Yes she is, fool.

Amos's mother grabs my hands. "Your brother is right, Amos; we thought you were dead once. Don't waltz into certain death. Be satisfied with what you are."

I don't respond. I just want this conversation to end before I get trapped into saying something that isn't true.

"Please," she begs. "I can't mourn you again."

I need to talk like them, act like them. "If you will excuse me, I'm proper knackered from my trip, I must rest now."

His father looks irritated. "Surely you'll come for tea?"

"Another time," I lie.

Amos's brother eyes me suspiciously as I'm escorted into a military Jeep bound for orientation. Perhaps he is right. Maybe I do have a death wish. What chance does an untrained Dreck from The Middle have? I feign optimism, and it helps. Would Cephas have really sent me if he didn't believe I had a chance? Or is this a last-chance ploy from a desperate old man?

Damn. His name is Derrick. Not Daniel.

My parents' executioner paces in the middle of the massive coliseum, his hands folded behind his back. The sun bounces off his shiny head. "Welcome to the last Canonization of the century," Renatus bellows. "As you well know, this year's winner will not only lead my third army, but they will have the privilege of taking my daughter's hand in marriage." I wince at the thought. It takes everything I have not to fling my ricochet at his exposed jugular. But what good would it do? He would head back to The Mountain, and I would be executed.

In the middle of the coliseum jut two massive towers. Each is over twenty stories high, both painted gold and made of steel. Renatus pans the crowd of about a hundred hopefuls, mostly soldiers trained from birth, but some intellectuals, some hopefuls, others just dreamers. I am somewhere in the middle.

"Behind me stands Sophocles' Towers," he explains. *Sophocles?* I wonder if he means The Riddle of the Sphinx in *Oedipus Rex*, written by Sophocles. My interest is piqued.

Renatus turns on his heel and crisply marches towards the towers. "Inside you will find a bounteous amount of challenges, puzzles, feats of strength. Your body and your intellect will be tested. The man who is to lead my armies and take my only daughter as his bride must prove his intelligence along with his fortitude. Brute strength will only get you so far. Is it one of you?"

My challengers size up one another. Next to me is a kid no older than nineteen. His hands and legs shake. Anxious eyes border on terror; it's obvious he doesn't want to be here. I hold out my hand,

"I'm Amos."

He turns to me, his soft, trembling hand barely clasping mine. "I'm . . . my name . . . my name is Kenan, I . . . I know who you are," he stutters. He has the body of an accountant or a politician, not a warrior. I wonder if his stutter is spawned from fear or if he suffers from a speech impediment. His thick black hair is shorter than most, which could just be preference, or it could be a small, silent gesture of defiance against Zion's tyranny. Either way, the boy has, no doubt, been forced into this by his parents. I turn back to the towers and wonder what kind of demented game awaits us inside. Renatus loves the sport of it all, so it is probably his design; it usually is. Months and outrageous sums of money are spent planning and preparing for this event. Soon thousands will be seated in these stands, watching us battle for our lives. It is Rome all over again.

You can't help but give Renatus your full attention. His cadence is soothing, his words inviting, his gestures charismatic. Most evil is veiled under such traits.

"What if no one wins?" a young soldier from the crowd yells out.

Renatus paces and nods. "Interesting question, young man. Have you forgotten this is Zion! You are Lazurites! That kind of pessimistic thinking isn't what made us great. I can already tell by your question that you have no chance. So, I will do you a favor and spare you. You may leave, soldier."

He just sits there confused, as if Renatus is joking.

"Leave!"

He finally does. And although he probably wouldn't have survived, I feel bad for the kid who must face his parents and explain why he was ousted, shaming his family.

The Lazurite way.

Well, one down.

"For the one cunning enough to survive Sophocles' Tower and its mystery, you will face one last crucible, a final audition if you will." Renatus purses his lips and feigns a long pause for effect. You can tell he has been waiting for this moment for some time. Concrete doors lethargically slide open. The faint sound of drums can be heard from somewhere inside the dark walls. I feel as if something terrible is about to be unleashed. Kenan's legs shake uncontrollably as he senses it too. Renatus makes no attempt to hide his jubilance. From the open doors emerges a mountain of a man. His legs like redwood trees. His arms like concrete pillars. He is seven foot one. He is dashing and stalwart. His blond hair long like Samson's. His eyes a lake of fire, his breath like brimstone. He is the harbinger of death. The usher of pain. A chaperon of destruction. His resume of slaughter is unmatched.

He is Legion.

CHAPTER SIX

We nosh at the communal mess hall. The food isn't great, but it's better than the dry, tasteless bars I'm used to consuming in The Middle. I examine the Lazurites around me. Most have perfect table manners. Gone is the bravado that was displayed at the coliseum before the arrival of Legion. Now some display the quietness of veiled fear. Kenan sits across from me, his eyes in his lap as he slowly eats; it is obvious he is used to much finer fare. He is not a wordy fellow, which for the moment is fine by me, as I too was rattled by Legion. My mind is filled with trepidation as I wonder what I'm doing here? Perhaps I should return to Reservation 9 and go back to peddling contraband for Boaz? Has my uncle really pinned all his hopes on me? How dare he lay such a burden upon my shoulders. My defeat and demise is more than likely in this grotesque competition; it will be the end of The Defiance and, with it, my father's legacy. If Silas were alive, would he have sent me?

But then thoughts of Sarai flood my mind, and I drown in them. Who would I be if I let her be forced to marry someone else in this room? Some barbarian. Although I doubt she would go along with it, and even if she did, surely she would make the poor chap's life miserable. Chap? Listen to me; I'm already sounding like a Lazurite. I set my food aside as the mere thought of it makes me nauseous.

Our orientation was wrapped up by a pudgy administrator with oily olive hair. For the next week we are to live in the bowels of the coliseum where we can train, study, become acclimated to the weapons we will be using along with simulators on what we might find inside the towers. The administrator marches in. I wonder how he keeps his balance; his feet are the size of a child's. "Listen up, now would be a good time to choose a bunkmate; tomorrow will be a long day."

I glance up at Kenan, and he just nods. I am relieved as he doesn't exude that pompous, prideful confidence of most Lazurites. I peer around and notice most have already shrugged off the fear of Legion. They smugly expect to succeed. Those growing up privileged aren't allowed to experience failure. Suffering is where pride and arrogance go to die. This is where I have the advantage of being the only Dreck in the room. Suffering is our birthright.

Two hours later I rest my head on a sliver of cotton that's disguised as a pillow. The bed is rock hard. The room has four concrete walls with no windows. It's not as bad as my place back home, though. I peer across the room where Kenan lies in his bed. His thin blanket flutters as he appears to be shaking underneath. Is he cold or scared? Most likely both.

"You okay?" I ask.

He doesn't answer.

"You know who I am. What's your story, mate?"

"My . . . my . . . father . . . he . . . is a senator," Kenan stutters.

"And you don't want to be here?" I guess.

He hesitates to answer.

"We're mates now. You can be honest with me. If I'm being truthful, I almost pissed myself when I saw Legion in the flesh."

"My father, he . . . he forced me. I'm . . . I'm supposed to make . . . make my family proud. But I'm not brave . . . brave like you, Amos. I'm scared."

"You would be a fool not to be. I'm scared too, but showing up while afraid is the definition of courage." I sound like my father. I miss him. I even miss Jude. My uncle? Not yet.

"Do . . . do you think you have a chance?"

"As much as the next guy, I suppose. We both do."

"It's bloody tosh if you ask me."

I notice that as he gets more comfortable, his stutter subsides. And he is correct; it is nonsense. The entire spectacle is. But I'm not here for the glory or the accolades; I'm here for Sarai. For me it's more than personal, and I'm hoping that gives me the edge. Kenan went on to tell me how his family lost almost everything in the second BitTender crash of 2085 and that their family name is still propped up by the legend of his two brothers, who both died fighting Drecks like myself. One of them even won this absurd contest five years ago. His father is sending a sheep to slaughter to bolster the family name. Are all Lazurites as ruthless as Renatus?

I roll over and think about my parents and how they met with Renatus under false pretenses, that they were to enter into peace talks, but once their convoy arrived, they were murdered. My father's weakness was that he was too trustworthy. Much like me, my mother was the skeptic of the family and had tried to talk Silas out of the meeting. So did my uncle. They were both convinced it was a trap, but my father was convinced it was worth it if it meant there was the slightest chance at peace. Therefore, his sacrifice would not be in vain, he told me. Renatus doesn't know the meaning of the word *sacrifice*. If history has taught me anything, without sacrifice, there is no peace. Without death, there is no penance.

I shake the painful past from my head, like a dog shaking water from its fur, and force myself into the present. Images of Legion submerge my brain. This giant was the most feared and fierce of Zion warriors. He would slay not individuals but swaths of men in battle. He had no desire for power or wealth, only a blood lust. Rumor has it Legion was orphaned at a young age, fending for himself in Zion's back alleys, fighting full-grown men for money at the age of twelve. Slaying elites at fifteen. Renatus took him under his wing, trained him, and honed him into the killing machine he now is. Sent him to school so he could learn to read and write. That he was nonverbal until Renatus acted as his father. Tomorrow I will visit the archives and view old footage of his battles and try to discover a weakness if any. He is Goliath.

I am David without a slingshot.

Cephas watches the yellow sun turn orange as it sets behind the mountain. He is perched atop his favorite rock, his Bible in his lap. By himself with nature is when he feels closest to God. No draggers to be heard or helldusters to be seen. Just the wind at his sore back and the last of the day's sun upon his leathered face. He is an impatient man who would rather be doing anything else other than waiting. But wait he does for Asher and the Canonization. Waiting on Jude and his techs, who are still trying to hack into the exoarmor suit. All in God's timing, he tells his people. He wishes he could heed his own advice. He is beginning to second guess his plan and wonders if it is his or the Almighty's? Sometimes to tell the difference one had to simply be quiet and wait.

"What are you doing?" Jude sidles up behind him.

"You scared the wits out of me, boy! What do you think I'm doing?" Cephas isn't in the mood for Jude's sarcasm.

"I don't know? Talking to yourself again?"

"What do you want, Jude?"

Jude holds up the exoarmor suit that Asher had brought them before he left. "Techs think they made a breakthrough."

Cephas, now interested, stands. "Has it been tested?"

"Not yet. I thought you would want to see it, if you're not too busy watching the grass grow or the sun die."

"Perhaps you should put it on for the initial trial?" Cephas pushes his tongue deep into his wide, wrinkled cheek.

Jude cackles and hangs the exoarmor suit on a branch of a nearby pine tree. "You want the honors?"

Jude hands him a stolen plasma gun, and Cephas takes aim.

"Maybe we should pray first?" Jude asserts, sounding serious for the first time today.

"I have been all day," Cephas responds, then fires the plasma gun. The energy ray hits the middle of the suit dead on. Instead of absorbing the energy, the suit dissolves into lava-hot particles.

"Um . . . I guess it was just a breakthrough in theory," Jude says, managing a smile.

Cephas peers to the heavens, "Theory isn't going to win this war."

"You think Asher is?"

"I don't know."

Then the whir of a helidrone. About a hundred yards in front of them. Cephas vaults up and begins to truck towards it.

"Where you going?" Jude asks, baffled as to why Cephas is heading towards the drone.

"The suit!" he mutters back.

Before Cephas can reach the exoarmor suit, a five-man Lazurite patrol appears.

"Cephas! Get back here!" Jude wails.

Cephas lumbers on until shots of plasma strike the trees, just missing his head and chest. He finally stops and turns, slogging back up the hill, wishing he would have exercised a bit more as a young man. He fires back at the patrol with his COLT 45, chafed that he is wasting his precious ammo. Jude bounds down the hill, whips out his crossbow, and lays down covering fire, just enough for Cephas to reach him.

"I brought the Jeep," Jude tells him.

They weave in and out of the trees until they reach the dirt road at the bottom of the other side of the hill, where Jude's Jeep awaits. Plasma shots explode around them as they hop in and Jude fires up the engine. Minutes later they are out of range and in relative safety, although the helidrone is still in the area.

"We lost the suit!" Cephas says irately, wanting more testing to be done.

"Maybe if you ran a bit faster?"

Sleep is a distant memory. We are marched into the middle of the coliseum. Rubbing my eyes, I trudge more than march. It's 5:30 a.m., and a stubborn morning chill lingers. Breakfast was divine—pancakes, sausage, and biscuits. At least for me and what I'm used to, I wonder what Lazurites usually eat? I heard a few complain that this morning's grit wasn't fit for a Dreck. This Dreck had seconds. The dour administrator impatiently taps his foot as we gather nearby.

"Good morning, prospects. Today, you are free to train and acclimate yourself to any weapons and simulators that you choose."

Different sections of the arena host a multitude of weapons and targets. Other sections are partitioned off with balance beams and hanging cement boxes that twist and gyrate.

"Just don't hurt yourself . . . yet," the administrator says with a wry smile, exposing for the first time his ivory-white teeth.

"What about the towers?" I ask. "May we go inside them?"

"The towers will be locked until the Canonization begins," the administrator answers. "What's inside them will be a surprise. With that being said, I suggest you familiarize yourself with our simulators. I will say this, balance and agility will be useful, cognitive acumen a necessity."

It is obvious that he is completely enjoying the cryptic nature of what he is telling us. The gaggle of hopefuls scatter to different stations. I walk over to the cement box suspended three feet off the ground by a large cable and nod to the operator. He lowers the box and swings the door open. I jump in and close the door behind me. A lone iridescent blue light illuminates cold concrete walls that are stained with blood. Above me on the ceiling jut about forty rubber spikes; I have to assume they will be steel when we enter the real deal. That explains the stale blood that streaks the walls. If three cups of coffee don't finally wake me, this will. The box suddenly spins and gyrates. The floor quickly becomes the ceiling. I see that the point is to avoid the points. There is just enough room between the faux spikes to place my palms; my feet are planted against the wall, the rubber nails inches from my face. The box performs a quick one-eighty, and my feet slide from the wall. I land on the rubber points, bending them over. If this was the real thing, I would be dead.

Well, that was a confidence booster.

I exit the box, hiding the defeated look on my face.

"How . . . how was it?" Kenan asks.

"Not bad," I lie. "Let's go see what's at the weapons station."

We make our way to the western corner where prospects practice with spears, swords, scourges, and yes, to my delight, a ricochet. Kenan eyes the ricochet, "Your weapon of choice?"

"That's how I took out Asher. Have you ever used one?"

"No."

"What's your preference, mate?"

He doesn't answer, just stares blankly at the ground.

"Let me guess, you've never used any of them?" I ask incredulously.

"Never."

I don't want him to win, but I don't want him to die either. That is if he makes it that far.

"Let's start with the ricochet. Grab it here and pull your arm back like this."

He does.

"No, hold it vertically. When you throw it, snap your wrist."

He throws it, and it dive-bombs into the ground. His hands weren't made for warfare. I don't know how a father could do this to his son. He's a blindfolded cow meandering into the slaughterhouse. The look in his eyes tells me he's quite aware of this fact. I should be brushing up, but instead I spend the next six hours teaching Kenan basic combat skills. Things my father and uncle had taught me. Hand-to-hand combat. How to use the opponent's energy and momentum against them. A sword is as foreign to him as a curling iron is to me. I go through every weapon one by one. Some he has never seen. I wish one of them was a shield, as I would tell him to run and hide and protect himself any chance he got. To just worry about surviving the first levels, then tap-out. Once inside, maybe I can protect him—if I can keep myself alive. Besides, if he somehow passed the towers, Legion would crush him under his big toe.

As I head towards the door, I spot an enclosed training arena to my left. I approach the glass door, and inside I spy Legion sparring with a couple of elites. Although *sparring* is putting it gently. Legion's gait is casual, like he is taking the dog for an afternoon stroll. An elite approaches him, swinging his stunclub. Legion ducks and slams his fist into his chest, crushing his exoarmor, along with his ribs. The elite drops to the ground and fights for air, his lungs punctured.

It's scary the way Legion asserts violence with barely any effort at all. What is even more scary are the words I notice scrolling in front of his face via a heads-up reader display. He is crushing elites while reading a book! I shake my head and turn away from watching any further carnage.

After a quick dinner, I make my way down to the archives. The archive room is cold, musty, and full of rats. Massive rats. Dinner back in The Middle. Luckily, I don't mind their company. Seems either the rest of the contestants are above being in such a deplorable room as this, or they don't care to do any research. Fine by me. I scroll through video after video on the giant holotube of Legion decimating his foe. For Legion, killing is just another bodily function.

I spend at least three hours watching old battles of previous Canonizations searching for a weakness. I sigh and take a deep breath, sipping the last of my stale coffee, which is now cold. He rarely repeats the same kill strike. I can spot no predictability in his movements. His training is impressive, his technique perfect. I can't visualize any weapon that could effectively counter his attacks. Very rarely does he take a blow of any kind. Out of forty battles, he only sustained three injuries from what I can tell. His left ankle, left thigh, and left shoulder. All surface wounds. Maybe I shouldn't have come down here? My confidence is now even more deflated. Two rats fight in the corner. I throw them part of my leftover dinner roll. Then I have a realization. I zoom in and watch those three battles in slow motion. Each time Legion was a tad slower than normal, readying a defense posture. Is he blind in his left eye? Are his peripherals off? That has to be it.

Think I found my slingshot.

On top of a Defiance reconnaissance ridge in Reservation 9, Cephas, Jude, and two other Drecks watch the horror below them through turn-of-the-century binoculars. Children scream as they, along with their parents, are ripped from their homes by two dozen Lazurite soldiers armed with plasma guns. Their black and gray exoarmor blend into the arriving dusk, making them look like ghosts, adding to the terror of the traumatized children. One father tries to resist and is immediately shot. At least two dozen families are being marched towards Zion transports.

"What's going on?" Jude asks through the side of his mouth. "They aren't Defiance."

Cephas reels in a long breath. "Word must be spreading that the lottery is just a guise for Renatus's cell harvest. His numbers are down, so now he is using force."

Jude spits in disgust. "It's the Nazis all over again."

Cephas raises an eyebrow. "Since when do you read history? Or read at all, for that matter?"

"Shut it," says Jude. "If we follow them to The Wall, maybe we can get some more men on the other side when it opens."

"We wait."

"Or maybe we ambush another patrol and swipe another exoarmor suit?"

"We wait."

"But we still might be able to hack into it," Jude implores.

"We wait," Cephas repeats.

"Do you think maybe your faith in Asher is a bit too much?"

One of the reasons Cephas keeps Jude so close is that he isn't afraid to question him or his leadership, which is a good thing. Sycophantic suck-ups and groupthink are the quickest ways to derail a noble cause. Cephas wants to stay the reluctant leader as long as possible; he needs Jude and people like him to challenge him, keep him grounded.

Cephas places a hand on Jude's shoulder. "My faith is in God, it is He who will decide if Asher is to be successful in our cause."

"But you chose him."

"Be happy I didn't choose you."

Jude bites his bottom lip. "I don't know why I argue with you."

"Because you enjoy it. Do you know what my wife used to tell me when we would argue?"

"I have a feeling you're gonna tell me."

"That it wasn't me she was arguing with."

"She was as batty as you!" Jude is confused.

Cephas taps the ragged and frayed Bible that rests in his coat pocket. "It's not flesh and blood that we battle, but angels and demons."

"So, is that why we are waiting? We're just supposed to do nothing?" Jude asks.

"No. We're supposed to assist the angels."

"And how may I ask do we do that?"

"We pray, among other things. Listen for God's will."

"I pray but hear nothing," Jude admits.

"Cause your trap is always running. Be still. Be quiet."

"It's hard when all I hear is the crying of children, the rumbling of empty stomachs."

"I didn't say it was easy."

Jude takes glimpses through his binoculars and recognizes one of the bawling children. "That's my niece!"

Jude scrambles to his feet and lunges down the hill, crossbow in hand.

"Jude, wait!" Cephas yells. "There's too many of them!" He nods to his security detail, who rush off after him.

Jude's left foot nicks a rock, and he tumbles down the hill but quickly pops his wiry body back up onto his heels. Before he can reset his momentum, the four Drecks tackle him to the ground.

"Let go of me! That's my niece! Let go of me!"

Luckily, none of the Lazurites below has heard or seen them.

Cephas shakes his head and looks out to the horizon. Families dragged to their doom, narcotics and trash slowly float from the sky like turkey vultures coming in for a soft landing, hope dissipating. Just another day inside his walled-off world.

"Be quiet. Be still," Cephas murmurs. His timbre dubious. His tone lacks the confidence it displayed mere seconds ago when these same words were uttered to Jude.

Maybe tomorrow will bring better news.

CHAPTER SEVEN

We are marched into the coliseum like a herd of prizefighters. I feel like we are in Rome during the second century. We are announced by name as the crowd cheers in jubilation. A giant video screen on both sides lists all one hundred of us and our odds of winning. As progressive and civil as the Lazurites claim to be, they no doubt have placed wagers on their favorites. I'm told it's what the Super Bowl used to be back in the days of the NFL. I peer up at the screen and see mine—*500-1*. Better than I expected, actually.

My name is finally announced. "Amos, the Slayer of the Son of Silas!" I pan the crowd. Everyone is standing in applause except for Sarai. She glares down at me in disdain. I'm the murderer of her beloved Asher. This is the first time I have seen her in more than five years. My eyes have never seen such beauty. I almost sink to the ground as a flood of emotions weakens me. I want to run to her. To tell her who I am. To exit this demented game and live the rest of my days with her in peace.

An elated Renatus is perched next to her in their luxury suite, where champagne and an array of delicacies are served. He sucks on his long fingers that are slathered in caviar. I can't tell if Sarai's loathing is because of me or her father's table manners. I peer around at my competitors, many of whom display confidence and bravado. Kenan shifts anxiously beside me, his hands shaking uncontrollably. So do his knees.

An hour ago, we were finally debriefed on what to expect once inside Sophocles' Towers. A series of twenty rooms in a maze-like configuration that shifts and changes every hour. Each room has a lever you pull once you have passed each challenge. Pull all twenty levers and you have succeeded. Then Legion.

If you survive the first level, there are surrender buttons in each of the upper levels if you are physically or mentally unable to pass that particular challenge. Press it, and you are officially out of the Canonization to be publicly shamed in true Zion fashion, but at least you'll live. But many of the elites would rather die than shame their family and be shipped off to The Middle to become a simple patrolman. I'm sure the irony is not lost on them that I'm that person in reverse. Groups of ten contestants were chosen at a time, five in each tower. Kenan and I were selected to go with the last group. A large holotube will show what is going on inside the towers so the crowd can enjoy with warped amusement our pain, our victories, and in many cases our demise.

As the first ten enter the towers, the rest of us are quickly ushered into a sealed waiting room with no windows, preventing us from hearing or seeing what is happening inside the tower as we wait. There is food, restrooms, cots, and a massive video board that will show the progress of each participant. I grab two cups of coffee and sit next to Kenan.

"I guess we wait."

"Reminds me . . . maaa . . . me of that line in one of Steven Seagal's movies. 'The anticipation of death is worse than death itself,'" Kenan stutters.

"Hard to kill," I reply, referencing the movie. "You're a 1980's fan also?"

"Still can't beat the movies or the music."

We spend the next six hours arguing over who would win in a fight—

Chuck Norris or Bruce Lee? *Star Wars* or *Star Trek*? It keeps our mind off what is happening outside these claustrophobic, concrete walls as contestant after contestant disappears from the board. Have they surrendered, or have they been killed? Based on the cheers inside the coliseum, I would say the latter.

"I'm going to get some shuteye," I inform Kenan and head over to a cot in the corner. As soon as I shut my eyes, I see Sarai. I have never seen her so revolted. I guess this is good as it proves she still cares for me. I wonder if she is ever happy. Does she feel trapped? Or has she capitulated to Zion's grip? Minutes before I enter that realm between sleep and consciousness, the administrator barges through the door.

"Group two, you're up!"

That didn't take long.

The spectacle has gone on for three days thus far. Once inside the towers, there are no breaks, no rests, no food, and no water. You either pass, surrender, or die. We are the final ten left to be called. Out of the first ninety, two have made it through the towers and wait for the main event, which is Legion. Kenan exits the restroom, or the *loo* as the Lazurites call it, for the fourth time in as many hours.

"My stomach is like a whirlpool, must be the food," Kenan tells me. But from how he is shaking, it is likely his nerves.

I point to the progress board. "Two have made it," I say with as much optimism as I can muster.

"Is . . . is . . . is that supposed to make me feel better?"

"That means it is possible."

"Maybe for you."

"I'm just a simple patrolman who made it to the Canonization. Anything is possible."

I meander over to the nourishment station and grab two plates of ground meat that my taste buds have yet to identify. I hand one to Kenan.

"Fill up now. We'll need it later."

"You assume I'll last that long."

I also hand him a gallon of water. "Hydrate."

"I already have to piss every five minutes."

I peer into his eyes and see a boy wanting to be a man, someone who wants to make his father proud, someone bred for something altogether different. Cephas would always tell me that God has a specific plan for everyone. That each one of us is blessed with gifts to carry out that plan. His is not this, is mine? The words of my uncle invade my brain.

"If God is with us, who can be against us? Fear not!"

Then the words of my father.

"Greater love has no one than this, that one lay down his life for his friends."

Why do I always hear their words, carry them on my shoulders? Is it a gift or a burden? Will I ever be my own man? Or are we simply a combination of those who came before us? It sounds like someone is knocking on the door, but I peer down and see it is Kenan's knees knocking together. He grinds his teeth, and it sounds like someone is using a metal file on hardwood. I don't want him to die simply for the blood lust of the crowd. No life is worth someone else's entertainment.

I place my hand on Kenan's shoulder. "Just stay alive, Kenan, and remember, once you reach the upper levels, you can tap out and go home. Don't worry about what your father thinks. His legacy isn't your burden to bear. Go home to your mother. There is no shame in surrendering. There are greater causes to die for. This isn't one of them. Trust me."

Again, I sound like my father. I might be talking to myself just as much as I am to him. Would my father want me here? Am I doing this for his legacy or Cephas's? If by some miracle I make it, will I fight for my uncle's cause, or will I take Sarai and run? The door unlocks with a thud. Kenan's face goes pale. My jaw clenches. The administrator lumbers inside, his boots trample the cold concrete floors, and everything seems to move in slow motion. As he smiles, spittle forms a nest on the corner of his lips. I can barely hear him utter the words. "It's time."

We strap on exoarmor suits with holes cut into them near the chest, back, and head—kill zones. Apparently, they want us to survive a little longer than if we had nothing at all; it prolongs the entertainment value, I guess. Next stop, the weapons station. A tall mountain of muscle with sunken blue eyes and large white teeth mumbles at each one of us. "Only one, chaps."

To my delight, there is a ricochet. Kenan eyes the assortment of killing paraphernalia and can't make up his mind. It's like asking a carpenter who has never seen a house before to choose his tools. I nudge him and nod to the thick stunclub. "Just worry about defense."

The gates slowly swing open, and we are birthed from the tunnel and into the bright morning sunlight. The crowd is on its feet for the final ten. I peer up to the sultan suite and see Sarai reading a book. We are separated into groups of five and are led to our respective towers. I can sense Kenan's relief when we are chosen for the same group. I have a feeling that relief will be short-lived.

Elite Lazurite guards escort us to the front of the tower. One of them murmurs under his breath, "Good luck, sheep." His cohort sniffs a cackle. I gaze to the sky and can't help but wonder if this is the last time I'll see the sun, the last time I'll see Sarai. I scan the exuberant crowd and for a moment can't help but feel sorry for them. Is this their source of joy? Do they really derive happiness watching others battle for their lives? Do they find solace in our pain? If Zion is paradise, why the Canonization? Empty lives desire such distractions, I guess. For Renatus and the ones who live forever, overcoming boredom must be a struggle. Things that are infinite are seldom cherished.

To my right, seated in the family section, is Amos's mother, father, and brother. His mother weeps and can't bear to watch. His father does his best to look proud and stoic. His brother, on the other hand, appears thrilled that I'm being sent to my doom. I wonder what Amos did to piss him off? *Or maybe he really doesn't believe I'm his brother?* I shake that thought and focus on more pressing matters. We wait for what seems like an eternity, and then the doors to the towers slide open. Surely, they were waiting for all bets to be placed. Wonder if anyone took me?

"In you go, chaps!" bellows a guard.

I take one last glance towards Sarai before we creep into the open door and enter the unknown. When all five of us cross the threshold, the door slides shut and then locks with a clunk. Complete darkness. I can hear Kenan's heavy, labored breaths.

"Take it easy, mate," I whisper to him. My sweaty palm grips my ricochet. I hear what sounds like a cat with metal paws tap-dancing across the cement, scampering in front of us, then behind us. Then red iridescent lights illuminate the room, and I see where the noise comes from—robotic battle drones. Slim rods of steel with scourges for arms and shoulder-mounted plasma guns. *Devilbots.* The five of us scatter and dive into different locations as they fire their weapons. Kenan lies on the ground, gripped in fear. I remind him he has a weapon. "Your stunclub! Turn it on!"

He activates it, and it comes to life, fizzling with electricity. Not a moment too soon as a devilbot whips his scourge in his direction; he manages to deflect it while stumbling backwards. In my peripherals I see one charging my flank. I roll to the ground and fling my ricochet. It cuts through the dead, stale air and decapitates the metal demon before returning to my hand. Another fires its plasma gun and barely misses Kenan. Before it gets off another shot, I slice it in two with another throw of the ricochet. Kenan nods thanks. A contestant to my right is not so lucky, as a drone takes him to the ground by wrapping his legs with its scourge, then finishing him off with a shot of plasma.

The crowd outside erupts with raucous applause. Succeed or fail, either way they are entertained. Four of us left.

"This way," I tell Kenan, trying to find cover behind a massive pillar.

Then to my left, a bot appears out of nowhere; it was hiding in the dark, it fires plasma at Kenan. I tackle him to the ground, and the plasma blast skims my left ankle. I grimace as it feels like I'm being stung by a hundred hornets.

"You okay?" Kenan asks.

For the love of all that's holy, I want to tell him to shut up and keep his head down. Instead, I grunt, "Yes."

A participant to my right uses his scourge to take out one of the final two bots. In the darkness, I can only see its crimson hellion eyes darting. It whips its arm, and the scourge wraps around my leg. It pulls me towards him. Kenan does not have an attack weapon, and the other two just watch, figuring to get me out of the way. From my back, I half-blindly hurl my ricochet. It misses the dancing devilbot, which pulls me closer. Its plasma gun readies. I stretch my left wrist out, which has the return signal attached, so the ricochet will slightly change course on its way back to me.

It's just enough, as it slices the bot in two. Kenan looks as if he's been holding his breath the entire time. He tells me he's sorry for not helping. I tell him to just breathe.

The four of us each pull a lever. One down. That wasn't too bad, but it was only level one. Four doors simultaneously open. We each step towards a different one. I give Kenan a look that tells him, "Don't die for this." I hope he taps out.

I tiptoe into the dark room, not knowing what to expect. The door slides shut, and the lights flash on. Next to me is the surrender button. On the ceiling is the second lever. All around me are protruding metal spikes. This is comparable to the simulation I failed earlier, but this time it's for keeps. The room suddenly twists and turns. I fall forward with outstretched hands palming the floor, which was the wall a second ago. Spikes inches from my head. The crowd outside gushes as if it is happening to them.

The room suddenly flips backwards. I stumble back and try to pivot on my left foot, but I don't quite make it as I roll to the side and onto a spike that slices my shoulder. Blood trundles down my shoulder and plops to the floor. Luckily, just a surface wound. Well, this is going well; two challenges—two injuries. It could have been a lot worse, though. The crowd blusters, living vicariously through my pain while no doubt slurping caviar and cracking crab legs. Not only do they hunger for violence, but apparently violence makes them hungry.

The room then starts to spin like a snowball tumbling down a mountain. Still on my stomach, I scamper on my hands and feet like a cat trying to keep pace. The lever spins below me, then above me, I reach out and just miss it. The room gyrates once again, and I roll around like a marble in a wooden box, just missing the metal spikes all while trying to track where the lever is. I am then shot from the floor to the ceiling. I begin to free-fall towards a bed of massive spikes. I reach out, and the tips of my fingernails scrape the lever, giving it just enough pressure to pull it down. The spikes retract into the floor as I flop to the ground.

Two down.

I don't want to think about what might be next.

I exit the sliding door and find myself on a different floor. A video screen on the wall displays the progress of the other contestants in both towers as well as footage of inside the coliseum. There is Kenan, trudging towards the exit. I'm glad to see he tapped out. It seems his neck is barely strong enough to hold up his head. The crowd chants, "Kenan the Coward! Kenan the Coward!" They throw apples and other fruit at him. He doesn't react as they bounce off his chest, oranges splattering against his forehead. A close-up on

Kenan's father shows him spitting in disgust as if he had just tasted something spoiled. Even he participates in this childish ritual. It makes me appreciate my father and the little time I had with him. I wonder what will happen to Kenan now. Cleaning toilets for Zion's elite platoons? Or a one-way trip to the front lines fighting my uncle's army or The Sons of Levi, perhaps? I feel for him, but glad he is alive. My father used to tell me, "Sometimes the best course of action is the obvious one, great leaders must recognize that fine line between never giving up and knowing what is impossible."

One day he'll have his day in the sun. How I know that, I don't know. If I somehow win this thing, I'll be certain he comes under my command. I can protect him.

I rip off part of my undershirt and tie it around my shoulder to help impede the bleeding. I check my ankle, and the heat from the plasma blast cauterized the wound.

Surviving the box of nails was more luck than skill. This room has four doors, one in each corner. I open the one to my left and am met with a gust of stale, damp air. Inside is a steel plank no more than thirty inches wide. Below it is an empty chasm so deep and dark I cannot see the bottom. I carefully traverse the plank until it stops at a steep wall fifty feet high. At the very top is a lever. Between me and the lever are a series of wooden pegs sticking out of the wall. Each one protrudes from the wall, then seconds later disappears randomly. After a minute of studying the pegs, perhaps it isn't random after all. I see a pattern emerge. Every other one on the left appears for four seconds, then disappears. The others are two seconds. The ones on my right are opposite but are three seconds and one second, respectively. At least I think so, but I am out of time as the plank begins to retract.

I jump to the first series of pegs. I need to use my right hand first to reach up and grab the next peg before it retracts. I only have a second to pull myself up with one arm until it's my left arm's turn. Surely it is no accident that the diabolical designer of these towers made certain that you could only hang on to one peg at a time. As a teen I used to climb tall oak trees for Cephas on reconnaissance missions, scanning for Lazurite patrols. The upper body strength gained from hours upon hours of climbing serves me well. I am finding that many things I used to curse my uncle for now behoove me.

I am halfway up and begin to feel a burn in my forearms and back. Blood from my shoulder and sweat from my brow slide off me and vanish into the murkiness. The void below me is my soul, deserted and cloudy. The pegs are Zion, my never-ending obstacle. The lever is Sarai, my goal, my purpose.

Once I pass the midpoint, the pegs become truly random. Speed is the only thing I have left to conquer this challenge. Each peg recedes into the wall just as my hand reaches for the next one. It's like playing whack-a-mole on steroids. I reach for the next peg with my right hand, and it shoots back into the wall before I can muster a grip. I fall towards the emptiness. I reach my arms out and I'm able to grab two pegs near where I began. I take a deep breath; my forearms are on fire, my grip throbbing. I have to start again.

Having the algorithm memorized, I quickly make my way back up the first half of the wall. Then I reach the randomized part. Something tells me to trust my instinct. I strangely feel as if I'm being guided to the top. I somehow know to grab the correct peg each time until suddenly I reach the top. I triumphantly grab the lever with both hands and pull down. Nothing. No doors open; the plank doesn't return. Did I miss something? Is there another lever? I peer around and do not see one. I'm sure Renatus and the crowd are enjoying a sadistic laugh at my expense. My wearied arms can't hold on for much longer. Then the lever itself retreats into the wall.

I fall into the darkness.

I wonder if Sarai is still watching.

I crash into a pool of frigid water and wonder if this was what was beneath me the entire time. Or was it because I pulled the lever? Or is this one of Renatus's mind games to give us a false sense of safety? Maybe the next challenge won't have such a soft landing? I can't help but think they wanted to exhaust our arms before figuring out how to swim our way out. Again, diabolical.

The room is dark. I have no idea how deep the water is. Thirsty, I slurp in a mouthful of water before spitting it out. Salt water. Of course. Seems they thought of everything. It's way too early to be this dehydrated. My adrenaline must have masked the burning sensation I now feel as the salt water mingles with the gash in my shoulder and cut on my ankle. I scan for a lever or some kind of exit. Nothing. Then something brushes against my leg; something is in the water with me. Whatever it is nudges me again. My eyes are beginning to adjust. Then I see it, a narrow fin slicing through the water. Now I know why it's saltwater. I have no idea what kind of shark it is, but I can only guess it is aggressive in nature and more than likely hungry. The cut in my shoulder further whets its appetite. Renatus's perverse creation now borders on surreal. I try not to panic.

Wish I had grabbed a sword or a knife of some sort. My ricochet won't work underwater. My heart just about leaps out of my chest when it bumps me again. It is toying with me. Where am I going to go? Like shooting fish in a barrel. I'm the fish.

It is behind me now. I paddle and turn. The ripples in the water grow larger as the shark picks up speed. Out of options, I grab my ricochet and hold the ends with both hands, with the blade in the middle facing down towards the water. I'll have to time it just right. My legs act like fast-moving scissors to keep myself as high in the water as possible. I look like a dancing dolphin. It dives down deep underneath me. With my arms raised high, the shark lunges up and out of the water. Its rows of massive teeth look like arrowheads used by Native Americans so many years ago. Just when it's at arm's length, I plow the blade of the ricochet on top of the shark's nose. The shark recoils, but quickly returns, its powerful jaws snapping inches from my face. I frantically repeat the blow behind its eyes over and over until it is finally decapitated. Blood swirls around me. My throbbing heart feels as if it's going to punch a hole in my chest. I catch my breath and hope this is the only one. Did I really just kill a shark?

I scrutinize the room, and still the lever is nowhere to be seen. Is it underwater? Of course it is. I inhale a generous amount of oxygen and dive for what seems like an eternity until I reach the bottom and feel around. Nothing. The murky water is so dark I can't see a thing. I might as well be blindfolded. After a minute, I kick my way back to the surface. On my fourth try I am already light-headed and dizzy. I suck in another deep breath. It feels like the room is running out of oxygen. Reaching the bottom again, my hands grope the floor until I finally feel the lever. I pull it, but it doesn't budge; it seems stuck, or I don't have enough leverage. About out of air, I bring my feet to the bottom of the surface to give myself more leverage and yank again. This time it moves. I rocket back up to the surface, almost passing out before I get there.

Now that the lever has been pulled, the water from the massive tank recedes. I ride the top of the vortex until the tank is empty. I lie exhausted at the bottom of the tank; next to me is a dead, headless shark. A humorous and bizarre sight if one didn't know the context. My father would always say, "An intact sense of humor makes any situation more bearable."

I am Asher the Shark Slayer. It has a nice ring to it.

CHAPTER EIGHT

The tower has been reconfigured, and I have searched for the next lever for over three hours. I find rooms that I have been inside already. Up seems to be down and down up. Stairs that lead to nowhere. Doors that have brick walls behind them. Since the episode with the shark, I have battled more drones, walked a tightrope with manufactured winds, and memorized a pattern of blinking lights, much like the game "Simon Says". My stomach rumbles, and my mouth is dry. On the walls are video images of people drinking crisp, clean water and eating steak and potatoes, which adds to my torture. I lick my cracking lips and check my shoulder. The bleeding has finally stopped. The faint sounds of the administrator rousing the crowd outside can be heard. My name is mentioned. "Amos, The Slayer of the Son Silas is still alive! Who would have thought? Anyone take the 500-1?" I wonder if I am the last one left. I walk back the way I came, and the room and the number of doors has seemed to change once again. I open one I don't believe I have tried before, and to my surprise another contestant emerges. Maven, I believe his name is. I have always been good with names. Something my mother taught me.

"We the only ones left?" I ask.

"Believe so, mate," he answers coldly, sizing me up.

"Seen the shark yet?"

He peers at me like I'm a Martian.

"The room with the pegs, when you get to the top, it drops you into a tank of water with a shark. Lever is at the bottom. How many you have left?"

"Three." Then he squints at me, checking out my ricochet. "You?"

"Two." I turn and poke my head into the room he emerged from, which leads to another hallway . . . have I been there already? "You know the way out of here?"

But instead of an answer, I feel a burning sensation around my ankle, and then I am upended and land on the back of my injured shoulder. He then drags me towards him with his scourge.

"What are you doing?" I yell. But I already know, he is getting rid of the competition. I pull out my ricochet and use the bladed curve to cut my ankle free. I roll to my left and pop up, barely avoiding the snap of his scourge. I fire my ricochet at him; he ducks, turns, and whips his scourge, catching the ricochet in midair. He pulls it into his left hand. Without the return sensor, it is no good to him, and he can't throw it my way; otherwise, it will just return to me, so he opens the door to his right, chucks it in, and closes it. I am now weaponless as he whips his scourge, just missing my forehead. I roll back and forth, barely avoiding being hit, and pop to my feet.

"Let's help each other, figure this out together!" I yell at him.

"There can only be one winner," he snarls.

I run down the hall behind me and take a left. I make my way back to the door that held the shark tank and jump inside. It has been reset. Water refilled, and a new shark, I can only assume. I kneel onto the plank and roll underneath it, grabbing the bottom of the plank with both hands, hanging suspended above the water as Maven swings open the door. Again, I silently thank my uncle for my strong fingers and calloused hands. The only light is from the scourge's electrified whip that hisses static. It looks like he is holding a coiled glowing snake. An angry one. He slowly walks across the creaking plank, looking into the darkness towards the pegged wall. His right foot steps onto the fingers of my left hand. The small metal studs protruding from his expensive elite army boots dig into my knuckles. I cringe and grit my teeth. He lingers there for a moment. Blood from my hand drips down and lands in my left eye. I rapidly blink, trying to push the salty crimson fluid from my stinging eyeball.

He finally lifts his right foot and continues forward. Just as his left foot passes my fingers, I grab his ankle and pull him off the plank. On the way down, he blindly whips his scourge in desperation; it just happens to wrap around my left ankle.

Dreck luck.

He now dangles below me as my fingers begin to slip from the plank. I'm not sure how much longer I can hold the extra hundred and eighty pounds I'm guessing he is. I can let go and take my chances with the shark below. But I'm weaponless. Maybe it will eat Maven first while I swim down and pull the lever? I peer down at him, and he smiles back up at me, enjoying my predicament, even at his own expense.

Lazurites.

I shimmy my leg, trying to shake him off, but he hangs on. I noticed that the scourge slid down a notch over my ankle and around my boot. I use my other foot and push off my left boot. The tail of the scourge slides down farther. I shake my leg again, and it finally uncoils and slides off. Maven falls into the water below, hurdling curse words back up at me the entire way.

If they replaced the shark I killed, I don't wait around to find out.

Cephas, Jude, and a motley crew of Drecks watch from a pirated signal on their battery-powered holotube as Asher finally finds the room with the second to last lever. Jude cooks what looks like a hotdog, but it is more than likely a large rat or small squirrel on a stick over the fire pit.

"Want one?" Jude asks.

"You're burning it," is all Cephas says with a nauseated look. This wasn't the first time he and his men have resorted to eating Mother Nature's scraps.

"I like it crispy, like chips."

Cephas wonders how he could think of food at a time like this. But then again, Jude was always eating. At a buck fifty he had a turbo metabolism.

"Must you smack your lips like that?" Cephas sniffs, the smell of burned rodent mixed with the gaggle of unbathed men was starting to get to him.

"Sure you don't want one?"

Cephas ignores him.

They watch as Asher struggles to find his ricochet as the rooms reconfigure again.

"Let's hope he doesn't need it," Cephas whispers regarding Asher's lost weapon.

"Two levers left," Jude snorts. "Cobber might actually pull this off."

Asher is inside an empty room except for two ropes, a lighter, and a note. Asher grabs the note, the words written are shown on the holotube:

Once the light in the room turns green you must pull the lever in precisely 45 minutes; otherwise, you will be surrendered. All you are given are two ropes and a lighter. Each rope has the following property: If you light one end of the rope, it will take one hour to burn to the other end. One caveat: They don't necessarily burn at a uniform rate. Good luck.

"That's easy. Just burn three-quarters of the rope," Jude squawks triumphantly while folding his arms, looking very proud of himself.

Cephas sighs, "They don't burn uniformly."

"So?"

"So, it could take forty-five minutes to burn the first half of the rope and fifteen for the second." Cephas sips his coffee. "I think I remember hearing this riddle as a kid."

"Alright, professor, what's the answer?"

"Let me see. I think you first light both ends of one rope and just one end of the other rope. The first rope will burn in thirty minutes. Once that is done, light the other end of the second rope, and voila, forty-five minutes."

Jude scratches his head. "How is that forty-five minutes?"

"Once the first rope burns, the second rope will have thirty minutes left, so simply light the other end, and the rest of the second rope will burn in fifteen minutes instead of thirty. Thirty plus fifteen is what?"

Jude doesn't answer.

"If brains were dynamite, you wouldn't have enough to blow your nose. Good Lord, who taught you your math, boy?"

"Your mom did."

Jude sidesteps as Cephas swings an elbow his way.

The light inside Asher's room flashes green. It's time. They watch Asher hold the lighter, looking unsure what to do. Cephas edges closer to the holotube, his dirty, long fingernails scratching his cleft chin. "C'mon boy, c'mon, you got this. Be your father's son."

With a smile and a small nod, Cephas watches as Asher does exactly what he just explained to his sometimes dense but jovial friend. Just as the fire on the last rope burns out, Cephas senses a new spark being ignited for The Defiance.

Asher pulls the lever.

"One more to go."

Jude throws another rat on the fire.

For two days I sat in the final room, which I have now deemed impossible. I have never been so thirsty. The last time I tasted water was more than sixty hours ago. The room is an empty box. The final lever is mounted on the ceiling fifty feet above me. There is no way to reach it. The flat, slick walls cannot be scaled. There is nothing else in the room. I have checked every nook and corner for any possible trapdoor or hidden device, but nothing. The room is locked, no way out. My skin is dry as a desert, my heartbeat and breathing rapid, all signs of dehydration. I can push the surrender button or die of thirst in this dark box. Or should I say casket? Either way, I lose Sarai. Confusion is setting in, another byproduct of dehydration. I sometimes wonder if this is a dream I am living instead of Renatus's sinister nightmare. Will I soon wake up and find myself back in The Middle, sifting through trash and delivering contraband for Boaz? I circle the 400-square-foot room again, rubbing my fingers against the concrete, searching for something . . . anything.

I finally slink down in a corner. I'm too dry for tears, but if my body could produce them, I'm pretty sure I would be bawling. My hands shake, and I picture Sarai in her faded Van Halen shirt and braided hair standing underneath our weeping willow. Gazing into her defiant, sable eyes made me feel anything was possible. If she was here now that she would figure it out, find a way. I should have danced with her on the boat the day we were engaged. Why didn't I? I have taken life's precious minutes for granted. I close my eyes and relive the bombing at the bazaar. Five children dead because of the explosive I sold to The Sons of Levi. I'm haunted by their mother's shrieks from losing what was most precious to them. Maimed families beyond repair. My tear ducts are able to extract what remaining moisture is left in my body to form one lone tear that evaporates before passing the corner of my mouth. Is Cephas watching and wondering if I am weak? Regretting his choice? I'm not him or my father.

What about Sarai? Is she watching, happily waiting for Amos's demise? I may never see her again. I should have done more to try and talk to her, tell her who I really was before entering this baneful game. She would at least know why I was here.

I'm empty.

I close my eyes and take a page out of my uncle's book; for the first time in my life, I pray. I don't know what else to do. I pray to be forgiven, to be washed. I pray for those in The Middle who are starving. I pray for the mothers of the children murdered at the bazaar. I pray for Sarai. For her happiness, with me or without me. I pray for Him to show me a way out of here. For wisdom, for strength.

And if that is not given, for peace.

To be honest, I don't even understand what I'm saying. I feel as if someone else is interceding for me, telling me what to say. I even pray for my uncle. For his leadership and discernment. For The Defiance.

I pray for The Wall to come down.

Something washes over me and through me. Fear dissipates. For just a moment I am okay with my fate, with what lies before me. A peace beyond understanding. I open my eyes, and then it hits me. My father's words, *"Sometimes the best course of action is the obvious one; great leaders must recognize that fine line between never giving up and knowing what is impossible."* Maybe that's it? Maybe pulling this lever is truly impossible, and that is the point? I'm sure Renatus would want whoever is to lead his third army to be able to discern the difference between what can and cannot be done. Someone bold but not reckless. All there is left to do is surrender. If I'm right, I pass. If I'm wrong, Sarai will be given to someone else. I will have failed Cephas, The Defiance. I stand and wobble towards the green surrender button. I suck in a deep breath as if the oxygen was courage, or better yet wisdom, and then push the button with my dry arid palm.

Nothing happens. Am I delusional to think this was the answer? Then a mechanical creaking. The ceiling starts to roll towards me. My disorientation takes over, and I just stare at it. Soon I will be crushed. I snap out of it and frantically try to open the door. It is moving faster now. Is this what happens if you surrender inside the last room? To be crushed for your cowardliness? I lie on my back and think about what to do; in a few more seconds I'll be pancaked. Lack of sleep, food, and water has turned my brain to mush. I'm exhausted. Wait a minute? The lever. I can reach it now. Cephas is probably shaking his head, and Jude is cackling, I'm sure.

Just pull the lever buckethead!

With just two feet to spare, I pull the final lever. The ceiling reverses course. The door unlocks. Lights flash. I hear my name and the roaring of the frenetic crowd. The blazing sun is blinding. I feel as if I've been in this tower forever. Cephas is rubbing his butt-chin, jump-starting a smile. Jude is doing a crazy dance.

I have done it, but all I want is water and to see Sarai's face. For a moment I have forgotten that Legion awaits me.

Sarai sets her book down. This is where she has a vested interest. Three contenders left. She assumes her father will come up with another plan to marry her off if neither is successful. As much as he adores Legion, even he knows he is too barbaric to marry his daughter.

Legion makes quick work of contender number one. Like watching a bull-riding match, the entire bout lasted about eight seconds. Legion made a show of not picking up a weapon. In fact, it was one hit. A mighty armor-crushing fist to the head. She noticed his gnarled knuckles were the size of golf balls. The contender didn't stand a chance, but does anyone? This fact mildly comforts her, and she wonders why her father had Legion return in the first place if he wanted her married off to the winner when there would likely be none. Maybe he secretly wanted her at home and alone? She is the last of his offspring, after all.

"Foie gras?" Renatus offers Sarai the rare delicacy.

She simply shakes her head; duck liver is something she never acquired a taste for. Nor does she agree with *gavage*, the method by which *foie gras* is produced. The ducks are force-fed grain via a tube down their throats. This causes the liver to expand and add a fatty texture. The overindulgences of Zion don't come without a price. To Renatus, everyone is a duck that only exists to please him. She'll take a market burger grilled by a Dreck any day. Her father smacks his lips as the coliseum caretaker mops up the blood from Legion's latest victim. Sarai hates how her father slurps his expensive wine instead of sipping it.

With overabundance, nothing is savored. She watches as Renatus beams with pride as Legion prepares for his next battle, guzzling water but keeping the blood on his hands. For a moment she is jealous. It was always about her brother; now it is Legion. A killer of his creation. A savage. It scares her to be his daughter. She is terrified that in her genes is the propensity to be like him. Or even worse, like her mother. Someone who idly sits by as evil propagates. *Her affluence is so great, and her shoe closets are so bountiful that perhaps she doesn't have the time to notice her husband's evil ways. Or that of Zion?*

The now raucous crowd cheers in delight as Legion gouges out the eyes of contender number two before pulling his limbs from his sockets. The Lazurites' cheers turn into a stiff golf clap as Legion circles his dead victim. Sarai can't help but think when you peel back Zion's snobbery and elitism, it really is just a culture of violence and self-gratification in the most primal sense. Their blood lust is unquenchable. The noxious odor just gets worse with each layer. She longs for the days spent lazily fishing with Asher while gnawing on homemade venison jerky far away from the ocean that now terrifies her. The simple kindness and companionship of Asher's fellow Drecks. That is before half of them became addicted to Zion's narcdrops. Enslavement, delivered by the pallet.

Next up is Amos, the butcher of her beloved. The back of her throat burns from the bile that has snaked its way from the pit of her stomach. Her mourning of Asher has been dwarfed by her anguish and animosity. Perhaps that will come later?

At this very moment, she is Legion's biggest fan.

I enter the arena and pan the crowd. Sarai is perched at the Seat of Sultans next to her father. I'm still exhausted from the towers. I feel like I have been asked to wrestle a bear after being hit by a bus. The blood stains are still fresh on the coliseum floor from the two "winners" before me.

Legion approaches. He towers over me by more than a foot. He is stronger than a Gorilla. Nimble as a Cheetah. His movements are surprisingly graceful for someone of his stature. Once more, I peek up at Sarai and wonder what she is thinking. To her, I'm a barbarian who killed her fiancé. I can see the venom in her eyes. I'm leveled by the mere thought of her revulsion towards me. I need to focus. Weapons fall from the sky and land on the arena floor. In typical Legion fashion, he doesn't reach for one. Why would he? His arms are like canons, and his fists are the size of bowling balls. Instead of exoarmor, we both don metal armor, similar to that of the Roman gladiators, by design, I'm sure. To my right is a spear, and to my left is a dagger. I don't have time to grab both. Conventional wisdom suggests I take the spear and try to take out Legion from a distance. But I have seen him grab spears out of the air and snap them like toothpicks; if I have any chance of beating him, it won't be by doing anything conventional. *"Fight like a Dreck."* My uncle's words replay over and over in my head.

Legion charges me. Strong and fierce. Possessed with blood lust. Always on the attack. His opponents try to retreat, play defense, but are usually swallowed up and quickly spit out by this behemoth. So I do what is unexpected, what he never sees. I charge him. He never has to practice defense. He is fast. I'm faster. I hear the *"whoas"* from the crowd as they don't expect my charge, and neither does Legion. He swings a mighty fist that I duck, then rolls to the ground. On my way back up, I stab his left ribs where his flesh is exposed in between his armor plating. The cut isn't deep, but blood trickles out, proving he is only a man. That he is human.

Silence.

This is the first time this arena has tasted Legion's blood. And now they want more of it. I was moving too fast to make the cut deep enough to do any damage. Now I think I just pissed him off. He releases a scream that sounds like peals of thunder. My eardrums literally throb. He dabs his index and middle finger against his wound. Blood drips from his fingernails like a melting ice cream cone on a hot day. He jams his fingers in his mouth and tastes his own blood.

He nods and smiles. "Not bad. I taste your blood next."

Legion spits out the blood and gallops towards me; his massive feet batter the dirt and rock of the arena floor. Saliva drizzles from his mouth. I swing my dagger at him, and he swats it out of my hand. He reaches back and punches me in the chest, sending me flying and leaving a massive dent in my armor. I feel as if I was hit with a sledgehammer. The wind knocked out of me, I suck for oxygen. He picks me up by my left arm, swings me around like he's performing the Olympic hammer throw, and tosses me against the arena wall. As I'm the last contender, he is toying with me as a cat does a mouse per Renatus's command, I'm guessing, prolonging the entertainment. The first two bouts were much too quick for Zion's liking. Before I can gain my bearings, he picks me up and slams me, sending puffs of dust into the air. I think I cracked two ribs. I won't last too much longer at this rate.

He lifts up his elephantine foot in preparation to stomp on me; before he lands it, I spin around and sweep his other leg, knocking him to the ground with a thud. He quickly rolls onto his stomach and tries to pound me with his gargantuan fists. I roll to dodge the blows. He finally makes contact. First, my nose breaks, then I'm whacked on the side of my head, I go dizzy for a moment, and everything fades to black. Seconds later I come back from my concussed state as Legion grabs the back of my armor and holds me up like a mother dog does her pup. He then tosses me across the arena. I finally roll to a stop. The crowd yells out their requests for the different sadistic ways they want him to finish me off. I can feel the ground shake as he hurdles towards me. I gather a handful of sand from the coliseum floor and fling it into his eyes. This gives me just enough time to roll out of the way before being trampled.

From the corner of my eye, I see Renatus sending Legion a quick nod. Playtime is over. Legion springs up and barrels towards me, his movements much more deliberate and concise than before.

Wait a minute.

His weakness.

I was so drained from the tower I forgot all about it.

I sprint to the corner of the arena, where more weapons have fallen. I grab a ricochet and a spear. Instead of strapping the ricochet's retriever to my wrist, I scamper towards the right side of the arena and slyly drop it to the ground and spurt back to the corner.

I toss the ricochet, purposely aiming wide left of Legion, and dart towards him. He doesn't track it for a moment as he knows, as everyone else does, that it will make a full half-circle before it starts to return to me. That is if I was wearing the retriever. Instead, it instantly tries to return to the retriever I placed on the ground to his right. Being blind in his left eye, he doesn't spot it coming straight for him. The ricochet hits him in the neck, and the electric shock stuns him for a moment, sending him crashing onto his back. Just as he hits the ground, I arrive and drive my spear into the chink in his armor between his chest and shoulder. It goes through his entire shoulder and into the dirt, pinning him to the ground. He struggles to stand but can't move. I run and grab the dagger, holding it above him. Renatus stands in shock, as does the entire coliseum.

Legion takes a deep breath and sighs. The flames in his eyes extinguish. He looks different. I no longer see a monster but a child. I see someone who only fights to be loved. Beneath the mountain of flesh is just an abandoned boy wanting approval, Renatus's approval. He is just another tool of Zion. A product of Renatus's manipulations and lies. Like the duck, he has been force-fed Zion's propaganda for the selfish gratification of the Lazurites. He waits for me to end him. Everyone does.

The crowd chants, "Finish him! Finish him!"

How quickly their loyalty turns. Legion, once revered, is now a loser. And Zion does not like losers. I think back to the tower when I asked for God's help. Do I see Legion differently because I have changed? Or is it simply the look of a man about to meet his demise?

I raise my dagger, and the crowd suddenly goes eerily silent. I'm not sure if it's out of reverence for their beloved Legion or if they are simply appalled. I know I am. Legion's shallow breathing sounds like ocean waves lapping up the sand. He looks to me as if he wants me to do it; that or he has accepted his fate.

"Do it. I deserve it."

I look to Renatus, then to Sarai. I can suffer her heartbreaks no longer. I simply drop my dagger and walk away, unsure if I have won or lost.

CHAPTER NINE

"**HE DEFIED ME!**" Renatus bellows, slamming his fist against the marble table. "Per the rules, only one man leaves the arena."

"Simply kill him," says Omar.

Sarai's ears perk; she doesn't want more death, but at least she wouldn't be forced to marry him.

"I can't kill him. Did you hear that arena? The crowd loves him. *Amos the Magnanimous,* they called him. *Amos the Vanquisher of Giants.*" Renatus spits on the floor.

Sarai senses a hint of jealousy in her father's tone. It is he who seeks the crowd's love and affection.

"It's not all that bad, my sultan," Omar says. "Look at it this way, you have a cunning and canny leader for your third army, a masterful and popular warrior for your only daughter, and you still have Legion. All in all, this is a win for you."

"Legion is a disgrace and will be sent to SeaPen."

SeaPen is Renatus's underwater penitentiary located just offshore from his magnificent compound. It is where his dissidents and political foes are sent, never to be seen or heard from again.

"SeaPen? But surely Legion is still an asset to Zion?" Omar asks.

Renatus waves off the suggestion. "Tosh."

Sarai peers into her father's eyes and sees the wheels turning. She knows Renatus is skilled at manipulating and transforming any situation to his advantage.

"Look, the populace is war-weary, and so are our soldiers. They need inspiration such as this, someone like Amos to lead them to final victory," Omar presses.

Sarai can see the annoyance in her father's ruffled brow, but then his expression changes, his cadence boisterous.

"A royal wedding for the ages," Renatus boasts. "The sultana and Amos the Magnificent, The Queller of The Defiance, a product of *my* Zion."

Of course he wants the credit, Sarai thinks before blurting out, "I will not marry that man. I'd rather die."

Renatus stands, "You are a Lazurite and a princess of Zion, and you are my daughter! You will do as you're told. Enough of this bloody palaver."

"Just a moment ago he was Amos the Defier. Now he's Amos the Great?"

"This discussion is over, my dear. Your mother has ordered another set of dresses. Don't disappoint her again."

"Would you force this upon Legion? Or your beloved Eleazar if he were here?" Sarai asks.

"Don't mention him, don't ever mention his name!"

"You wouldn't. Not your wounded prince or your mighty warrior. I will not be a second-class citizen."

"They would do it without question; it's for the good of the Lazurites and for the honor of Zion. You will bloody marry Amos. With him, you will bear me grandchildren."

"I'd marry that savage he defeated before I'd marry him!" Sarai yells, the anger stirring her to tears. Before they reach the surface, she glides out of the room. Once in the hallway of the grand palace, she falls to her knees and bawls. Tears for Asher, tears for Eleazar, tears that her father treats her like property, tears that she is simply a prop for Zion. Tears soon cease, but before they disappear, they turn into resolve.

Resolve quickly turns into a plan.

I have never seen such opulence. Crown molding made of gold. The white and gray swirls of the marble floors remind me of a hurricane's eye. My feet feel unworthy to walk on it. I keep reminding myself I'm not a Dreck, I'm a Lazurite warrior and the winner of the Canonization. I'm afraid Renatus will see right through me for who I really am as his elite guards escort me into his library. His bookshelf and desk are made of dark bocote wood, which smells like dill. I can see my reflection from the hardwood flooring's bright sheen. His bookcase contains volumes on war, physics, chemistry, language, and genetics. There is an entire section dedicated to genetic disorders alone. His walls are covered with pictures of him and Eleazar fishing, swimming, and posing on the beach. There are even a couple of Legion. None of Sarai.

"Congratulations, Son," Renatus strides into the room, his hairless head as shiny as the floor. He has the aura of an immortal.

"Thank you, sir," I manage to reply. *Sir?* I am immediately disgusted that I have addressed the butcher of my parents as sir. I need to think big picture. I am here for Sarai. There is a time to deal with this monster, and now isn't it.

"Drink?" He pours two bourbons, undoubtedly more expensive than a year's wages back home and surely not the stuff he is dropping in MiddleLand.

I accept, even though I hate the stuff. "Yes, my sultan."

"Knock off this sultan rubbish. The winner of the Canonization and the defeater of Legion can call me by my name." He hands me the tumbler, and I quickly down it, trying to calm my nerves. It is surreal standing here in the same room with him.

He eyes me and does his best to feign friendliness. But there is something less than friendly that lurks beneath his next question. "So, speaking of Legion, you let him live. Why?"

I knew this was coming, and quite frankly, I'm not sure what his intentions are with me. Was I called here to be sent to my death or to his underwater prison for defying his rules? I answer carefully.

"Legion is a legend. I grew up watching him. He was always one of my heroes. I thought him too valuable to Zion and your army. Valuable to you. I meant no disrespect."

Renatus is leery of my answer. He sniffs the air as if he can smell the truth.

"Being a leader of men means doing what is difficult, things you don't like doing. Even if that means killing men like Legion. When the greater good is involved, there will always be sacrifice."

"I agree, but being a leader also means circumventing the rules at times for the greater good, does it not?"

His blue eyes narrow ever so slightly. Did I go too far with that comment? His lips part, and his ivory-white teeth gleam. What is it with the Lazurites and their teeth?

"Yes, I suppose sometimes it does. Another?"

I nod, thinking it might be rude to decline. But this time I nurse the drink, not wanting to lose my bearings.

"So, Amos, tell me, who is it that taught you to be the warrior that you are, the leader I think you might become?"

Another tough question, as I'm sure he knows Amos's father was a mere commoner and that Amos himself was a simple patrolman.

"I guess you can say reading. Ever since I was a child, I was fascinated with the great warriors and leaders throughout history. Sun Tzu's *Art of War*. Washington. Patton. Alexander the Great. And it helps to have an older brother," I say in jest. I wonder who Renatus idolizes? Hitler and Stalin?

"Now, Amos the Magnificent." Renatus's bronze arms and long fingers wave in the air. His movements and mannerisms are almost deity-like. He is light on his feet, robust for his age.

I peer at the ground and force a blush.

"Now, Son, don't be humble. None of those men you mentioned were humble."

"Those who are humble are often underestimated. I believe this helped lead me to victory." I sound like my uncle and my father. Again, I hope I haven't crossed the line.

He studies my every move, slowly digesting each one of my words. But he is a closed book. I can't tell what he is thinking. "Your victory was brilliant, I'll give you that. Also a bit lucky."

"Doesn't luck favor the bold?"

"I suppose it does."

"What will become of Legion?" Not sure why I asked that.

Before he answers, Sarai strides in. Seeing her up close for the first time in five years wrecks me. I cannot help but open my mouth in awe of her stunning beauty. I breathe in her fragrance. I want to collapse into her arms. Tell her who I am. She tilts her head as she peers into my eyes. I can't look back. I can do nothing but stare at the floor.

"Ah, your prize," Renatus blurts as if I just won a painting at an auction.

Then she does something Renatus or I do not expect; she bows.

"Welcome to Zion's great palace, Amos the Magnificent."

Renatus about chokes on his bourbon.

Sarai's trainer and confidant, Hagar, fires up the Jeep. Sarai lies in the back under a blanket as they pass the guards and exit Renatus's compound.

"This all seems a bit dodgy, you sure you want to do this?" Hagar asks nervously.

"The only thing I'm sure of is I'm not marrying that man."

Sarai's cousin is a captain in Zion's first army. She convinced him through his back-channel negotiations to set up a meeting with her and The Sons of Levi. Her plan was to have Amos meet her at her cabin retreat in the woods. Once there she would give The Sons of Levi his location, and they could take him out. If and only if they harmed no one else. The move was reckless and severe, even for her. But desperation breeds such things.

Dusk is setting as she tries to steady her head from the bumpy ride. She thinks back to just hours ago when she stood outside her father's library waiting to meet Amos. How she had to steel herself and bury her hatred. But his eyes surprised her, and she thought she had spotted kindness. There was a familiarity about them as well. She couldn't quite spot it, but for just a moment she felt at peace. But she almost gagged when she bowed before him. As soon as she left the room, she scampered to the nearest loo and wretched until she was run dry. Her throat throbbed, and her stomach burned. It will be hard to keep up such a charade.

She closes her eyes and sees the weeping willow. The wind causes its twine-like strands to flog against her body. Lasso her soul. They beckon her to where Asher awaits, back against the trunk, reading one of her poetry books he hated so that he could speak her tongue. She always knew what page he had left off on from the marks his garbage-stained hands left from spending the day digging through her father's trash drops. She can feel the scar on the back of his neck where she hooked him from one of her overzealous casts while fishing on their favorite pond. He would then try to repeat one of the poems, never quite getting it right. She would smile, and soon enough he was making up his own verses, a mix between a 1980's love ballad and a 1990's rap song. The words would trundle out of the side of his mouth because of his signature half grin.

"We're here," whispers Hagar, not loud enough to rustle her from her daydream. "Sarai, we're here."

Then the weeping willow suddenly catches fire, and the long strands are like fast-acting wicks slowly disintegrating to ash. Her daydream has turned into a nightmare. For some reason Asher didn't notice the fire, nor could he hear her screams telling him to run. After a moment, he too was in flames.

And then gone.

Her eyelids opened like a creaking door. Her breathing was heavy.

"You okay?" Hagar asks her.

"Fine. Bad dream is all."

"I still think this is a bloody bad idea," Hagar tells her again.

"There are no good ideas anymore. Just bad options. Thank you for doing this, Hagar. I know it's risky for you. I didn't know who else to ask."

"Did I have a choice, my sultana?" he jokes.

"Shut it."

Truth was, Sarai felt bad for asking him to do this. If Renatus found out, Hagar could be sent to SeaPen or worse. But he was her only friend and the only one she trusted inside of Zion. He had always been like an uncle to her. He gave her encouragement and words of affirmation that her father didn't. Nor her mother. One had a God complex; the other was a narcissist. *Peas in a pod.*

It was less than two weeks ago that the man she was about to meet had tried to kill her. In a world of walls and blurred lines, how quick your enemy becomes your friend.

I'm baffled. Why would she act like this? I'm the killer of her beloved. Does she no longer care for me? The real me. Is she now a true Lazurite caught up in the pomp and opulence of Zion? I search her eyes for a clue and see desolation. Has she capitulated to the Lazurite way? Has her sorrow and Renatus's constant pressure finally scraped away the spirited and robustly autonomous woman I once knew?

"I'm not sure what it is you like yet, tea?" she offers me.

"Sure, please." I don't particularly like tea, but I'm confused and trying to be as congenial as possible. She pours me a cup as if she were a servant working in this secluded getaway in the woods. Renatus said this is where we are to get to know each other while planning the marriage. Something he wants done right away. Zion needs a royal wedding, he had insisted. A massive celebration for his people. A spectacle. It is just us and four lone sentries in the front of the quaint cedar log cabin. The inside is modern but not as ritzy as the castle. I like it. A fire is crackling in the fireplace, and the bronze leather couches are more comfortable than anything I have ever sat on.

"Hungry?" Sarai asks me. "Apologies, I didn't bring a chef, so you'll have to suffer my cooking."

I suppress a smile; she has always been a horrible cook.

"How about I cook?" I suggest.

"Tosh."

She is even speaking like them now. I know how much she despised their fake pretentious language. Is she not her because I'm not me? Should I tell her now? Will my cover be blown? Will she want to run off with me to spite her father? I want nothing more than to disappear, just us. Then there's The Defiance. My uncle. My people. I am my father's legacy. They are starving and being harvested for their LifeCells so the powerful can live forever.

Maybe we should eat first.

Twenty minutes later she brings a salad and two overcooked burgers. A side of pickles and black olives.

"Let's nosh," she announces.

The meal is tolerable due to the expensive wine that was on hand. I finish my glass as she finishes her second. I can tell she is doing everything in her power to calm her nerves. It's obvious she doesn't want to be here, but it seems she is steeling herself for something, adding to my confusion. After thirty minutes of small talk, her next question levels me.

"So, when you vanquished the son of Silas, was it a gentleman's duel? Or did you stab him in the back?"

I don't know how to answer that. I pat my face clean with a silk napkin and stand. "Fancy a walk?"

She sighs and guzzles the last of her wine, and with a hint of sarcasm, she replies, "Whatever you wish, Amos the Excellent."

"Just Amos, please. We don't have to walk. We can talk right here."

"I think I could use the air. Air in here is a bit stiff."

She is talking about me. I need to loosen up, but not too loose.

We stroll along the river through a herd of trees. A buoyant mist begins to fall as if the clouds are sneezing.

"So, defeating Legion, you must be proud of yourself?"

"I was lucky."

"I heard this Asher was a cunning warrior and a mighty adversary. Was he an easy kill? Did you do it alone? Were you lucky then too?" I can feel the venom in her voice. She is having a harder time hiding it now. Maybe it's the wine, or maybe one can only bury rage and love for so long. I can no longer see her like this. Her deteriorated spirit, her anguished heart. Her counterfeit feelings. Her fabricated words. No longer will she have to kiss the hand of a dragon. I have to tell her. I can't wait any longer. I never could hold a secret for long. We stop, and I turn to face her.

"I have something to tell you, Sarai. It's going to sound crazy I know. I wouldn't believe it if I were you, but you must believe me."

She already looks skeptical.

"Sarai, look into my eyes. Hear my voice. It is me. It's Asher."

The rain turns into a deluge.

She didn't slap me; she punched me square in the nose.

Sarai ignores the sting on her knuckles and the pain in her wrist as she wallops Asher a second time. A third time.

"How dare you! Who are you? What kind of a person are you?"

Asher grabs her arm. "It's me! It's really me. Listen—"

"Let go of me, you sick monster. You couldn't hold a candle to him. No Lazurite could!"

"Listen to me, I was sculpted!"

"Shut your mouth!"

It's just all too much for her as her knees buckle. The sheets of rain drench her hair and mat it to the dirt, which was quickly transforming into mud. Asher bends down to wipe her hair from her eyes.

"Don't touch me! Get away from me!" she bawls.

"Sarai, please! You have to believe me. I was sculpted as part of Cephas's crazy plan for me to win the Canonization, to lead one of your father's armies and be a spy for The Defiance. And to marry you . . . that is why I agreed, that is why I'm here. I'm here for you Sarai. Look at my eyes. Look!"

She does, and they so much look like Asher's. But she still can't believe it.

"Look at my neck." Asher bends and shows her the scar on the back of his neck where she had hooked him with a fishing hook. "Our tree, the willow. That is where we were to get married. My proposal, the fish, it swallowed the ring. No one else knew. Our casting contests, I would win, but you always caught more fish. It's me, Sarai. Look at me, look into my eyes, hear me. We are eternity mates."

"Then dance with me," she asks, trying to trick him.

"Not a chance."

She contemplates his answer as Asher hangs his head and wipes tears. Sarai puts her index finger underneath his chin and lifts his head parallel to hers. She scans his eyes and sees it.

Love.

Kindness.

Sorrow.

Tribulation.

Affliction.

Loss.

Restlessness.

These aren't the eyes of a Lazurite. They are that of a Dreck. They belong to Asher. He belongs to her. They freeze, afraid that any movement or words will shake them from this dream, and they will awake separated once again. In Zion's world, love is fragile and easily spooked. She moves first, slowly edging her chin to his. She shudders from his warm breath. They kiss softly. A redemptive kiss never thought possible trumps the first time their lips had touched. Their faces are slathered by the heavy downpour. An embrace five years in the making.

"I feel as if I've stepped out of a nightmare and into a dream," she whispers.

"Then don't open your eyes."

"But how will I see you?"

"I have seen you every day for the last five years. Your beauty is more than I remember. It's more than I can take."

"I can't breathe when you say such things. I thought you were dead, I had died inside."

"Death can't separate us."

"I can't believe it, how? How did you do this?"

"I don't know. I can't believe it either."

"How is Cephas?"

"The same."

"And Jude?"

"Still alive. Eats like a horse, still has the metabolism of a hummingbird."

Sarai giggles. *It's Asher, alright; that is definitely his sense of humor.*

"I would visit our willow every chance I got. I could feel you on the other side."

"That's because I was there. Even when I wasn't," she responds.

"I'm not sure it is possible, but you have grown more beautiful."

"And you are a liar. Now what?" Sarai asks, still dazed and astounded.

"We get married," Asher smiles, the words coming out as if they aren't real.

"Well, you have already proposed."

"And what about you? What have you been doing? How is Zion? Your aunt, do you ever speak to her?"

But she doesn't want to talk about any of that, at least not now. She wants to use her lips for something other than words as she again pulls him in. After a minute Asher suddenly pulls back and breaks into a loud and uncontrollable laugh.

"What? What's so funny?" she smacks his shoulder.

"Tosh? Did you actually say tosh?"

It's four in the morning, and Asher still embraces her tightly. Other than kissing, they both agreed long ago anything else would wait until they were bonded in marriage. *Marriage.* Sarai still can't believe they are finally to be married. With her father's blessing, no doubt! She smiles at the irony. *It doesn't hurt that Amos is handsome*, she thinks. She can feel his strong chest slowly rise and fall on her back as he sleeps soundly. The air traversing his now swollen nose from her whacking him makes a soft whistle in her ear. Her joy overrides her guilt. Her bones tingle as her love for him is marrow-deep. *Is this real?* She wonders. *Is he really here? Is this really him?* Her facial muscles are fatigued from smiling as they haven't been used for a long time. She slides her fingers between his, her soft palms grate against his hardened and calloused knuckles. As he swaddles her tight, her heavy black curls engulf him. The sparrows are up early this morning, just starting their love songs. *They must be singing for us.*

Then she hears a rustle, too loud for birds, then two muffled thuds right outside the cabin. She pops up and suddenly remembers. *Sons of Levi.* The last few hours had been so surreal and euphoric that she had forgotten all about it. They are here to take out Amos. No, Asher. Her love. She vigorously shakes him.

"Wake up! Wake up!"

His eyes creak open, "What? What is it?"

"We have to go! Sons of Levi are here!"

"What?" Asher jumps up and grabs his ricochet. "What are you talking about?"

"I hired them, to, to take you out."

"Are you serious?"

"Yes, I know it was wrong, but it was when I thought you were Amos, the man I was forced to marry, the butcher of my eternity mate."

"Put on your exoarmor."

They both slip into armored suits. Sarai grabs her scourge. The cabin goes dark.

"Power has been cut. How many are coming?"

"I don't know! Wait a minute, I'll simply go out there and tell them it's called off, to abort."

"You really think they're gonna leave you untouched? A chance to take out or kidnap the sultana? I know The Sons of Levi. Trust me, they would not pass up that opportunity."

"I wasn't thinking straight. I was too pissed off!"

"There's that Lazurite temper," Asher jokes.

"Remember that," she replies with a grin.

They creep to the door and slowly open it, leading into a family room and sitting area. Gunshots ring above them. They both hit the ground and crawl behind a bookcase.

"Was that gunpowder?" Sarai asks incredulously.

"Yes! Our suits are useless against bullets."

"Where did they get guns?"

"Probably me."

Sarai sees movement in the corner. Then she watches Asher roll to her left and fling his ricochet. It spins across the room, taking out a Levite. Asher rolls across the room behind a desk and peeks up, scanning for movement. He is tackled from behind, a knife at his throat. Asher fights to keep the menacing blade away from his Adam's Apple.

Sarai whips her scourge, snapping the knife from the intruder's hand. She swings it again, wrapping it around the Levite's leg and yanking him to the ground. She quickly reaches around behind him, delivering a forearm to his temple, knocking him unconscious.

"Nice work! Where'd you learn to do that?"

"I don't sit around in the castle all day eating bon-bons."

"It's like we were never apart," Asher is referring to their facetious banter.

More bullets whiz by them as Sarai sidles up next to Asher.

"Now what? We're pinned in." Sarai states as she spits.

A Levite takes cover behind a large steel safe. Asher leans his head around the desk, and it is almost blown off.

"We're sitting ducks. We have to move. His lead will blow right though this oak," Sarai whispers, finding it ridiculous that they are crouched behind a two-hundred-year-old oak desk donning advanced technological armor rendered useless by weapons almost as old as the desk itself.

Sarai peers up and spots a massive chandelier made from the antlers of a mule deer, native to the area. She nods to Asher, who clutches his ricochet. She watches him say a short prayer and snap his wrist. The ricochet cuts through the air and snaps the chain off the chandelier. The cluster of sharp antlers comes crashing down, impaling the final Levite assassin.

"Good idea," Sarai states plainly as if she expected no less.

"What did you expect? Aren't I Asher the Great?"

She swiftly kicks him in the shin but catches his face as he bends down and pulls him into her.

"Okay, Asher the Great, should I straighten the nose back for you?" She makes a mental note to herself to start calling him Amos in public.

"I don't know. I think it adds character."

He pulls her close, lips almost touching. She tilts her head to the side and amusingly bends his crooked nose to the left with her index finger before planting one on him. Doesn't matter if they're fishing or fighting. After five long years, they quickly return to being two peas in a pod.

"I can't believe you were going to have me assassinated!"
"You didn't think I would marry a Lazurite, did you?"

CHAPTER TEN

I have seen footage of Prince Charles and Princess Diana's royal wedding. It pales in comparison to what Renatus arranged. The streets are filled with people. Rose petals rain down like confetti. Two massive Shire Horses pull our golden carriage, and their hooves clack against the red carpet that overlays the concrete. Traditionally, in a royal Lazurite wedding, we would have left in the carriage, but Renatus wanted a grand entrance. A spectacle. I prefer Sarai in her faded jeans and ripped Van Halen T-shirt, but she is stunning nonetheless in her Lazurite white wedding gown with red stripes. The train alone is over twenty feet long. Gold flecks glitter from her arms and traverse down to her midsection. Her makeup is a burnished chestnut, just a shade darker than her eyes. Her magenta lipstick with purple hues reminds me of a smoky sunset. Her charcoal hair is twirled into fancy knots and tight braids that must have taken the hairstylist hours to assemble. Butterflies dance in my stomach.

I, on the other hand, am dressed in formal military garb. Black and white with a red sash. I was also forced to don a ridiculously tall red top hat.

"You look good in red," she whispers to me.

"You better take this hat before I accidentally throw it in the trash," I whisper back.

The carriage stops in front of a red and gold carpet that leads to a weeping willow overlooking the ocean. Not the same weeping willow, but I wink at Sarai, as only we know the significance. We are escorted to the willow, where Sarai stumbles and almost trips. She has never worn heels before. Her mother is embarrassed, but it just endears her to me even more.

Renatus himself stands to officiate. Even today is about him. We would have preferred a church and a pastor, but both are banned here in Zion. I can tell there is a tinge of perplexity in Renatus's demeanor, as I'm sure he is somewhat bewildered as to how accommodating Sarai has been. I can't help but wonder if he will find us out. I asked Sarai to act defiant, or at the very least look hesitant. But she said she can't help herself. Her joy cannot be suppressed, and she doesn't want to wait. Nor do I. There are Lazurite guards everywhere you look. Helidrones hover above us, flashing their lights and dropping rose petals to the ground. Renatus lifts his hands to silence the crowd. He himself wears a ten-gallon hat, also red.

"Today, my only daughter, the beautiful sultana, will marry Amos the Great, the crusher of the mighty Legion, the Slayer of the Son of Silas, and now husband to my Sarai and soon-to-be commander of my third army!"

The crowd roars. I think how Sarai must feel that her own father gave me a greater introduction than her. I think of Legion, now rotting in Renatus's aquatic prison. He did nothing wrong. He dedicated his life and skills to Renatus and Zion.

"Do you, Sarai the sultana, promise to serve Zion and all it stands for? To put Zion first and above anything else?"

"Yes."

I find it interesting that our marriage proclaims have nothing to do with us and everything to do with this false utopia.

"And you, Amos the Great, do you promise to serve Zion and all that it stands for? To put Zion first and above anything else?"

"Yes, sultan."

Squinting, I pan the crowd, and all I see is a hazy frost of gold and diamonds. I'm just part of another Zion event. Another excuse for the masses to be overly dressed and to gorge themselves. I am told that there was only one person bet on me to win the Canonization. Probably has the tallest hat in the crowd and a new suit.

"And now your vows," Renatus orders us.

Our vows are generic enough. Something typical of a forced marriage for two people who aren't in love, something Renatus would expect. Again, we mention service to Zion and Renatus. We are saving our real vows for a secret ceremony of just the two of us, under *our* willow. The one thing that is real is our kiss. Doves are released, as are butterflies, and soon we will dine at a banquet with enough food that would feed The Defiance for months. My people are suffering as the world around me is falling apart, but for me, in this very moment, everything is falling into place. I have Sarai. Next, I will be commissioned as commander of a quarter of Zion's army and firepower. If Cephas had a jovial bone in his body, he would surely be doing a happy dance right about now. I'm certain Jude is.

I'm a Dreck turned prince.

Sarai and Asher stand underneath their weeping willow next to The Wall. Asher didn't have to steal a military Jeep to get here. He just had to ask for it. Alone and dressed like Drecks. Sarai is in her cutoffs and has a faded Def Leppard tee. Her hair is down, even a bit messy. Asher is in acid-wash jeans and a Hawaiian shirt that Magnum PI would be jealous of, his faded *Star Wars* hat on backward. Overhead are drones releasing narcdrops and trash into The Middle. For a moment they put aside the suffering of his people and the wickedness of hers to soak in this moment. They clasp each other's shaking hands, both more nervous than they were at the royal wedding. Which, ironically enough, The Wall is being used as a screen to show nonstop videos of the ceremony. This is for real.

At first, Asher was concerned for Sarai's safety, and that The Sons of Levi had agents nearby. They tried to kill her here, after all. But she wouldn't have it any other way; they weren't about to get married anywhere but beneath their willow.

"I like your shirt," Asher says, looking for something to say. When an anticipated moment finally arrives, sometimes one doesn't know what to say or feel.

"Pour some sugar on me," Sarai banters back, singing some of the lyrics to Def Leppard's most popular hit. She too has waited for this moment for so long she also can't help but to be nervous.

Asher peers down at her feet and breaks the tension.

"No heels?"

"Shut it!"

The wind is still; the strands of the willow hang listless as if the tree is giving them a moment of silence, honoring their long-awaited vows. Sarai squeezes his hand.

"I'll go first." She takes a deep breath and closes her eyes, still believing this is all a dream. "When we first met, I found you a bit annoying as to how persistent you were. But you knew all along what I didn't know at first; we were meant to be together. You were simply following a path you knew to be true. It just took me longer to figure it out. Your fall not only wrecked your head, but it wrecked my heart. Since that day, I've been falling towards you. You awe me to the point I can't stand on my own two feet. Your words level me. I am astonished by what you do, who you are, who you will become. I mean, how are you even here right now? Are you kidding me? The Canonization? Legion?" Sarai wipes the moisture from her eyes. "You once said you would go through hell and back for me. For most it's just a saying, an expression of love, a cliche. But you, you actually did it. I'm yours forever. I will always offer you the respect and service you deserve. Even though you can't cast a fishing line worth a damn."

Asher grins. "I'm supposed to follow that?"

"You better. You've had five years to practice."

Asher makes a show of removing his hat and replacing it with the massive red top hat. Sarai laughs and quickly smacks it off his head.

"Funny."

This time, Asher closes his eyes; his hand is on hers, the other on his heart, as if it might burst from his chest.

"As you know, my fall was no accident. It is a metaphor for you and me. No pain or destruction can keep us apart. No wall, no car accident, no family, no war can separate us. Not even death. Our souls are bound together for eternity. How did I know the first moment I saw you that you were the one? I can't put it into words. It's like trying to describe the beauty of a sunset being pulled into a vast ocean to someone who has never seen it or how the tall pines appear after being covered with fresh frozen snow. Pure and quiet. Just looking at them can cleanse your soul. How does one know there is a God? All one needs to do is stand atop a mountain and watch a bald eagle soaring or gawk at the night sky while walking in the desert. Or watch a child be brought into this world. Life created, not your Father's way but from the Father above. But for me, all it takes is to gaze into your eyes, and I know. I know beauty, I know love."

Asher opens his eyes and wipes the tears from Sarai's cheeks. The winds pick up, and the willow's strands smack against each other as if they were clapping. She watches as he nods to his left at something long and narrow wrapped in cloth.

"What's that?" she asks.

"Fishing poles."

"Sounds great, but we forget about our first dance as newlyweds."

"Not a chance."

I stand in front of five thousand earnest Lazurite soldiers. Well, most of them earnest, as many were conscripted. This is my first introduction to them as their commander. Some stare at me in awe as the defeater of Legion, others in scorn as I'm not from royal blood. If they are to follow me, I need to earn their trust and their loyalty. I march back and forth, holding my ricochet in my left hand.

"Let it be known, mates, that I will not ask of you anything I'm unwilling to do myself. On the battlefield, I will drink what you drink, nosh what you nosh, sleep where you sleep. I will be with you on the front lines. Your victories will be yours. Your mistakes will be mine."

I pan the crowd and witness their puzzled countenance as they aren't used to hearing such words from Lazurite leadership. They are used to their commanders dining on delicacies and sleeping in cushy, warm accommodations while they eat oat bars and shiver under thin blankets.

"There are no stupid questions or requests. Mother dies, you go on leave, Wife goes into labor, two-week pass. Chaps make no mistake, we will attack with an iron fist, but we will not lead with one."

That is where my first decision made some waves. I only kept five out of the original twenty captains. I choose fifteen new ones not yet indoctrinated in the Lazurite way of leading. Low-level men, servant leaders, much like the men my uncle used to tell me about, the men Jesus chose—fishermen and tax collectors. And even though he refused profusely at first, I select Kenan as one of my captains. A reluctant leader like myself. He thinks his stutter will hold him back, I told him actions speak louder than words.

"Suggestions are encouraged. I don't care about your rank. Stripes on your arm have nothing to do with intelligence. The best idea wins. I have an open-door policy when it comes to this army and its leadership. I want your unvarnished opinion. With that being said, orders are still orders. But you will be part of the decision-making process."

A shaky arm is raised in the back.

"Yes, soldier."

"Our rations, they are not enough. They are never enough."

"I will do everything in my power to change that. And your rations will be my rations until then. If I'm to expect you to die with me, I can surely grow skinny with you. Any other questions?"

They seem too stunned to ask.

"Good, then let's get started. Today we are going to do something new. You all already know how to use plasma guns and pulse-grenades. Weapons of Zion. Our exoarmor protects us from these types of arms. We have the technological advantage . . . for now. Soon, The Defiance too will have exoarmor. It's only a matter of time, my spies tell me," I lie. "We must learn alternative warfare, adapt. We must train to fight future battles. We must use weapons that can penetrate exoarmor."

I pull a fifty-year-old 9mm Ruger handgun from my belt that I pilfered from the archives. "Does everyone know what this is?"

Someone yells out, "A handgun, lead, and gunpowder."

I nod.

Another asks, "I thought those were banned?"

"They are, but just because they are illegal doesn't keep them out of the hands of those who shouldn't have them. Our army doesn't have them, because we don't need them. But the black market is full of them, many going to The Defiance, The Sons of Levi. Does anyone know what a lead bullet will do to exoarmor?" I ask rhetorically.

An exoarmor suit hangs on a tree to my left. I pull out the handgun and riddle it with bullets. They all see the suit flying in the wind like a massive piece of Swiss cheese.

Another question. "Are you bloody saying these weapons are no longer banned and will become available to us?"

I lie once again. "Not yet, but maybe one day soon." It's a risk as if word gets back to Renatus, I could be in deep.

My captains take over and begin training their platoons on specifics. We train with old-school weapons. We do a deep dive into hand-to-hand combat, a lost art. With all else being equal, it could come down to the ability to fight with your hands. Besides, the close proximity to your enemy or training partner makes it more personal. Maybe one thinks twice before taking out someone who was once their brother—before the existence of The Wall. It's tougher when it's your bare hands as opposed to a plasma rifle from two-hundred-yards away. When you can see their pupils, smell their breath, taste their sweat, it becomes real. It makes one think what it is they are fighting and dying for.

As I walk towards my command center to study maps and upcoming attack plans, a wiry man with a flat nose and narrow chin in his thirties approaches.

"Sir Amos?"

"Yes, soldier."

"My name is Darius. I'm a lead scout for reconnaissance."

"What can I do for you, Darius?"

He slowly pulls down the front of his shirt to reveal the smallest of tattoos. I peer at it closely. It is a pelican.

"Cephas sends his regards," he whispers.

Darius is part of The Defiance and my contact. He sneaked across The Wall two years ago and has integrated himself into Renatus's army. After I won the Canonization, he asked for a transfer here. He will be my go-between for any communications between me and my uncle. For just a minute I relish my role of prince and commander. Darius reminds me why I'm here.

"Is there anything you have for me?" Darius asks.

"No. Not yet," I reply.

"Nothing?" A look of skepticism washes over him.

"It's too early," I tell him. I'm not yet privy to useful information to pass along. At this point, I'm more concerned with gaining the soldiers' trust.

I spend the next week training my soldiers to use guns, spears, swords, knives, and clubs. I'm teaching them under the guise that one day The Defiance will have exoarmor.

But I'm really training them to fight against their own army.

My first patrol is two days away. Meanwhile, we have been slurping up every indulgence Zion has to offer. Sarai and I have just returned from fishing off her father's one-hundred-and-twenty-foot yacht. As we change in our quarters, her chefs prepare our freshly caught tuna and mahi-mahi. She wraps her arms around me, her fingers tracing the humps on my spine.

"Let's just eat in here tonight," she says seductively.

"Your father is expecting my presence."

"'Expecting your presence'? Don't you sound all regal?" she says in jest. "Next, are you going to ask if we should nosh?"

I'm starting to sound like them.

After a small pout, Sarai slips her slender frame into a black glittering dress fit for a princess. I don what I think they call a tuxedo, but with red and gold stripes. I oddly find myself liking our attire as uncomfortable as it is. The gold cuff links, the expensive watch tattooed with diamonds. Polished Berluti handmade shoes. I have to remind myself it's elitist snobbery. That many of my people back in The Middle don't even own shoes.

Thirty minutes later we dine. Tastes and textures I didn't know existed. Someone plays Mozart on the grand piano behind me. Crystal. China. Silver. Unwarranted extravagance. But my taste buds do not complain as the chefs are truly talented. My unrefined palette gulps down what is Napa's finest. There are some delicacies on the table I don't recognize.

"Did your third army receive you well?" Renatus asks, licking his greasy lips as he ingests something slimy.

"I believe so. We had a good week."

"And your captains? You have them selected?"

"Most of them." I had one change his mind.

"You are moving fast. I like that," he smiles. The glare from the chandelier that beams onto his shiny bald head is almost as bright as his shoes. "Just be certain you can rely on them."

He pokes a thin sliver of fish with his fork and holds it up. "Do you know what this is?"

I shake my head.

"Fugu, better known as Puffer fish. A rare delicacy but dangerous. Its skin contains a toxin a thousand times greater than cyanide. If not prepared correctly, it can kill you instantly."

I make a mental note not to have any.

Renatus continues. "Be sure you can trust your captains as much as I trust my chefs!"

"I plan on testing their war readiness. We are planning a low-level patrol in two days."

"Good. I take it you are finding your accommodations more than sufficient?"

"Very much so."

Renatus peers at his jubilant daughter, who is rubbing my leg underneath the table. "I see you two are getting along?"

"Yes, Father," Sarai replies, still staring at me.

The haunting music drowns out any thoughts of back home. The guilt of knowing my people are starving and my soldiers are hungry while we leave plates half full is slowly dissipating. I'm beginning to find the Lazurite way of life to my liking, and it worries me. What worries me more is that in two days, I'm tasked to hunt down my own.

I walk a fine line between gaining Renatus's trust and serving The Defiance and their cause. I take another sip of wine and look to Sarai. She is whom I choose to serve right now; at this moment, she is my cause.

Is there still room in my heart for my uncle's?

After a three-day caravan and four-day march, we set up a base camp on Reservation 17 on the other side of The Wall. It is south of Reservation 9, my hometown and Defiance headquarters, and just north of former New Mexico. I purposely steered clear of any known Defiance hot spots. I'm hoping for a quiet week. If we encounter The Defiance they will most likely hide or run from an army of this size or resort to guerrilla warfare tactics and just prick and prong us from our flanks while disappearing back into the woods. I also sent Darius out ahead of me to warn any Defiance of our presence. Besides, this is a training mission, and I will not order a full-scale attack. Instead, we will set up a defensive posture, as I don't want to be attacked either. It's weird being back inside The Middle. It hasn't been that long, but it feels like ages since I left.

My men light fires and set up tents, though there is not enough for everyone. So, I decide to sleep outside and shiver with a third of my army who will also bear the elements. Food being sparse, I too will have only a half ration for supper. I wonder why Renatus doesn't supply us the way he should. Is it a test? Or are he and his cronies slowly bankrupting Zion? Maybe paradise isn't as solvent as he has others to believe. Or maybe he is just being plain sadistic. I have also heard rumors that the good stuff goes to his elite first army, and we get the scraps.

For the most part, Kenan has kept quiet, but the men under his command follow orders and do not overtly show ambivalence towards him, because he was shamed as a coward during the games. He takes a page out of my book and hands his tent over to his second in command. His men take notice. The conscripted are usually the lowest rank and traditionally forced to cook. Some of them traverse through the sea of dirty and parched troops and pour them water. An elite Lazurite soldier, one who probably has aspirations for the Canonization one day, snatches the entire jug of water from a conscript and then shoves him to the ground before spitting on him. The elite believe they are the top tier in this caste and see conscripts as mere peasants. I immediately jump to my feet and approach the elite. As he turns to me, I sweep his leg, he lands on his side, and I rest my boot on the back of his neck.

"What's your name, soldier?" I demand, gritting my teeth.

"Jarrod, son of Senator Raza." He spits out as if that will help his cause. As if I should be impressed.

"I don't care if you're a son of Renatus; no one soldier is better than another." I peer over at the crowd gathering and raise my voice. "In my army, no man will be judged or gain merit based on where they are from, their bloodline, or who their father is, is that clear? Every man here will cook, every man here will clean. How you treat what you consider the least of these is how you treat me." The last line is something my father used to say.

I see nods around me and smiles from the conscripted. Jarrod says nothing as my boot applies more pressure, "Is that clear, soldier?"

"Yes, sir."

I remove my boot and help him up. I then grab two jugs of water and pour Jarrod a cup. "Now drink, then get some rest."

I walk the line of men, pouring them water. I stop at a man who must be in his fifties, rail thin for a Lazurite obviously conscripted.

"What's your name?"

"Samuel," he hacks, pulling his long pearly white bristly hair into a ponytail.

"How old are you, Samuel?"

"Sixty-one." Teeth are missing—again, not very Zion-like.

"You married?"

"Yes, sir."

"Amos, call me Amos. For how long, soldier?"

"Married at eighteen, so forty-three years," he says proudly, but also sadly.

"Forty-three days for me," I say with a wink. "We'll talk later mate. I think my cup could be filled with some of your wisdom."

He peers up at me, stunned, wondering, *Who is this Lazurite prince actually talking to me, asking me personal questions? Asking for my advice!* I bend and whisper into his ear, "When we return, you can take your leave. I will put in for an honorable discharge at full pay."

As I walk away, he staggers to his feet. "Sir Amos, my wife is dead. I think I'll stay and fight for you."

"Don't fight *for* me, fight *with* me."

The tough old bird gives me a resolute nod before plopping back down and lighting up a smoke. I pour my troops fresh water for the next hour before lying under the winking stars next to my new comrades. Occasionally, I catch a glimpse of the red beacons attached to the trash pallets being air-dropped into my homeland. I find it hard to believe that not too long ago, I made my living rummaging through Zion's litter. I have noticed a few of my other captains have given up their tents to the men underneath them. Whether it is sincere or they are just trying to impress me, I'm not sure. But either way, my example is starting to catch on. I try not to be too optimistic, as giving up a tent is a far cry from getting them to fight against Zion and their own people. I need a miracle. I'm not sure what I'm trying to achieve is possible: Gaining Renatus's trust, the third army's loyalty, doing my job for Zion, and keeping casualties to a minimum for not only The Defiance and my people but also for my army, most of which are just boys, barely eighteen. As I close my eyes, I pray that God will send me a solution to the impossible.

At 2:34 in the morning, one arrives.

"Wake up, Amos! Wake up!" Kenan bellows in my ear. I pop up to the sound of men running around, confused and scrambling for their weapons.

"What's going on?" I ask calmly.

"There!" Kenan points to an ancient military Jeep. It has extra steel armor welded to the front, back, and sides. It smashes through our horses and Jeeps, heading straight for me.

"Suicide bomber," I yell, grabbing my ricochet. Sons of Levi, no doubt. My men, finally gaining their bearings, fire their plasma rifles at the incoming Jeep, which does little to slow it. I have no shot with my ricochet.

"Pulse-grenades!" I order.

As it gets closer, I stand my ground. I don't want my troops to see me run. One of the soldiers tosses a pulse-grenade; its shock wave tosses the Jeep into the air, and when it lands on its side, whoever is driving detonates its payload; the Jeep is lined with TNT. The massive explosion sends me hurtling to the ground. Pieces of dirt, shrapnel, metal, and earth rain down like hail, pelting my back. I pull myself up as the black, acrid smoke clears. I see at least twenty of my men lying dead. Pieces of them scattered like a spilled box of toothpicks. I shake in anger and shock. I can smell burned flesh and singed hair. It reminds me of the bombing at the bazaar, and I wonder if I'm cut out for this sort of thing.

"Now what, sir?" Kenan asks.

I have to regain my composure. I must act, I must think. This isn't The Defiance. These are tactics The Sons of Levi employ. Besides, Cephas knew I would be here. Then I hear screams from my left flank. Arrows fly from the forest and impale four more of my third army.

"What do we do, sir?" Kenan hollers again.

"They're in the forest," I say obviously, "Kenan, take fifty men to the west and ride around the outside of the trees." I tell another captain to do the same but on the east side. I gather twenty of my own men, and we hop on horses, "I'll meet you in the middle."

"Perhaps you should stay, let your men take care of it," Kenan stutters.

"I'll meet you in the middle," I respond firmly, wanting them to see that a true leader doesn't lead from behind.

As we charge into the forest, I wonder if I have a traitor in my midst, as how else would The Sons of Levi know I'd be here. It's ironic to call someone else a traitor of Zion, considering who I am.

I duck and charge forward. I'm in the front, as I said I would be.

Some Levites are on foot, some on horseback. Our horses mow down their foot soldiers as we begin to catch up to their riders. Arrows take out two riders to the left of me. Their lead rider, donning a contorted metal mask, stops on a dime and turns. He pulls an ax from his leather satchel and hurls it at me. I pull on the reins, and my horse skids to a stop and rises on its hindquarters, chest in the air. The ax slices into its chest, and it flops on its side, sending me rolling to the ground. I pop up and fling my ricochet, sending it slicing through the air. It hits the back of the rider wearing the metal mask, and the electrical current jolts him off of his horse. He is up in a hurry, his long and lengthy body taking massive strides through the forest, only stopping to hurl daggers at us.

"Take him alive!" I command my men.

I slide off my horse and scamper towards him, dodging the sharp knives. His feet get tangled in the underbrush, and he falls to the ground. I arrive at the same time as some of my men. He flails to his feet, but he is surrounded.

"Take off the mask," I order, having a good idea who it might be.

He obliges. It is the leader of The Sons of Levi, Dagger. I check his left arm and spot a Liberty Bell tattooed on his arm just to be sure. He spits in my face.

"Die you Lazurite cell pirate!"

My men handcuff him and start to beat him.

"Enough!" I yell, wiping his bloody saliva from my face. "Where are the others?"

"You honestly think I would rat out my men? You Lazurite fascists are dumber than I thought."

I motion to my men. "Take him."

"Freedom will be ours!" Dagger screams as he is being dragged to a horse.

At what cost? I wonder as he and his men have killed countless innocent women and children in the name of freedom. He has the same endgame as me, but his methods lack morality. I fear his scorched-earth campaign will dislodge the seeds of freedom that have been delicately sowed into those who still wish for it. "Don't trample the flowers while killing the weeds," my father used to say.

I look to the sky and project a silent thank you. Dagger is my solution, my miracle. Renatus will be elated with his capture. I will have earned my men's trust. I have served Zion without hurting The Defiance. One day I may be able to convince Dagger the error of his ways, and perhaps he will become an ally. But for now he is a terrorist heading to SeaPen.

And a part of me is happy for what he tried to do to Sarai.

CHAPTER ELEVEN

"**B**loody brilliant, mate!" Renatus congratulates me. "Your first mission and you have impressed me. I can't tell you how long The Sons of Levi have been a thorn in my side, and Dagger is a barbarian of the purest sort."

It has been so long since I have heard a compliment or have received accolades of any kind. Not since before the death of my father. Cephas would spoon-feed them at best, usually with undertones on what you did wrong. For a kid, that's chocolate with a squeeze of lemon. We stroll along the sandy beach in front of his palatial estate. He puts his hand on my shoulder.

"Proud of you, Son."

He means it. I clear my throat and watch the ocean waves lap at my bare feet. The soles of my feet being scrubbed clean by the sand. "Thank you, sir."

He stares at me and can practically read my mind; it's uncanny. "You have the look of a man on the verge of a request," he guesses correctly.

"Yes, yes, I do. My men . . . they . . . our provisions are meager, sir. Food is scarce, so are tents," I say, unsure why I'm stuttering. I can sympathize with Kenan.

"Ah yes, ever since the BitTender crash, Zion hasn't been the funded paradise it was set out to be. This war has gone on far too long. But I will see to it that you have what you need for certain victory."

"Thank you, sir."

"Renatus, please," he insists and then stops. "Do you know why I put up The Wall?"

I swallow hard. "No."

"My scientists had created a gift, something wonderful for all, but like all good things, this gift was abused, it wasn't cherished. Second-life rights were supposed to be an insurance policy, a second chance. Instead, so many used it as a way to squander their first. A society bereft of morality. When one doesn't fear death, what is cherished?"

For a moment I forget about his hypocrisy. He then pulls from his pocket a necklace with a dolphin pendant.

"This belonged to my son, Eleazar, before he drowned in these carnivorous waters. Treachery usually accompanies such beauty. He loved dolphins."

I'm shocked. Renatus won't even speak to Sarai about his Eleazar. Yet he confides in me. He covers his mouth and peers at the sand. His eyes are sad, even warm. For a moment I forget who he is.

"Eleazar was born with a rare chromosomal disorder. His seizures would scare the wits out of me. He was brave but wounded. Always wounded. One day, when you have a child, you will understand that there is nothing you won't do for them. Nothing."

"The most beautiful things in life are the most delicate," I respond with something I came up with, not just another one of my father's regurgitations. Renatus's wiry hands pat my cheek.

"You are a warrior-poet, Amos, a true prince of Zion. Now come, let's eat with your beautiful wife. As for tomorrow, we catch marlin."

I'm excited at the prospect of fighting such a fish.

"And I have something for you, a reward for your obedience to Zion," Renatus smiles and leads us to a back storage garage away from the beach. He opens the doors and flicks on the lights. Inside is a harem of Ford Mustangs.

"Your wife told me you were a car guy, that you like the ponies?"

"Yes, yes I do," I respond with my jaw to the floor. I spot a 2099 Jet Black Cobra with white racing stripes. The electric engine has twelve-hundred horsepower. I open the door and gently get behind the driver's seat as if unworthy to sit behind such a machine.

"Zero to sixty in two seconds," Renatus brags. "Go ahead, Son, take it for a spin."

I start up the engine and grip the thick steering wheel. My hands have never harnessed so much raw power. Amos's Lazurite blood has begun to seep into my marrow. I think I'm becoming one of them. I'm sinking in Zion's quicksand, and I can't feel the noose around my neck. I'm not even trying to escape.

I'm finding the breath of a demon warm and the bosom of a dragon quite snug.

Before our fishing trip, I head to the main pool for a morning swim. I considered taking one of the Mustangs for a morning drive, but I really need my exercise. Instead of coffee, I grab a Newer Coke from the mini fridge, stocked full at my request. The pool is indoors and reminds me of the Roman pool at Hearst Castle. I have never been there, but I have seen pictures. The pool's bottom is an iron blue with red stripes. The water is crystal clean. I down my soda and dive in. The water is just the right temperature. Not too cold, but cold enough to still be refreshing. Lights twinkle above me. Six different waterfalls cascade into the pool. The length is a stunning fifty yards. Four different diving boards of various heights grace the deep end. This is my first time swimming in anything other than a lake. Later will be my second time on the ocean.

I turn for another lap, and I hear, "Asher."

I lift my head, and it is Darius. He peeks around to be sure no one else is here.

"What are you doing here, Darius?" I try to hide my annoyance. Every time he shows up, it reminds me why I am here. It reminds me of my uncle.

He whispers, "You were supposed to meet me last night, remember?"

"I got held up. You need to leave."

"I need to report back to Cephas. You promised me troop movements, The Wall openings, planned EMP drops, and drone counts."

"I don't have that yet," I lie.

He is on to me. "But you have access. You should at least know some of these things by now."

Truth is, I do know. Telling him will escalate this war; selfishly, I am not ready for that. That will lead to time away from Sarai. It means time we can no longer spend together in relative harmony and peace.

I can tell he doesn't believe me. "I'll find you tomorrow, and the next day, and the day after that."

I throw him a bone. "Tell Cephas I have captured Dagger, and that I'm still gaining Renatus's trust."

As he slips out, I return to my laps. I feel guilty about lying to my uncle, but the truth is, I am not ready for this. I never wanted it. I can't live up to his expectations or my father's legacy. I mean, every time I close my eyes, I see the bombing at the bazaar. I hear the wails of the mothers who lost their children. I can feel their anguish. How can I lead like this? How can I empty myself for Cephas's cause when this is what I'm full of? On my twentieth-something lap I hear a splash. I open my eyes and see the slender frame of Renatus streaking through the water.

"You like to swim?" Renatus asks, popping his head out of the water.

"First time in a pool, but yes," I reply.

"It's the best exercise you can get. I'm in here every morning. Doesn't take long to get one knackered."

"I have noticed."

We swim our laps, side by side, and I can barely keep up with him. After thirty minutes, my arms burned, and my legs like rubber. I wonder if Renatus has gone bald or if he shaves his head to be faster in the water.

"So tell me, Amos, how did you do it? How did you beat the mighty Legion?" Renatus asks, his breathing steady, not a hint of exhaustion.

"I studied him. Found a weakness," I respond, trying to catch my breath.

"I didn't realize he had one."

"Doesn't every man?" I say, trying to sound wise.

He smiles. "Yes, yes, they do. A good warrior knows his own weaknesses. A great one knows his opponents. What is yours, Amos?"

I think long and hard and wonder if it is a trick question. If I say none, he knows I'm lying; if I tell him the truth, he may deem me unworthy to lead his army.

"I'm too trusting," I lie.

I don't dare ask him his, and I doubt he will reveal it, even though I know that pride and overconfidence are among them. But then he surprises me.

"Mine is that I'm dauntless. An intrepid man makes mistakes."

He has nothing to fear, for he has made himself immortal. For now.

"So, what was Legion's weakness?" he asks again.

"He is blind in his left eye."

"And how did you know?"

"I went to the archives. I watched all his previous matches."

He nods as if telling me well done.

"What is it you hope to accomplish here, Amos?"

"To take down The Defiance. To win the war. To bring peace to Zion."

"Maybe your weakness is that you are naive?" Renatus responds after a pause.

"I don't understand."

"There will never be peace, young Amos. It isn't possible. It doesn't exist in the hearts of men. As long as there are people like us and people like those in The Middle, there will always be war. Once we defeat The Defiance, someone else will rise in its place. Maybe even our own people. You see, they want what we have. It's pure and simple avarice."

Renatus sounds as if war is a good thing, something he relishes. But he is correct; war has always existed and always will. My uncle tells me there is only one that can bring true peace. Just thoughts of being in The Middle, living in my tiny hostel among the Drecks, and digging through trash seems like a lifetime ago. I peer down at the clear water and see my reflection. For a moment I'm startled. I have forgotten that I don Amos's face. But it is more than my appearance that has changed.

Renatus puts his arm on my shoulder. "We have to cover each other's blind spots, mate. I'll try not to be so fearless, and you don't be so damn trusting."

Why do I feel at home? Why do I feel as if I have my father back? I know it's wrong, but my flesh wants to stay in Zion, where I can foster my relationship with Sarai unfettered. A burden has been lifted when I can be with her with Renatus's approval as opposed to his constant interference. Is this how evil is birthed and morality dies? Slowly, while dining on lobster and sipping fine wine?

"And what happens when we win? When The Defiance has been defeated. Does The Wall come down?"

"There has always been a wall, Amos, just not a physical one." Again, he studies me, then smiles. "Let's go catch a big fish, shall we?"

The sea doesn't want us out there today. Renatus's forty-five-foot fishing boat surfs the fifteen-foot waves as we make our way to the fishing grounds. The cold saltwater splashes over the bow, instantly soaking us.

Renatus, with his shirt off, soaks in another wave of icy water. It rolls off his smooth head and onto his shaved chest. He is loving it.

"People don't spend enough time outdoors!" he whoops.

A wave hits our left side, sending me sliding towards the railing. Renatus reaches out and snatches me before I go overboard.

"I got you, I got you." His tone is that of a worried parent. He holds my arms tight. "You okay, Son? You okay?"

"I'm fine."

But I'm not fine. I'm taken aback by his sudden concern, his worry for me. He covers his mouth.

"Sorry, I just. Eleazar drowned in these waters, and I . . . seeing you almost go overboard, I just. Never mind. Remember, wide stance and loose knees will help get your sea legs." He puts his arm on me. "You almost had a trip to The Mountain, Son."

I see some humanity in him; perhaps things aren't so black and white? After our boat slices through another wave, I finally find my balance and inhale a large breath of fresh sea air. Something about being on a boat that makes me feel instantly free. An hour later we have reached the fishing grounds. The seas have calmed a bit. We both cast our lines as I look out at the vast ocean and wonder how I got here? Not too long ago I was just a refuse rat, digging through the trash and living in a cold, damp cement hostel.

Renatus stares out at the vast ocean, the sun reflecting brilliantly off the water. "I love being out in creation."

I am surprised by his term. "Creation? You believe in God?"

"Surprised?"

"A little," I reply.

"Yes, there is a God, Amos. But I believe he rules by absenteeism. That is where we step in. Both my parents and sister died when I was young, then my son. Where was God then?"

I don't have an answer for him; Cephas would.

Renatus stares at the horizon, then at me, "Perhaps that is why we are here, to pick up where He left off? Maybe that's what protocol is for?"

What Renatus says next makes it even worse.

"Now that we have Dagger, we need to work on getting Cephas."

I simply nod.

Renatus shakes his head. "Cephas, the great leader of The Defiance, if people only knew him as I did."

Now I'm curious. "What do you mean?"

"The meeting with Asher's parents. Silas, the peacemaker and his wife. Silas and I were both ready to broker a peace deal, end this bloody war between Zion and The Defiance. Things were going well and agreements were being made. Then, out of nowhere, Cephas and his band ambushed us and broke the temporary ceasefire. I looked into Silas's eyes, and he was genuinely surprised. He had not backstabbed me. It was Cephas who went behind his back and attacked without his knowledge. But the way Cephas tells it, you would think it was the other way around. If only people knew the real Cephas, he wouldn't be loved as he is."

It can't be, can it? He has to be lying. But why would he? I can see if he knew I was Asher, but why would he lie about this to Amos? Did Cephas really betray my father? Is that why my parents were killed? My head is spinning.

I am so lost in this thought my fishing pole is almost ripped from my hands.

Renatus yells, "Fish on!"

The banquet is impressive. The dance hall and ball are grandiose. Sarai wraps her hands around Asher's neck, trying to get him to dance, lips a nickel's width apart.

"How was fishing?" Sarai asks, never taking her eyes off of his.

"Incredible. Two-hundred-pound beast fought for a good forty minutes before I hauled her in," Asher replies, still on a high from the morning's festivities.

"I would have reeled her in in thirty," Sarai replies, tongue in cheek.

"I have no doubt you would have."

Sarai sees something in his eyes that just isn't quite right, "You sure you're okay?"

"Great." Asher lies.

Renatus dances with Joanna with such poise and grace that Asher takes notice. His feet slide elegantly across the floor as he twirls her, slowly leading her into a dip.

"Your dad has some chops."

Sarai smiles, "Perhaps you should take lessons from him."

"Not a chance."

The grand hall is replete with senators, generals, and other members of the elite. All dressed to the nines, with their wives laminated in diamonds. Crystal chandeliers and gold flaked trim on the crown molding. Opulence drips from the ceilings, and vanity oozes from the walls.

Sarai's white, gold, and red dress is something out of a fairy tale. She, like Asher, is getting used to such attire. She, like Asher, is getting sucked into Zion's extravagance, Zion's lies. It is not so much the riches as it is the only way she and Asher can finally safely be together; that is what she treasures. Conversations with her father are even pleasant now. She no longer loathes her mother's company. Her ripped Van Halen shirt is tucked away in the back of her dresser.

For the first time in her life, Sarai feels like she has a father. Sure, it's perhaps proxy love through Asher, but it is still love, love that she had never had from him before. Renatus didn't come out and say it, but he spoke to her in kindness, actually paid attention to her. Things are almost normal.

"When is your next patrol?" she asks, not wanting him to leave again so soon.

"Five days."

She thinks about what Asher might do if he and his army come face to face with The Defiance soldiers. His people. Drecks. She wants to ask what his plan is for her father's third army. Is he training them to fight against Zion? Is he trying to gain their loyalty per Cephas's plan to be used to overtake her father and the Lazurites? Or has he switched allegiances? Her father can be pretty persuasive. But she doesn't ask. She fears that if the words are spoken, it might pull them back into reality from the clutches of Zion's paradise. She has Asher now and doesn't want that to change. The fact that Asher hasn't offered her any of this information tells her he feels the same. The bliss of ignorance. But this isn't ignorance; it's willful obtuseness. Does she think that perhaps a peace deal can be brokered? Maybe she can convince her father to end the war and open The Wall, and then she and Asher can remain this way, on an island, just the two of them. No Defiance. No war. No Wall. Including the abolition of second-life protocol. She has no plans of outliving the many children or grandchildren spawned from the man she now holds. Zion's wool is thick. Its web sticky.

As the music stops, Renatus approaches them.

"What? You two don't like to dance? Is the music not to your liking?"

"Ash . . . uh . . . Amos refuses," she almost said Asher.

"Dodgy footwork?" Renatus asks with a smile.

"I value your daughter's toes," Asher responds, taking a sip of his wine.

"Perhaps we'll remedy that one day," Renatus says in a tone that sounds more like a demand.

"Perhaps we will," Sarai agrees, elbowing her husband in the ribs.

"Now, if you two beautiful ladies will excuse us for a moment." Renatus grabs Asher by the arm and whispers into his ear.

"Be up early. I have something to show you in the morning." His words have more gravitas than normal, almost as if they are life changing.

Sarai overhears and fears that they might be.

After a quick workout and a light breakfast consisting of cream cheese and smoked salmon, I take a shower. Until I reached Zion, I had never experienced a hot shower or bath. It's divine. I have trouble getting out, but I don't want to be late. I meet Renatus out front. He is in the driver's seat of a freshly waxed Jeep. He checks his watch.

"Right on time."

"What kind of soldier isn't?"

He smiles and rams it into gear as we take off with a lurch. Our armed entourage consists of four other Jeeps and two helidrones tracking our every move.

"Where we headed?" I ask.

"The Mountain," he replies bluntly. From his look I can tell he wants the rest to be a surprise, so I don't press him on what exactly is *The Mountain*.

Twenty minutes into the trip we encounter a torrential downpour. I peer into the back and spot the Jeep's vinyl top.

"Should we stop? Put the top on?"

Renatus looks to the sky and raises one hand while driving with the other. "Don't shelter yourself from the storms of life, Son. Absorb it, relish it. It's okay to get soaked in it; the sun always returns."

Once again, Renatus impresses. He guns it on the muddy road, the tires spin, and the back end hooks to the left, a smile on his face. An hour later we reach the base of The Mountain. We pass through the first fenced checkpoint and make our way up a windy, bouncy road until we are almost halfway up. We stop when we reach the five-foot-thick steel door. It reminds me of NORAD, or at least how it was portrayed in the movie *WarGames*, another 80's classic. More helidrones and armed elite patrol the door. The men stand to rigid attention when they recognize who is driving the Jeep.

"Good morning, sultan," one of them says while saluting.

Renatus ignores him. The door rolls open, and we drive through. I wonder what is inside. *New weapons, perhaps?* We hop out of the Jeep, still dripping wet from the rain. He hands his coat to a guard, grabs a towel, and wipes the rain and mud off his face. He throws me a towel and leads me to an elevator that takes us twelve stories underground. He is silent, with an eager smile of anticipation about what he is about to show me. The elevator door opens, and then it occurs to me where we are going.

"This is where it all happens, mate," Renatus whispers proudly as if anything above a murmur would awaken his harvest. "The second-life protocol."

Thousands of bodies lie in cryogenic chambers waiting to be used for Zion's elite. They float inside the pink translucent fluid like they are unborn babies in amniotic fluid. My body shakes. I'm not sure if I'm cold from the rain or just have the chills from what lies before me.

"How does it work?" I ask, already partially knowing the answer.

"To spare you all the technical rubbish, basically we harvest what is called their LifeCell. It immediately kills them, and it is the basis for regeneration. Resurrection, if you will." Renatus scrutinizes my expression. "Why so shocked? They're only Drecks, mate."

"Just amazed at the technology, at what you have created," I lie.

He rests his hand on my shoulder. "You are part of the elite now Amos. Because of this, and your loyalty to Zion, I offer you eternal life."

It is risky saying this, but I say it anyway. "What if I don't want that?"

"What? Protocol?"

"Yeah, what if I didn't want to use another's LifeCell?"

He licks his lips. "Respectable. Did you know when I first came to power, I ran on the second-life platform. I truly wanted to make the world a better place. To heal people, to bring back the lost, those gone too soon, like my son. I truly thought we could engineer protocol to use a manufactured or synthetic LifeCell, if you will. I believe we still can. That is the hope anyway."

Again, I feel as if I'm being swaddled into Zion's bosom. Its comfort and security. It's strange to think that I could be invincible. We approach a control station where numerous doctors and techies amble about. Renatus approaches one of them.

"What's this week's count?"

"One hundred and seventy," he answers after checking his chart. I can only assume he is talking about their harvest. *Harvest.* I'm even starting to think like them. This isn't a harvest. It's murder. They are Drecks, my people. But I begin to wonder, am I still one of them?

"Any matches?" Renatus asks.

The doctor simply shakes his head. Renatus turns to me and nods to follow him. As we stroll through the line of cryo chambers, I try not to look at their faces, afraid I might see someone I recognize. We stop at one chamber harboring a small child, a young boy.

"You see, my son, Eleazar, was born with a cellular disorder. When he, when he drowned, we recovered the body. But protocol hasn't been successful. I'm told we need a LifeCell with the same chromosomal disorder as my prince." Renatus peers at his frozen, lifeless son. His eyes become moist. His teeth grind. He quickly snaps out of it and pats my back.

"We shall keep trying."

We?

To my left is the processing center for new arrivals. Through the glass I can hear the screams of a mother and the groans of a father as their children are ripped from their arms. Will they be a match for Eleazar I wonder? I cringe. Six months ago the scene would have panged me greatly.

"We are Lazurites!" the father screams, "You can't do this to us!"

I peer over at Renatus. "Lazurites? I thought you were only harvesting Drecks?"

"And enemies of the state," he responds. "They were caught smuggling Bibles and other contraband into The Middle."

And I used to be the one on the receiving end. How far I have come.

Or fallen.

"Why not SeaPen?" I ask.

"SeaPen is for much bigger fish, excuse the pun, mate."

But I know the real reason. Now that he hasn't found a match for his beloved Eleazar in The Middle, he is starting to see if his own people will yield a match.

As we turn the corner and walk back through the next row of chambers, I see something that finally shakes me from my complacency.

In an instant I remember who I am and why I'm here.

In the two chambers to my left, frozen in time, are my parents.

Sarai poses in front of the full-length gold-trimmed mirror; this is her third outfit. She smiles, thinking about the six-course banquet they will attend tonight, and perhaps she will convince Asher to dance. Then back here and her intimate time with him. It took a while, but she has gotten used to how he looks now in Amos's skin.

A few months ago she wouldn't even have dreamed of wearing such ornate and gaudy attire. Now she fancies it. She used to scoff at wearing jewelry, but now she is so layered with gold and diamonds that she glitters and sparkles. She is becoming her father's daughter. And she has never been happier. She turns as Asher shuffles through the door.

"Ready to nosh?" she asks.

His face is pale, his walk cadaverous.

"Asher?"

He trudges past her, removes his ricochet from his belt, and places it on the bed. It sinks into the goose down comforter. He slowly sits next to it.

"Asher? Are you alright? What happened?"

He looks at her, their massive bedroom, her lavish dress. Her adornment of what was once mined from the earth. He scowls.

"What are we doing?"

"I don't understand. We're going to dinner. What's wrong? Did something happen today?"

"What are we doing? Who are we, Sarai? What are you wearing?"

Sarai's worry is becoming ire. "Have you been drinking? What are you talking about? Does this have to do with what my father showed you?"

"Where's your Van Halen tee?" he asks, still looking like he has seen a ghost.

"Asher, tell me what's going on."

"Your car accident, back in The Middle. It was no accident."

"I'm not following."

"I found the wreckage, Sarai. The break line had been cut. It was not an accident."

"Cut? By who?" Sarai starts to breathe rapidly.

"Who do you think? Your father."

"That's crazy. Look, I know he is many things, but—"

"Think about it, Sarai, you were with me, a Dreck, on the other side of The Wall. He kills you, transfers you to Zion, implements second-life protocol and problem solved."

Sarai shakes her head in disbelief.

"Do you know where I was today?"

She just stares at him, fear and anger boiling inside her.

"The Mountain. You know what happens inside The Mountain?"

"Yes, protocol."

"And do you know exactly what is involved?"

She shakes her head. "What are you getting at, Asher?"

"Your father, the rich and powerful of Zion, not only want to live forever, but they sacrifice the innocent to do so."

A tear streams down Sarai's face. She has ignored the rumors this entire time, but deep down, she knew the truth.

"Drecks Sarai, they are kidnapping and harvesting Drecks for their LifeCells. Killing them. Children. He is rounding up children so he can find a cell match to bring back his precious Eleazar. He's even harvesting his own people now."

"I don't believe it."

"I have been there Sarai, I have seen it! We have been coddled in Zion's grip for long enough. It's time to fight."

Her heart is pounding. "There has to be another way, a way we can end this without war . . . a negotiation maybe? My father can be reasonable. Let me talk to him."

"Your father is a despot and a murderer."

"You have to let me try. I don't want to lose you and me. Not again."

"How can you defend him?"

Sarai squints back tears. "I . . . I'm not. I'm not defending him. I just . . . I feel war with him will cause me to lose you again. I love you more than I hate my father."

Asher grabs her shoulders and leans in. "Sarai, my parents are alive."

"What?"

"They're in the belly of your father's hungry mountain. He told me he is keeping them like a trophy, and that Cephas is next."

She sees the anger and determination in his eyes; there is no going back. She touches his cheek, and he wipes the tears from hers.

What now? she wonders, a question to herself as well as to Asher.

"I'm going back to The Middle. I need to speak to someone, then I need to see Cephas. I need to know the truth."

"The truth about what?"

"My parents. Your father said it was Cephas that betrayed them and ambushed *him*, not the other way around."

"Do you believe him?"

"I don't know. But I think I know a way to turn the tides in our favor, or at least give us a fighting chance."

"I'm coming with you," Sarai demands.

"No."

"I'm coming; you can't stop me. You know that."

"Listen to me, Sarai, I can be gone under the guise of a mission or another patrol; if you're gone also, your father will get suspicious. You need to stay here, for now, and act normal. I'll be back for you shortly. I promise."

With that, Asher kisses her passionately. She returns it with vigor. She grabs his face and kisses him like it might be their last. He finally pulls away.

"We're Drecks, Sarai, we always will be."

And just like that, he is gone.

Act normal. Sarai doesn't know what that is anymore. She wonders if this is the second time she has lost him as she realizes he is no longer a prince of Zion and she a sultana. She has been living her dream all the while blind to the nightmare that is Zion.

It's time to wake up.

The fire snaps, its many tongues lick the air. Cephas leads a Bible study as men from his inner circle participate around the percolating campfire. They talk about fear and anxiety and how in Christ there is freedom from both. But even as Cephas spouts these words, he is anxious over Asher's lack of progress, that The Defiance will fail, that maybe he has already failed his people, his nephew, betting it all on a crazy and somewhat outlandish plan that many of his leadership didn't agree with. He taps his cleft chin with his right index finger. Jude liked to joke that he had a massive dent in his chin, that his mouth was in a car crash.

Cephas wraps it up with a prayer. After a round of amens, Cephas keeps his eyes closed and continues to pray silently that God will take away his urge to sip the DemonTonic. His cravings have been worse than usual lately. Usually, they would break bread together, but bread, or any food for that matter, is scarce. Rats are now on the menu. Just as Cephas sighs and turns to retire for the evening, one of his commanders speaks in an insubordinate tone.

"Maybe we should all stay and discuss contingency plans?"

"Contingencies for what?" Cephas scolds.

"If your nephew fails," the commander responds plainly.

"He just needs more time!"

"More time? If you haven't noticed, sir, we are starving, our numbers are shrinking, and Zion's army is growing. And all we do is gather around this stupid campfire and do nothing about it."

Cephas takes a deep breath and holds his tongue, choosing words carefully. "Sometimes, God's plan doesn't align with ours, at least not on our timelines; we need faith and more patience."

"We have been patient for long enough. Your absurd plan is failing. When is the last time you even heard from Asher? My spies tell me he and his new bride are living the high life. Fat and happy while slurping Zion's milk. In fact, Darius tells me Asher tells him nothing, nothing about Zion troop movements or The Wall openings. No intelligence of value whatsoever. He will not even meet with him!"

Cephas's face turns beet red. A little piece inside him can't help but think that maybe his commander is correct. *Is his plan lunacy? Can Asher be trusted? As Asher never believed in The Defiance or its cause, did he truly only accept this mission because of Sarai? How could I have been so stupid? Of course he did it for Sarai.*

The commander turns to the twelve others. "I put forth a vote of no confidence in Cephas as leader of The Defiance."

Cephas grits his teeth; he wasn't expecting this.

"You think I like my current position, commander? That I like watching my men starve? Or die on missions I send them on? The weight upon my shoulders is almost unbearable. This wasn't something I asked for. It was thrown upon me. But I have done my best. You look at me like I'm a tired old man, and maybe I am. All I can say is that I have not made my decisions based on fear. That is all I have to offer. But if you think you can do better, then let's vote."

Before he can respond, Jude bursts into the room, out of breath. His skinny legs dance around like his feet are on fire.

"Lazurite soldiers are approaching!"

"What? How many patrols?" Cephas asks.

"Not a patrol. My scouts tell me five thousand men, half of Zion's army, are at our doorstep."

"How close?"

Before Jude can respond, the sound of plasma rifles and screaming Drecks can be heard. Then the smell of gasoline and smoke. They are being flushed out with fire.

"Head for the tunnels and exit the rear!" Cephas orders, referring to the series of secret tunnels that eventually exit two miles north of their compound.

The defiant commander refuses to move. "We stay and fight!"

"It's suicide to stay down here. We escape and fight another day," Cephas pleads.

"All of our weapons and intel are here! We must guard them, otherwise we will have lost everything." The commander refuses to move. Cephas shakes his head as he, Jude, and the rest of his leadership head towards the tunnels.

Minutes later they are met by hundreds of other Drecks escaping through the vast array of underground tunnels, carrying anything they can grab on their way out. The smoke is thickening, causing Cephas to choke. Twenty minutes later they reach ladders that lead to camouflaged manholes in the center of a thick forest. They quietly emerge from them one by one and gather in the thick dark brush, hiding from Renatus's first army. Cephas and Jude stare at what used to be their headquarters, now lighting up the night sky in a massive fireball. Most of their weapons and intelligence were stored there, along with the little food they had left. How had they been found? Do they have a mole? Did Asher know about this attack and not warn him? Was he too busy prancing around with Sarai? Attending banquets and balls? Driving fancy cars?

The Defiance's headquarters is not the only thing burning. Cephas seethes as he watches everything they have gathered and worked for turn to ash. The tonic is calling him, reeling him in. *Maybe I should step down.*

"Now what?" Jude asks solemnly.

Cephas's head sinks. "I don't know. I really don't."

Just when he thought things couldn't get any worse, a thought hits him.

Amos.

Did he die in the blaze, or did Renatus's army find him in the underground prison?

If the latter, then the ruse is up.

CHAPTER TWELVE

The last time I walked through these doors I was a contraband mule. I am returning as a false prince. Boaz dons three gold rings to match his gold Rolex. His abundance is evident by his waistline, which stretches well over his small feet. One of the few here in The Middle that aren't starving.

"Business is good," I state, tapping his bulbous stomach. He knows who I am, not the real me, but who Amos is, as he surely has watched the Canonization. His flabby, wrinkled jowls flap in fear.

"I barter for used goods. I am excellent at finding deals," he lies.

To get what I'm here for, I have to frighten him. "Don't lie to me Boaz."

I pace his massive family room lined with expensive furniture as my muddy boots taint his silk Isfahan rug. His hands tremble in fear, causing the light to bounce off the diamonds embedded in his Rolex.

"I'm not lying," he stutters. "My business activities are all completely legal."

I approach him with a menacing gait, but inside I can't help but laugh and wonder what he would say if he knew I was Asher the Dreck, his ex-contraband mule.

"I know you're the largest supplier of contraband east of The Wall. That your items come across in the garbage drops. I know you hire poor Drecks to rummage through the refuse and underpay them." That last part was a jab just for me.

I get within inches of his sweaty brow and bantam green eyes. "I know that you pay off patrolmen to look the other way. Do you know what the offense is for supplying arms to The Defiance, to The Sons of Levi?" His eyelids shutter as he knows he faces death.

"Please, please, I'll do anything, I can pay you, please."

I sit and practically melt into his suede leather couch. "How about some tea?" It's not the request he was expecting.

"Yes, yes, of course."

A minute later he returns with two steaming cups. I sip mine; his cup clatters against the plate as his hands still shake like the tail of a rattlesnake.

"Sit," I tell him, staring at the teacups, "Is this china?"

"I . . . I believe so, yes."

"Do you have any family, Boaz?" A question I have asked him in the past as Asher, but he never answered.

"An ex-wife. Three of them, actually," he admits.

"Any children?" Just as I ask the question, his white Persian cat jumps into his lap.

"No, never had the time, I suppose." He shrugs, stroking the purring feline now nestled comfortably into his massive girth.

I stare into his greedy eyes. "Well, you are a busy man. Tell me Boaz, what do you think your purpose in life is?" Again, I sound like my father.

"I don't, I don't understand," he stutters.

"Is it to line your pockets and fatten your belly? Or is the purpose of life to serve others, serve a cause greater than yourself?"

He doesn't answer. He looks confused by the question, as if he has never considered it.

"Do you think it's possible that a simple Dreck, a contraband mule can rise up to become a great leader? A liberator for an entire nation?"

He leans in; now he bores into my eyes, my soul. There is a hint of recognition; his fear dissipates. I almost think I saw a smile. *Does he recognize me?*

"Perhaps anything is possible," he replies.

"I'm glad you feel that way," I stand. "Perhaps we can work out an arrangement. Give me what it is I came for, and I'll let your little operation continue. It will be our secret."

He wasn't expecting that. The corner of his lips rise. "Anything. What is it that you want?"

"I want the myth, the legend. I want the map to the Fort Worth Armory."

He is taken aback. "I don't have any such map. As you said, it's a myth, pure folklore."

It's a gambit. I am unsure if he even has it. Or if it even does exist, for that matter.

"And if I did, I probably would have sold it already," he forces a chuckle.

Or he is saving it for times of desperation. Right now, I'm desperate. I need to make it very clear that he is as well. I abruptly stand.

"Very well, Boaz, before your execution, tell me how your stay at SeaPen was. I have never been there."

As I head towards the door, he pops up. "Wait."

I turn and feign boredom, tapping my ricochet. He leaves the room and returns a few minutes later with a rolled-up, tattered piece of paper that looks more like an ancient scroll.

"I present to you, The Fort Worth Armory."

I grab the map and try my best to hide my excitement. Within my grasp is quite possibly The Defiance's last hope, assuming the armory actually exists and the map isn't a fake.

"If this is a fake, *I'll be back*," I say it in my best Arnold Schwarzenegger voice.

"It's the real thing."

"Oh, and if anyone asks, I was never here."

Again, Boaz squints like he's experiencing deja vu. I can tell he knows that something is very odd about my visit, about what I'm doing here. He stares at my ricochet, "Tell me, Amos, where is it that you are from again?"

I smile, and instead of answering, I hold up the map. "Careful Boaz, you may yet become a good man."

Darius went ahead to set it up. I leave my third army at camp two miles behind. We are back in The Middle under false pretenses of another patrol. What I really did was move my army from an impending ambush Cephas had planned last week. Along with Kenan and a dozen other elites, we ride on horseback to the edge of the woods.

"Are you . . . you . . . sure this is a good idea?" Kenan stutters, wondering why we left our muscle behind.

I tell him that I am meeting an informant who is easily spooked. I hop off my horse. "Wait here."

I traverse deep into the woods, my boots trampling through brush and fallen branches. After seeing my parents cemented in that frozen womb, I am a believer now. I will fight for The Defiance and what they stand for, regardless of my uncle. Regardless of the mistakes I have made in the past. Cephas is right though. I need to forgive myself for the bombing at the bazaar. I need to move past it.

Dusk approaches as I spot the flicker of a flashlight in the distance. Three flashes, then one. I mimic it with my own light. Another another half mile, I arrive to find Darius. Next to him is a man whose face is covered with a black hood.

"Clear?" Darius asks.

I nod, and Darius slips off the hood. Cephas eyes me with what feels like a permanent scowl. Although his heart has changed, his appearance hasn't. He peers at me, my exoarmor, my black and gold Lazurite sash. My face is freshly shaved, my clean skin smells of soap. He sees I have been eating well, sleeping comfortably. It's evident he hasn't.

"So, this is what a prince of Zion looks like." His tone derisive.

"Uncle, I have something—"

He interrupts. "My men tell me your army has moved. Last week I had a perfectly planned ambush, and somehow your army knew not to be there. Did you tell them?"

"Yes," I answer plainly.

"YES?" His face turns crimson, like a bad sunburn.

"I will not let you kill my boys."

"*Your* boys?" Cephas replies furiously. "These are Lazurite killers. You are not one of them, Asher. I sent you to do a job."

Now my voice raises. "That's correct, you did. You sent me to earn their trust and convince them to fight *for* us. That can't happen if they're dead. Wasn't that the plan?"

"It was until my spies told me how much you and your bride have been living it up while we starve! Enjoying it no less. And what about the intel you were supposed to provide Darius? You have given me nothing!"

"Nothing!" I yell back. "What about Dagger? He is out of play."

"You are assuming that is a good thing. We didn't agree with his methods, but at least he kept Renatus busy. How about anything of consequence?"

"Consequence? How about winning the Canonization? Defeating Legion? No progress? How long do you think it takes to earn the trust of an entire army? So much so that you convince them to turn against their own people, their own leaders, their way of life, and commit treason that is punishable by death? Not to mention earning the trust of Renatus! You have asked the impossible, yet I am delivering."

Cephas's head sinks. His gaze lowers to his feet. "You're right Asher, I'm sorry, it's just that I need . . . *we* need every win we can get. I guess I have become impatient. Times are bleak, Nephew."

"When aren't they?"

He looks up at me with his bloodshot eyes, and I wonder if he's back on the tonic. I have never seen him so hopeless. So angry. He reminds me of the old Cephas.

"I have something to ask you, Uncle, and I want the truth."

"Of course."

"The meeting with my parents and Renatus, where they were supposed to discuss a peace treaty. Who did the ambushing? You or Renatus?"

Cephas sighs with a hint of shame. "He told you?"

"Yes."

"And you believe him?"

"I don't know what to believe anymore."

"Yes, it is true."

"And without my father's knowledge? Against his orders?"

Cephas raises his voice. "Look, you need to understand, I saw an opening, a way to take out Renatus and perhaps end this war once and for all. Your father was way too trusting. You can't trust a man like Renatus."

"And apparently you can't be trusted either," I snap.

"Please, Nephew, I didn't mean for your parents to get killed. I was doing what I thought was right at the time. It's just one of many things I hope you can forgive me for."

I see that he is truly remorseful, and my tone softens. "Yeah, well, guess what, Uncle. They aren't dead."

"What?"

"They are in The Mountain, frozen in time. And we are going to get them out. All of them."

He says, "It's not gonna be easy."

"It never is."

"We had a bit of a setback."

"Of course we did!"

Cephas's voice is sullen. "Two days ago they found our headquarters. Burned it to ground. We lost everything, Asher. Weapons, food, intelligence. Men. Good men. I became complacent about our safety. I thought us untouchable in our compound."

"Jude?" I ask, surprised by how much I miss him.

"Jude made it. Stringbean is too skinny of a target." Cephas forces a slight smile.

"I'm sorry, Uncle. You're right. I could have given Darius more intel. But the attack on your compound, I had no idea. If I did, I would have told you."

"I know. Tell me you have good news, Nephew. Tell me this isn't a social visit."

I hand him the rolled-up map. "The Fort Worth Armory."

He snatches it but peers at me with his usual skepticism. "It doesn't exist." But then he realizes it's our last hope, that it must exist. "Does it?"

I feel like we have switched roles, at least for the moment. "My prayer is that you'll go and find out. There is a food and supply depot twenty miles east of here my army uses to re-supply. I'll give you the key."

"And if we find the weapons? Then what?"

"Go to Sector 304 on the western side of The Wall. I am hoping to have it opened before you get there. I will then bring my third army to meet you."

"So, you have a plan already to open The Wall?"

"It's in the works."

"And your third army, you have gained their trust? You think they will follow you, Nephew?"

"I think so."

"*Think so? Hoping?* It's not breeding a lot of confidence, Son."

"Have faith, Uncle," I say with a smile, regurgitating his own words back at him. "Besides, we're out of options."

And with the flip of a switch, he is back to being Cephas, the strong and hopeful leader, cantankerous, yes, but also wise. He places his gnarled fingers on my shoulders; dried blood and dirt sleep in the cracks of his knotty knuckles.

"Tell me, Son, you didn't kill Legion. Why?"

"I don't know, I just, I—"

"You felt something, didn't you? In the towers, after you prayed."

"Yes."

"Can I be honest with you?"

"When aren't you?"

"I didn't think you'd pull it off."

"We haven't won yet. We still need a miracle."

"I never thought you would get this far, but here we are. You won the Canonization, you somehow defeated Legion, you now command Renatus's third army, you are a hero of Zion, and now you stand here handing me a map to what I thought didn't exist. How's that for a miracle?"

"Why did you choose me?" I have been wanting to ask that for a long time.

"I didn't." He points to the sky. "I take my orders from a higher command."

"What is He telling you now?"

"To pray for another miracle. You may no longer be welcome in Zion."

"What do you mean?"

"Amos."

He doesn't have to explain. Either Amos died in the fire when they burned down Cephas's compound, or he was rescued and is now regaling Renatus with quite the tale.

There is only one way to find out.

After nearly seven days on horseback, Cephas, Jude, and a remnant of The Defiance reach Reservation 23, the former Lone Star State. Their rations were depleted two days ago. Cephas gingerly slides off of his horse and can't remember the last time he was this sore.

"We make camp here tonight and then enter Fort Worth first thing in the morning."

Cephas peers at his exhausted and famished men. "But first things first, we need food." Then he adds sarcastically, "Even Jude is hungry."

"Already on it." Jude approaches with two compound bows and hands one to Cephas.

Thirty minutes later Cephas and Jude are crouched behind a fallen tree, forty yards in front of them is a majestic American elk. His massive antlers sport eight points on each side. Jude tosses a leaf into the air, and it blows away from the elk, doublechecking that they are still downwind.

"Winds are good," Jude whispers.

If the winds are just right, an elk can smell you from a thousand yards away. Good thing, as neither of them can remember the last time they bathed. Not that Cephas has anything against hunting with a firearm, but he loves the purity of using a bow and arrow. He liked the fact that a thousand years ago you could make do with what they were doing today. He felt a connection to the past, with his ancestors before gunpowder existed. He remembers teaching Asher how to shoot a bow before the ricochet became his weapon of choice. He used to say, "You draw back, and sometimes they hear you. Winds change, and they'll smell you. Look you in the eye for just a moment. They see you have no malice; you're doing what nature intended, and so are they. I think the animal can sense it, can look into your soul, and forgive you. Can't do that with a gun." Besides, ammunition was best saved for the war.

"You want it?" Jude asks, knowing full well Cephas does.

Cephas draws back, exhales, and releases. The arrow slices through the air and hits the elk behind the shoulder blade about a third of the way up from the top of the front leg; a perfect heart shot. It runs on pure adrenaline for about forty yards into the woods before falling.

Cephas glances over to Jude. "I killed it. You gut it."

An hour later, after gutting and skinning the massive animal,

Cephas and his emaciated men ravish the tender elk meat.

"Where did Asher even get the map?" Jude asks.

"Boaz."

"Boaz? He can't be trusted."

"He'll do anything to save his own hide. Remember, to Boaz, it wasn't Asher he was speaking to; it was a prince of Zion, The Vanquisher of Legion, it was *Amos the Great*!" Cephas says in a sing-song tone. The fresh elk meat has lifted his spirits and lightened his mood. Not to mention the map he now grips in his oversized paws.

"Hah! I would have loved to have been there. To see that greedy mercenary shake in his fat boots!"

Cephas peers up at the dazzling canopy of stars. "Some men have their treasure here on earth, some will have it in heaven."

"If that's the case, we must be rich up there!" Jude jokes, watching a star streak across the sky before staring into the crackling campfire.

Cephas is silent for a few minutes. Then, "Why do you follow me, Jude?"

"It's not so much you as it is the cause. God has a purpose for everyone. Some are meant to be leaders. Some are meant to follow. One is not better than the other, especially in our case, eh?"

"Ain't that the truth," Cephas snorts.

"Never been to Texas. You think it's there? You think it actually exists?"

Cephas scoots closer to the fire and warms his hands. "I don't know, but I don't think the Almighty is sending us on a snipe hunt. And if He is, there is a reason behind it. Get some sleep, as for tomorrow we find out."

"If we do find it, do you think there will be enough weapons to make a difference?" ponders Jude.

"There used to be a saying that 'Everything is bigger in Texas.' Let's hope that rings true of the armory."

I'm apprehensive as I return to Zion West. Did they find the real Amos alive? Or was he killed during the fire? It's a risk, but I must return. I still need to gain the hearts and minds of my third army. Giving them a week off should help. I need to find out how and where I can open The Wall. If Cephas is successful and the Fort Worth Amory exists, I will need to let them in. Besides, it has been two weeks since I last saw Sarai, and my heart aches.

As I approach Renatus's oceanside compound on horseback, she sprints towards me. Before I can dismount, she leaps onto my horse and lands in my lap, kissing me before any words are spoken.

"I wasn't sure you were going to return," she says hesitantly.

"You're the one place I'll always return to," I reassure her.

"How did it go?"

I don't want to go into details. Just knowing she is on board is enough for me.

"We shall see," I reply. "Your father, how is he? Has he asked about me?"

"Once or twice, in fact I think he is very keen on seeing you. Is something going on?"

Again, I don't tell her about Amos, I don't want to worry her.

"Nothing."

"He did say he wanted to dine with us tonight upon your return."

"Good, I'm famished," I smile at her, hiding my worry, but she's not buying it.

"What is it, Asher?"

I look out to the ocean and watch the powerful waves crash upon the rocks. I want to turn the horse around and take off with her on it. To leave this place, return to The Middle with her. Hide somewhere and simply just live out our lives.

"You ever wonder why we worry?"

She looks at me like I have lost it.

"I mean, if God has a plan for us, and if things were meant to be, why do we worry? Fear shouldn't exist, right?"

"But bad things still happen," she retorts.

"Yes, but is that meant to be, or is that our freewill in action?"

"I don't know. What are you getting at, Asher?"

I touch her face. "Sarai, if anything happens to me, it's up to you."

"What are you talking about?"

"Cephas can't do it alone. He needs someone on the inside, someone strong, someone who doesn't believe in all of this Lazurite nonsense, someone who will stand up to Renatus, someone who understands the Lazurite people as well as my people."

"That's not me, Asher. I'm not equipped to be that person. I'm not a leader. Besides, nothing is going to happen to you."

Yet, she is that person. She doesn't see what I see. I hold her tight as if her body could absorb my vision of her. Like life, the wind picks up and swirls decaying leaves around us, blowing them indiscriminately across our feet, and I think of my uncle, my parents, The Defiance, Renatus, my own floundering emotions and realize that, ironically, The Wall and Sarai are my only two constants in life, the only two things I can rely on. The former I hope to bring down; I only pray I don't lose the latter in the process.

Three hours later we dine on imported delicacies prepared by world-class chefs. I am dressed in casual wear, so is Sarai. Renatus, in full military garb, takes notice, but hides his annoyance.

"Feel good to be back?" Renatus asks me.

I grab Sarai's hand. "Nothing like Zion," I lie.

"And tell me, Amos, did you have a productive patrol? Accomplish anything of note?"

"More of a training mission than anything else."

Renatus wipes his greasy lips and snorts, "I am sure you heard by now, my first army discovered The Defiance headquarters and burned it to the ground."

"Yes, I heard. Congratulations."

"Victory is close, young Amos, can you feel it?"

I simply nod.

"Tell me, Amos the Great, what training is your army doing? I thought those troops were already top-notch." His tone is derisive. Does he know? Or is he just in a surly mood?

"We are still meshing. Their training isn't complete. As you know we have a lot more conscripts than professionals. I need more time. More weapons."

He licks his fingers and smacks his lips. "I did hear you cleverly avoided an ambush. You have great instincts, Amos the Great, much like a wolf."

Someone inside my army is reporting on my every move. Why am I not surprised?

"Are you a wolf, Amos the Great?"

My leg begins to shake, Sarai gulps her wine, and I wonder if she too finds this line of questioning odd, or if this is just Renatus being Renatus.

"I don't understand the question, sir."

"I told you not to call me SIR!" He slams his fist angrily against the table. Sarai grips my hand; she knows something isn't right.

"Sorry Renatus, military habit."

"Do you know Zion's policy on treason?" he asks rhetorically.

"Death," I answer quietly.

"Turns out, boy, that our weaknesses are the same," he says.

I look to Sarai and then back to him. I shouldn't have come back. He knows. I reach down for my ricochet. I left it in my room! There are six armed guards in the room with us. I don't have a chance.

Renatus swigs his wine. "Yes, Amos, they are the same. We are both too trusting. And apparently both fearless."

"What are you talking about, Father?" Sarai finally asks.

He stares at me, his face burning red. "I would like you to meet somebody."

Ten elite guards open the double doors, and in walks the real Amos.

"Amos, meet Asher, son of Silas."

CHAPTER THIRTEEN

What was once a sprawling metroplex, Fort Worth, is now stained with empty, dilapidated buildings. A few helldusters battle the morning nip by standing over a garbage can fire, eagerly awaiting the next narcdrop. They wearily eye Cephas and his entourage as they enter what was once a bustling downtown. Not too far from here was the home of the Dallas Cowboys. America's team in fact participated in the last Super Bowl ever played. They lost to the San Antonio Raiders in overtime.

Cephas sighs and thinks about what a different world this used to be. Sports, games, hot-dogs, BBQs, and family. Now it is starvation, murder, oppression, and The Wall. A world where children no longer play outside, at least not outside Zion. To his right was what used to be a megachurch where families could worship freely. Now Bibles are burned at the altar of Zion. Jude shakes him from his melancholic thoughts and points to the map.

"Just on the outskirts," Jude informs him.

Three hours later they approach a farmhouse that sits on ten acres of picked-over apple trees. Cephas studies the map.

"There, near the barn."

"Think it's vacant?" Jude wonders aloud.

His question is answered immediately as a scrappy seventy-something man whose beard is as long as his arm comes limping out of the farmhouse, aiming a shotgun at them.

"What can I do ya for?"

Both Cephas and Jude grip their pistols underneath their coats.

"Just passing through," Cephas answers plainly.

"Y'all better keep on going. Nuttin' here."

"Now what?" Jude whispers to Cephas.

"We come back later."

"Don't go pilfering any of my apples either," the old man crows.

Just as Cephas and his crew turn to leave, the old man raises an eyebrow.

"Wait a damn minute, are you... Cephas? Leader of The Defiance?"

Cephas ponders the question carefully. If this man is a Lazurite sympathizer, then a truthful answer could be deadly, but if he's a Dreck, then that's a different story. Before he can say anything, Jude blurts, "Yes, he is. He's the one and only Cephas, commander of The Great Defiance."

"Idiot," Cephas whispers.

"Just look at him, he's a Dreck for sure," Jude mumbles, squinting from the morning sun.

The old man lowers his shotgun. "Then I'd be honored. What's mine is yours, hoss."

"Funny you should say that," Jude says through an oversized smile.

"Don't got much, but you're welcome to it."

"Maybe so, or you may have everything," Cephas says cryptically.

"How so?"

"We believe that somewhere on your land is the Fort Worth Armory."

"Heck you say! Armory is a myth. Everyone knows that!" the old man squabbles.

"Maybe, but can we check your land anyway?"

"If you think you can find it, and it helps defeat those Lazurite butchers, then be my guest."

After showing him the map, the old man, limping slowly, leads them to his barn.

"What happened to your leg?" Jude inquires.

"Shrapnel. I was part of the first resistance when The Wall was fresh. But I'm the lucky one. My family not so much."

Jude lowers his head. "Sorry to hear that."

"Grab some shovels," Cephas orders.

After four hours of digging inside and around the barn, Jude's shovel clanks.

"Think I got something!"

Cephas and his crew rush over. "Dig around it."

A few more minutes of digging reveals a massive slab of rusted metal. A chain connected to both ends.

"This is it! This has to be it!" Jude dances around while shaking his fists.

"Settle it down stringbean, we haven't found anything yet. Could be an old grain storage locker." Cephas feigns aloofness and points to the chain, "Pull."

It takes all of them to pull the heavy slab across the barn floor to reveal a secret opening and a stairwell that leads underground. The smell of history burps from the underground chamber.

"What in the Sam Hill," the old man mutters in disbelief.

"I told you this was it!" Jude scampers in circles.

Even Cephas can't hide his excitement as they grab lanterns and make their way down the stairwell. No one has inhaled this musty air since the Civil War. The room is fifteen hundred square feet, much smaller than any of them anticipated. They scour the entire room only to find two rusted muskets in the corner.

"There's nothing here," Jude utters in shock.

"This is why you let legends be legends," Cephas growls.

The old man picks up one of the muskets. "What'd I tell ya? A myth. Y'all are welcome to stay for some coffee and apples."

Jude picks up the other musket, and it nearly crumbles in his hands. "I knew Boaz was a selfish lying rat!"

Cephas places his hands against the wall as if he needs help standing. The veins in his forehead hammer against his wrinkled, leathery skin as if they are trying to punch their way out. His knees wobble. The Christian in him wants to pray; his flesh wants to strangle Boaz. The last hope for The Defiance is now extinguished. His headquarters destroyed. His weapons gone. His men nearing extinction. He thinks about having a drink.

But Cephas doesn't know how bad it really is.

SeaPen is two hundred feet under the surface of the Pacific Ocean on the coast of Point Reyes near Renatus's palatial palace. Talk about keeping your enemies close. We arrived in a small cargo submarine that docked with a cement tunnel leading to the prison. This is like Alcatraz, but underwater. Inescapable. As I'm escorted to my cell, we pass the mess hall where lunch is being served. The inmates don heavy coats made from iron that are locked to their bodies as a way of limiting their movements. Their boots are so heavy that it seems to take massive effort just to walk, a great but inhumane method of crowd control. You are not allowed out of your cell without these weighted duds.

I spot one inmate who walks unencumbered as if the heavy coat is nothing but threads of cotton. His massive frame and height are unmistakable. He peers up at me; it is Legion. I nod at him, but he acts as if he doesn't know me. On the other side of the room, eating alone, is Dagger. He glances up, and his hatred for me seems to dissolve into surprise. He must be thinking, *Why is Amos here in handcuffs?* Most residents here are political dissidents and foes of Renatus, and if they knew my true identity, I would fit right in. But right now I feel like I'm a policeman forced to live with the ones I arrested. To them, I'm just Renatus's cohort. I have a feeling I won't last long here.

My cell is a six-by-six tempered glass square. Actually, it's not much smaller than my hostel back on Reservation 9. My mattress, or more like a glorified blanket, lies in the middle of the floor. A small toilet in the corner, no privacy as the glass is on all four sides. I feel like a fish in an aquarium. Except that I have an anchor wrapped around my neck.

"Welcome to your castle, Amos the Great," the guard snickers as he shoves me into my cell with more force than necessary.

I lie on the cold blanket and think of Sarai. Is she okay? Does her father know she knows who I am, and is she being punished? Will she join me here? Or something even worse?

I wonder if Cephas found the armory, and if he did, was there anything there? And if so, who will open The Wall for him now that I'm in here? I have failed. Failed Cephas. My father. The Defiance. Sarai. Was this really all for naught?

Suddenly a guard appears with a visitor. *Renatus.*

The guard quickly cuffs me to a pole in the middle of the room and leaves as Renatus enters.

"Oh, Amos, or Asher, that is your name, right? Asher, son of Silas?" he says with a mocking tone.

"Does it matter now?"

"No, I guess it doesn't."

"Where's Sarai?" I ask.

"Doesn't matter," he answers plainly.

"Please, she didn't know. She didn't know I was Asher. I fooled her too."

"We'll soon find that out."

"Just please leave her be. You can do what it is you want with me," I plead.

"I know we can, Asher," he says in a deviant tone. "If I wasn't so affronted, I would be impressed with what you have accomplished. Surely Cephas's idea. Didn't think the old man was this clever."

"Who says I'm done yet?" I say defiantly.

"Tell me something, Asher, if you had lost the Canonization, or not have defeated Legion, then what? What was your backup plan?"

"I didn't need one. I have faith," I say, not sure where the words came from.

"Now you sound like your uncle," he scoffs. "Cephas. He sent you to the wolves, Son. Sent you to die. Yet you still have allegiance to him and his misguided cause. He didn't care for you; he used you. If you cooperate, I will spare you, Asher, perhaps even reinstate you, as you found the Zion way of life pleasing, didn't you?"

It is tempting, as he is taking advantage of my weak state of mind right now. I pray for strength.

"You and Sarai could pick up where you left off, Son."

I simply shake my head.

"I was like a father to you. I was prepared to give you everything. My only daughter! Your own army. Riches beyond what any Dreck can imagine. Eternal life, boy!" He slams his fist against the glass. "You were like a son to me."

"You take what you want when you want it. You have no regard for human life. Not even your own daughter's. And yet, you seemed so surprised by my betrayal. What a sight, the great Renatus has hurt feelings."

He punches me square in the jaw. I spit blood.

"You're going to hurt while you're here, Son. Now the degrees and levels of pain will be up to you. But I recommend talking sooner rather than later. You will tell me where Cephas is and the rest of The Defiance. You will give me a list of the other spies, such as yourself. Along with the remaining compounds we are yet to find."

"I know nothing. And what I did know I have long forgotten," I say blankly.

Renatus stands and smirks. "Trust me on this. Your memory will be refreshed. Cheers."

"Calm down, Cephas!" Jude implores.

Cephas has finally lost his temper. He kicks and throws rocks against the wall of the underground bunker that is the legend of the

Fort Worth Armory.

He looks up and growls, "Why? Why?"

"It's just a setback is all."

"A setback? We are finished, Jude. Do you understand? *Finished!* We have no weapons, no men, and no place to go!"

Cephas turns and begins to storm up the stairs.

"Where ya going?"

"To find some tonic," Cephas answers with hopeless eyes. He then grabs the old man. "You have anything to drink?"

"No, but there are pallets of the stuff a mile west," the old man answers.

"Well, that's great! Just great! One setback and our fearless leader quits," Jude chides him.

"One setback? One!" Cephas barks back.

"Okay, maybe a few, but this lack of faith is pathetic!"

Cephas stops, picks up a rock, and flings it at Jude. Hard enough to scare him, but slow enough that he can dodge it. Jude easily sidesteps it. The rock crashes into the bunker wall. A piece of the ancient wall chips away. Cephas squints at it.

Jude continues on his rant. "What did you always tell us? 'Have faith, God has a plan! With God on our side, what is there to fear? Who could be against us? That—'"

"Shut up!" Cephas barks and trudges over to the wall he had just pelted with the rock. He rubs his fingers around the small indentation. He grabs another rock and chips away at the wall until he finds a rusted metal ring attached to it. He pulls on it. A loud creaking noise reverberates through the room as Cephas pulls open a door hidden within the rock wall. Jude is too shocked to speak. Not wanting to be disappointed again, no one says anything.

They all file one by one through the door. Cephas shines his lantern, illuminating the massive room to reveal hundreds of wooden crates. Jude scampers over to the first one and pries it open with a crowbar. Inside are twenty Springfield Model 1861 rifles.

"It does exist," Cephas whispers.

Jude forces open crate after crate. "There are thousands of them!"

Cephas also finds a crate full of Civil War-era hand grenades. In the corner are two Gatling guns. Cephas's guilt for his diminishing faith is quickly drowned out by his excitement and thanks. What lies before him can turn the tides of this war in their favor. Exoarmor was not designed to protect against lead and gunpowder. Technology put the Lazurites in power, and it will be technology that will be their undoing. At least that's what Cephas hopes will happen. Jude dances around like a kid on Christmas morning. Cephas is cautiously optimistic. He feels like a desert receiving its first rain. He only hopes it's not a mirage.

"They need to be cleaned, cataloged, and tested, there is a lot of rust on these," Cephas orders, hoping that the two-hundred-and-fifty-year-old weapons are still viable.

"We'll need a way to transport them," Jude adds.

"I have two wagons you can hook your horses up to," the old man offers. "Would go with ya, but got a bum leg."

"We will never be able to repay your kindness. On behalf of The Defiance and freedom-loving people across this land, thank you."

"No thanks required, just win!" the old man spits.

"Ammunition?" Cephas queries, almost forgetting the guns are useless without it.

Jude replies, "About ten cases worth. Twenty-thousand rounds."

"Then we must not be wasteful."

"I'll throw rocks if I have to," Jude says.

"Let's hope it doesn't come to that." Cephas can finally speak with a hint of confidence, "These weapons were used to win America's first Civil War. They will now be used to win its second. Lord willing The Wall will come down, and Zion will fall! We will once again be a united country. We will once again be free!"

After a few hoots and hollers, his men anxiously return to inspecting the weapons.

There is almost a spring in his step as he sidles up next to Jude and places his hand on his shoulder.

"Didn't I always tell you to have faith?" Cephas says, tongue in cheek.

"I can't believe you threw a rock at me."

"Like I had any chance of hitting you, stringbean."

Renatus paces around the oval table of his brightly lit war room. He is starting to come down from his adrenalin high of punishing Asher. If he weren't so busy, he would have been there for his interrogation. His assistant, Omar, is near the center, along with a couple of generals and a few elites.

"We are yet to extract any information of use. Key word being *yet*." Renatus turns to one of the generals, "How long before you are ready?"

The general clears his throat. "We're ready now, sir."

Renatus peers up at the ceiling and then addresses his head scientist. "And what about project Anti-Armor?"

The nervous scientist carefully chooses his words. "We are operational, my sultan. We have five thousand units so far."

Omar raises an eyebrow. "Project Anti-Armor?"

Renatus pats him on the head. "You will be briefed on it later."

Before Renatus can discuss his next topic, Sarai bursts in, her hands cuffed behind her, two elites in tow.

"I demand to know where Asher is!"

One of the elites speaks up. "I apologize, my sultan, she ran past our—"

Renatus waves him off, "You may be my daughter, but you are now a traitor to Zion and in no condition to make demands."

"What will become of him?" Sarai spits.

Renatus wiggles his fingers in the air like he is playing an air piano, "He will be interrogated, then put to death, a traitor's death."

She falls to her knees, "I beg you to spare him. I beg you, Father. Please."

"If I showed leniency to every traitor, there would be no Zion. Besides, SeaPen isn't big enough."

A tear slides from her cheek. "And what about me?"

Renatus takes a deep breath and then turns to the men seated at the table. "Leave us. We will reconvene tonight."

All except for his main advisor, Omar, march out of the room. None of them can even look at Sarai. Renatus steps towards her.

"You, my dear, I have had much tolerance for. But this is unforgivable. Asher's fate will be your fate." He waves to the two elites behind her. "Take her, please."

She is dragged out, kicking and screaming. "Father, please! Do what you want with me. Please spare Asher!"

The door shuts with a thud. Renatus stares at the ground and rubs his head, conflicted.

Omar sidles next to him. "You know, she still may be of use to you."

"Apparently you don't know my daughter. Whatever information we don't get from Asher, we definitely won't get from her."

"Not quite what I mean, my sultan."

"I'm listening."

Omar is not sure if he is out of line, but he is always willing to take risks to gain Renatus's favor. "She carries the gene, correct?"

"Yes."

"If she ever had any offspring, there is a chance they would carry the same genetic disorder."

Renatus's eyes widen. "Yes, yes, another wounded one."

Omar places his hand on Renatus's shoulder, then quickly removes it. "You could finally have your son back."

Renatus wonders why he hadn't thought of this.

"I'm sure they have already consummated the marriage, but just for good measure, send her to see Asher."

"Sir? It is she who carries the gene, not Asher. It could be anybody."

"Again, you don't know my daughter Omar. She would not be with just anybody. Send her to SeaPen and give them some alone time."

"Of course, my sultan."

Renatus inhales a breath of new hope; perhaps one day soon he can have his wounded prince.

I scream as an electric current surges through my body. The electrodes are connected to my forehead, arms, and legs. My tormentor takes great pleasure in my interrogation. He is a stout man in his forties with long flowing hair and scanty snake-like eyes. I wonder if he always aspired to be a tormentor when he was a child. Or was it Zion that perverted him? Renatus's lies have a way of warping one's soul. This man has been hearing them since his birth.

"Where is Cephas and the rest of The Defiance?" he asks again.

"I told you, I don't know, I haven't been in contact with them for months."

He sighs and presses the button, sending high voltage roving through every fiber of my body. I clench my jaw until my teeth almost crack. My fingernails dig into my palms until blood drips from them, splatting onto the cold cement floor. It finally stops, and I close my eyes and pray that I will not break. I cannot break. I must not fail The Defiance any more than I already have.

"Tell me exactly which reservations The Defiance operates out of?"

"I don't know," I moan, finally catching my breath.

"I'm just warming up here, mate." He smiles at the puddle of urine underneath me. "Seems the prince of Zion has soiled himself." He taps his fingers, teasing the button. "Are you sure you have nothing to say?"

"Guess I should have used the loo before we started," I say sarcastically through bloody teeth.

His eyes narrow. "Just bloody tell me, mate. Everyone eventually breaks. Save yourself the pain."

"Then you'd be out of a job. Besides, it looks to me like you are enjoying yourself."

He smiles. "Well, you are right about one thing: I do enjoy this. But as long as there are enemies of Zion, my job is secure."

He zaps me again. Maybe I shouldn't have provoked him, but at this point I don't think it matters. My fate is decided. I have a feeling even if I do talk, Renatus will either end me or keep me in this underwater dungeon forever. When I begin to foam at the mouth, he stops the agony.

I take a deep breath. "I have something to say."

He grabs his pen and paper and leans in. It takes me a few minutes to gather the requisite amount of oxygen to speak.

"Tell Renatus that I am Asher, son of Silas, and I will never betray The Defiance. Tell him he was outwitted by a simple Dreck from Reservation 9 and that soon, along with his precious Wall, he will fall."

"Very well, son of Silas," he states nonchalantly as his plump finger holds down the button that is responsible for my misery.

I writhe in pain and see that he doesn't plan on stopping this time. My agony is acute. I ask God to take this cup from me, or at the very least numb my pain. After what seems like an eternity but is probably only a few seconds, a wave of peace flows over me. I no longer feel the excruciating pain as I close my eyes and see a bright light. For a moment I am on the pond fishing with Sarai. Frogs croak in the midday sun as they jump from lily pad to lily pad. A light breeze fans my face. Then I hear her voice. It's not her angelic timbre I expect, but one of fire.

The door swings open, and Sarai marches in, flanked by two Lazurite guards.

"That's enough!" she barks.

My tormentor pulls his hand from the button and stands. "My sultana, to what do we owe the pleasure of your company?"

I open my eyes and wonder if I'm dreaming or dead.

"I need to speak to the prisoner alone," Sarai demands.

"My sultana, you must appreciate that I have been given strict orders by Renatus himself that no one is to see or talk to the traitor of Zion."

She hands him a small tablet. "I am here on direct orders from my father."

My tormentor does a retina scan, and the electronic tablet unlocks. He reads it and then immediately bows.

"Of course, my sultana. Please forgive my insolence."

"Bring him to conference room 14B," she orders.

Five minutes later I'm escorted to where Sarai waits for me. It was smart on her part as surely everything said in the interrogation room was being recorded. After my escorts leave, she rushes to me.

"Are you okay? What did they do to you?"

"I'm fine now that you're here. Just a little voltage, that's all. Not like touching The Wall or anything. What are you doing here, Sarai? You shouldn't be here."

"I'm here to get you out."

"Did Renatus suspect you? Does he know you knew who I really was?"

"It was Renatus who sent me here."

"What?"

She shakes her head. "He said, he said to come see you and be certain I spend some *alone* time with you."

"*Alone time*? I don't get it. Why would he want—"

"I have no idea. Maybe he was feeling generous? Doesn't matter, we need to get out of here."

"Perhaps we should heed his advice," I say jokingly.

She punches my shoulder, "You have just been tortured, and our lives depend on finding a way out of here, and *that's* where your brain goes?"

I can't help myself. "With all that electricity they've been pumping into me, I'm a bit amped up and ready to go, if you know what I mean."

She can't help but smile. "You're shameless."

"I know."

She grabs my hands, "One of your insiders asked me to send you a message. I have no idea what it means, but he said it is of the utmost importance. 'Dallas may be hot, but Fort Worth is hotter.'"

I can't believe they found it and that it is real. I wonder how many weapons were there. I would have loved to have been there to have seen Cephas's and Jude's faces. A part of me thought Boaz had given me a fake.

"What does that mean?" she asks.

"It means we have a chance . . . if we can get a portion of The Wall open."

"Your third army awaits you near the western end of The Wall," she informs me.

"How does that matter now that they know who I really am?"

"Your true identity isn't public yet. Renatus doesn't want to be embarrassed. If your army hears it from you and not someone else, I believe you can still convince them to follow you. Fight for you. After all, you convinced me to fall in love with you, didn't you?"

I grab her face. "That was my greatest miracle."

We kiss like it was the first time; it's always as if it's the first time . . . or the last.

"How do we get outta here?"

"I'll tell them I'm escorting you back to Father for further questioning."

"And if that doesn't work?"

She pulls from her coat pocket my ricochet and hands it to me. Attached behind her back is her scourge. It was a huge risk to smuggle those weapons in, but why would they scan the sultana? Even at SeaPen. I'm awed by her bravery.

I smile. "What else you got hidden in there?"

"Just the courage of a Dreck."

"Or their recklessness."

"Let's go find out."

As soon as we leave the room, an alarm blares. We are found out.

"Why the alarm?" I ask.

"I was allowed to see you but specifically told not to leave the interrogation room."

"I guess our decision is made for us," I say, activating my ricochet.

"I guess it's time to be reckless with a pinch of courage," she responds, activating her scourge.

We exit the room and enter the hall. Two Lazurite guards immediately confront us, aiming their plasma guns. I flick my wrist, sending my ricochet flying as we both hit the ground, avoiding the initial blasts from their weapons. The ricochet swats one of them in the neck, sending an electrical pulse through him as he folds to the ground. Sarai whips her scourge at the other guard, wrapping it around his leg, and pulls him to the ground. We drag them into a utility closet around the corner.

"Get undressed and put on their exoarmor," Sarai whispers.

"Why? The armor is synced to their DNA, it won't protect us," I respond.

"I know, but with their helmets, we can pass as guards."

Good thinking, as long as we don't get shot at. We undress and slide into their exoarmor. Mine is a little tight. Hers is a bit loose. A minute later we exit the closet disguised as Lazurite guards and lock it. We stroll down the hall, feigning to look for ourselves as other guards pass us. One of them stares awkwardly at our ill-fitting suits but continues on.

"What's the plan?" I whisper.

"We make our way to the docking station and steal a transport sub."

"You know how to operate one of those things?"

"Father used to take me and my brother for some underwater sightseeing. Every now and then he would let us take the wheel."

I stop. "We need to do something first."

"What?"

"Release the hounds."

"We don't have time for that," she pleads.

"You know as well as I do that no one here deserves to be here. Besides, chaos will behoove us." I think of Legion. And surely this place is loaded with Defiance spies or Lazurites who are Defiance sympathizers.

She thinks for a moment. "Control room is to the left."

We approach the control room and tap on the window. They see our outfits and our black and red guard helmets and we are buzzed in. We make quick work of the two unsuspecting guards and force the operators into a corner.

"How do I open the cells?" I ask one of the operators holding up my ricochet.

"It's biometric," he stutters.

I lead him to the control panel where his retinas and handprints are scanned, giving us access to the system.

"Open all the cell doors," I order.

The operator hesitates. "You won't get away with this, you Dreck vermin."

"Is that supposed to offend me? You really need to work on your insults," I laugh before placing my ricochet near his neck, where he can feel the sizzle of the blade. "Open them, now!"

Gritting his teeth, he does.

Sarai holds up her scourge. "And a transport keycard."

The operator opens a locked cabinet and hands her a keycard to operate one of the transport submarines. We exit the control room and are engulfed by chaos. Inmates fighting guards. Multiple fires have started, and we are immediately drenched by the sprinkler system. From the corner of my eye, I spot Legion. He is going in another direction; his gait is as if he is taking a leisurely stroll through the park; no one dares approach him. I yell at him, but either because of his want or because of the pandemonium, he doesn't respond. I wonder if he even knows what is happening.

"We have to go . . . now!" Sarai yells over the blaring alarms.

We sprint through two sets of doors and make our way to the underwater loading dock, taking out two more guards in the process. As we turn the corner, I hear a familiar voice.

"Stop!"

Behind us is Dagger, aiming a plasma rifle he must have pilfered from one of the guards.

"Gimme the sub key," he demands.

"Your rifle is useless against our armor," I lie.

"Not if it's stolen," he replies.

I look to Sarai.

"The indicator light on the back of your helmet is red; it never synced to your DNA," he answers as if reading my thoughts.

I take off my helmet, and he instantly recognizes me.

"My lucky day. I get to take out a prince of Zion as well as escape this hell hole."

"Listen, I was sculpted. I am Asher, son of Silas. I am here to take down Zion."

"Poppy-cock!"

"Listen to me, Dagger, why do you think I'm in this place? Renatus found me out. Why else would a prince of Zion be trying to escape SeaPen?"

"Well, Cephas is crazy enough to pull something like this."

"I know our methods have been at odds on how to fight this war, but now is the time to work together, The Defiance and The Sons of Levi. Together we can win this war. We have never had more of a chance, now is the time. Our end goal is the same after all."

"Considering your soft tactics, how do you plan on defeating Zion?"

"Fort Worth Armory."

"A myth," he scoffs.

"Cephas has the weapons in hand."

"You know how to drive one of these things?"

Sarai removes her helmet, "I do."

CHAPTER FOURTEEN

The three of us load into the transport sub. Sarai inserts the keycard and takes the controls. Dagger sits behind us, still aiming his plasma rifle at me.

"You still don't believe me?"

"I don't trust you," he responds.

Sarai seals the hatch. "We're airtight."

The sub then disembarks from SeaPen. From a viewing window we can see five or six other subs also departing. I wonder if Legion is in one of them.

"So, the armory is real . . . I'll be damned. How many weapons?" Dagger asks me.

"I don't know the details yet," I reply.

"So, if you're Asher, and we are fighting the same enemy, why did you arrest me and bring me to Zion?"

"You tried to kill me, remember?"

"Don't forget me as well," Sarai quips.

Dagger chuckles. "Oh yes. So you really want an alliance with The Sons of Levi?"

"That depends."

"On what?"

"Tactics."

"Zion has no rules of war. Why should we?" Dagger snorts.

"Because we aren't Lazurites, and if we act no different from them, what are we fighting for?" I say.

Dagger nods to Sarai. "She's a Lazurite!"

"You think I would be here if I wasn't against everything Zion stands for?" Sarai barks back.

"Do you know how many children I have seen those cell-pirates kill or kidnap? How many families torn apart?"

"Then why would we do the same?" Sarai says.

"You all think I'm a bad person, disagree with my methods. But you don't know me, who I really am. Don't judge my character during times of war."

"What a man does during adversity is how character is defined." Maybe I am my father's son.

Dagger studies my eyes. "It was an accident, ya know."

"What?"

"Those children, at the market. The bomb you sold my people. It was an accident."

"Just because you didn't mean to do something doesn't make it right," I respond angrily.

"Maybe."

I can no longer relive the nightmare of that day. Instead, I focus my attention on Sarai. I am in awe of her. Her eyes radiate a humble confidence as she steers the sub towards the surface. I hadn't stopped to think how hard it must be for her to be the enemy of her own parents, fighting against them. Even worse, knowing what they stand for. She didn't have the advantage of virtuous parents. Yet, she still manages to do what is righteous. She is a true leader.

Then I spot a missile heading straight for us.

"Bank right!" I scream.

"Where'd that come from?" Dagger yells.

"Must be a patrol sub; news of our escape is already out," I say as Sarai turns the sub hard right.

The missile is quickly catching up to us.

"We're not gonna make it!" Dagger hisses.

His assessment is correct.

"Get us as close to the surface as you can," I tell Sarai, hoping we survive the blast and don't drown.

We continue our turn and dart almost straight up. But we don't make it. The missile clips the back of our sub and explodes. The rear third of the sub is blown off. For a second, I black out.

I'm cold. So cold.

I feel like I'm floating.

Again, I'm overwhelmed by a sense of peace.

Then I open my eyes. I am thirty feet below the surface of the Pacific Ocean. Below me, what remains of the sub sinks into the abyss.

Sarai.

Where is she?

I frantically look, but visibility is near zero. The saltwater stings my eyes. My lungs burn. I have no choice but to swim to the surface.

"Sarai!" I frantically shriek.

Her brother drowned in this same ocean, I will not let it take her also.

"Sarai!"

I bob up and down in the increasingly angry ocean, searching in all directions. I am only about three hundred yards from shore. I yell her name as a wave punches a glass of salt water down my throat. I gag it back out. To my left I spot an arm floating towards me. I fervently pray it's not Sarai's. My arms slice through the water as I finally reach the floating limb. On the shoulder is a tattoo of the Liberty Bell. It's not Sarai's. It's Dagger's.

"Sarai!"

My muscles, already weak from Zion's version of electric shock therapy, are scorching as I battle to stay afloat. I refuse to swim to shore without her. Then I hear a faint sound fight its way through the rolling waves.

"Asher!" Sarai yells.

She is fifty yards to my left.

"Here!" I wave my arms and begin to swim towards her.

"I'm fine! Save your energy; swim to shore."

It takes us about ten minutes to finally reach land. We ride a giant wave that takes us the last fifty feet. Exhausted, we crawl to each other and embrace, our feet still partially in the freezing water.

"Thought I lost you," I manage to stay.

"Not possible. We are eternity mates, remember?"

I smile until I see Dagger wash ashore, what's left of him.

"So much for an alliance with The Sons of Levi," I mutter.

Sarai stands and looks out to the horizon. We are not far from where her younger brother Eleazar had drowned. I know that she still feels responsible.

"I hate the ocean."

It takes us eight days to reach the western section of The Wall near my old stomping grounds. My third army awaits me. I am hesitant. Do they know who I really am? How will I be received? Sarai and I wait on a ridge about a mile out before approaching their camp.

"It's too big of a secret to keep. They must know," I tell Sarai.

"You're right. After your escape, it would now behoove my father to tell them, even if it is embarrassing."

"Maybe this isn't a good idea," I lament.

"Maybe, and there would be no shame in turning back, but this moment is what you have been working towards. I'm not sure we can win without them, even with the armory."

I ponder for a moment; my fear is acute, but who am I if I don't practice what I espouse? I remember what my uncle has taught me. *If God is for us, who could be against us?*

"Let's do this. After all, we're Drecks, right?"

Sarai's smile does little to hide her apprehension. But what we do now we do together. Her satiny arms pull me tight into her embrace. Her silken hair is a soft-landing spot for my hardened cheeks, for my spirit. Her maternal yet robust hands clasp mine. They hold me up. They are an anchor for my soul.

"Whatever happens next, I want our fate to be the same. I cannot be separated from you anymore," she tells me in a rapturous whisper.

We hike down the hill, and the six sentries watch in awe as we march towards the camp center.

Dead silence.

They all stand and watch me jaunt towards them. I scan their eyes and see a mix of fury with a pinch of bewilderment. Before I can speak, one of them yells.

"The traitor has returned! Crucify him!"

With that, the mob rushes me.

"Traitor!"

They kick me.

"Low-life Dreck!"

I'm punched.

"Crucify him!"

I am dragged to a pole. They tie my arms behind my back. Rocks are hurled at me.

"Stop!" Sarai screams. "Stop! And hear him out!"

Another yells, "She is in on it! She is with him!"

She is grabbed and tied to an adjacent pole.

"She is a sultana of Zion! Let her go!" I howl.

"She's a traitor!"

Another rock smacks me in the temple. I am dizzy for a moment. *Bad idea!* Did I really think a simple Dreck could convince a Lazurite army to fight against Zion? Was I that naive? Was Cephas that blind? Then Kenan runs in front of me with his hands in the air.

"Stop! Stop this now!" Kenan bellows without a stutter of any kind. "We have fought with this man, bled with him, we have learned from him, he has led us unlike any commander we have ever had. He has treated us fairly, even graciously. I don't care if he is Amos or Asher, I say we let him speak!"

My captains contemplate for a moment, then one of them cuts me loose.

"You have five minutes," the captain tells me.

I nod my thanks to Kenan and stand on a high stump. I pray for the requisite words, my father's wisdom, and my uncle's pugnacity.

"What you have heard is true. I am Asher, son of Silas. I have deceived you, and for that I'm sorry. If there was any other way I thought I could have shown you the truth, I would have done it." I take a deep breath, "What is genuine is how I feel about you as you have become my brothers, some of you my friends. But what I say to you now is true. You and the rest of Zion have been told a lie; that second-life protocol has been outlawed. But that is not true. Not if you're rich or powerful."

"You're lying!" someone from the crowd wails.

"I have seen it for myself. I have been to The Mountain. I have seen how it's done. It takes another human life for the protocol to work. Your brothers and sisters are being harvested then sacrificed so the elite can live forever."

I see shock on the faces of those who believe me. I peer down at my muddy boots and wipe the blood from my forehead.

"Zion is dying. You may not see it, but it is rotting from the inside, slithering towards Gomorrah. Its decadent shell is decaying. What is it that you fight for? For Zion? Why? What virtue is it that is here? Do you know what transpires on the other side of this wall? These are people of your same heritage, your same blood; they used to be Americans just like you. Your brothers, your sisters. Now they are oppressed, starved, and murdered. Your trash is dumped onto our homes, our parks where children used to play. Renatus's drugs have been infused into our society. Children are ripped from their mother's arms and dragged to The Mountain so Renatus can try to give life to his own son. Once, there was a dream that was America, where life, liberty, and freedom were for all to have. Religion is now outlawed, and why do you think that is? Because Renatus believes he is a deity and the only one to be worshiped. You think you're free? YOU THINK YOU'RE FREE? You're not free!"

Some of the conscripted soldiers cheer and raise their weapons in defiance. It has begun. I need the others to follow suit.

"Do you think Renatus cares about you and your children? You only fight to keep his belly and his coffers full! What do you think will happen once he runs out of Drecks? Whose LifeCells do you think he will pilfer then? It will be yours and your children's. Believe me when I say Zion will break, and The Wall will come down. We will be free once more, and a country divided will be united again! Who's with me?"

Silence.

"Fight for Zion, and you'll be on the wrong side of history. Fight with me, and you can tell your children and grandchildren you were part of something special. That you were emancipators. That you redeemed a broken country! Who's with me?"

Silence.

The older conscripted man I had saved from bullying steps forward and slowly begins to sing "The Dreck's Dirge." His voice a whisper at first. By the third verse, his lament has reached a thunderous crescendo. Others begin to join in:

> *"They took our freedom, and with that our soul*
> *With Zion's tonic, we are no longer whole*
> *One day it will finally fall*
> *The oppression that is The Wall*
> *As Drecks, we have no more hope*
> *We hung ourselves with Zion's rope*
> *Second Life used to be for all*
> *That was before The Wall*
> *Now we live in a giant cage*
> *Where no one can hear our rage*
> *There was a day we used to stand tall*

That was before The Wall
We are now deemed a lower class
Forced to live with Zion's trash
Happier times I can recall
That was before The Wall"

Silence.

He then barks at the top of his lungs, "I'm with Asher! Asher the Liberator!"

With that, many of my army roars with approval. They chant my name.

"Down with Zion!" they whoop.

Sarai gives me a smile and winks as if to say she knew I could do it. I wait for them to stop.

"It won't be easy. At this very moment, Renatus's first army marches towards us. Some might say we are inferior to them. That would be a miscalculation on their part. I have trained you to fight them in a way they don't expect. With weapons their exoarmor can't defend against. Let me be clear, no one will be forced to fight. There are no conscripts in my army. Those who are afraid or do not wish to participate may leave now with no reprisals. But remember this, my brothers: Fear is a choice. Fear is a feeling. We have righteousness and God on our side; whom shall we fear?"

A large contingent of elites gather. One of them spits in disgust. "You're a liar and a traitor to Zion. We will not follow you!" The elites, realizing they are outnumbered, turn and begin to march away.

"You're losing them, sir," Kenan says nervously.

"I don't want them anyway."

I now have my army, but I still need to figure out a way to open a section of The Wall so Cephas and his armory can join us if we are to have a chance. I sidle up to Kenan.

"Didn't you say you were a computer tech in a previous life?"

Renatus is still aghast. As he paces the war room, he thinks over and over about how Asher had duped him again, how he would capture him again, and his treasonous daughter. Livid, he tosses a chair across the room, "How did he escape SeaPen?"

No one answers. Renatus shakes his head, calms himself. *It's time to end this war once and for all,* he thinks. Maps and drone footage laminate the room. Omar points to the screen.

"My scouts tell me Cephas and a pitiful band of what is left of The Defiance is massing near the western portion of The Wall."

"And Asher?" Renatus inquires.

"My spies are reporting he now has your third army under his command," Omar replies.

"And my daughter?"

"She is with him."

Renatus stands, bile smolders in the back of his throat. "It's time we end this bloody war. Split my first army. Send the majority after Asher. Take the rest, along with a squadron of helidrones to take out Cephas."

"You think he'll stay where he is?"

"Open a portion of The Wall. Section 309 should do it."

"Snare him? I like it." Not wanting to go through protocol again, Omar continues his sycophantic ways. "What about prisoners?"

"Take none. Annihilate them . . . all of them," Renatus spews with a wave of his hand as if The Defiance was just a fly on his neck.

"And the sultana?" Omar asks.

Renatus looks down at his palms, almost as if one of them holds the right decision. "I want her alive for reasons you already stated."

"But what about the third army? Our plasma weapons are useless against exoarmor."

"Already taken care of." Renatus stands and presses a button on the table. In walks a Lazurite guard wearing exoarmor carrying a silver plasma rifle. It's four inches longer and has more girth than your average plasma rifle. He hands it to Renatus.

Renatus strokes the weapon as if it were a cat. "Just out of production, Gen2 Plasma, renders exoarmor inoperative."

"I thought that technology was still years away?" Omar says in awe.

"It's amazing what one can accomplish when one has the screws put to them," Renatus tells him, referring to the threats he made to his science and technology group.

"So that's what the Anti-Armor Project is? Has it been tested outside of the lab?"

"It's about to be." Renatus smirks, then aims the rifle at Omar who is donning exoarmor. After watching the sweat bead on Omar's forehead, he then turns the new weapon on the guard and fires.

The plasma penetrates his armor, killing him.

"With this new weapon, Asher and his third army do not stand a chance. Victory is ours; soon, mate, this war will be over. The Defiance crushed."

Omar peers down at the dead guard. "Shall I bring him to The Mountain?"

"And what? Waste a perfectly good LifeCell?"

Cephas and his remaining army shroud themselves under a canvas of trees about two miles from Sector 304 near the western section of The Wall. Helidrones hover in the distance, flying search patterns. After another good cleaning, they load their rusted Springfield rifle muskets. Jude and a few men wheel a Gatling gun in between two large boulders.

"The Wall is still closed," Jude points out the obvious.

"He'll have it opened, we have to give him more time," Cephas replies. "In the meantime, use the Gatling to take out any drones that get too close."

A fierce wind arrives that causes his hungry men to shiver, but it's no match for Cephas's thick, leather-like skin. Jude, on the other hand, who is all skin and bones, shudders.

"Want my coat?" Cephas asks.

"That smelly thing? You kidding?" Jude says.

Cephas sniffs his coat, then shrugs. "Suit yourself."

"What if Asher doesn't succeed in opening The Wall?" Jude asks.

"Has he failed us yet?"

"That's my point. He's gonna run out of luck at some point."

"Then we find another way. And it's not luck, my friend."

"I know, I know, divine intervention."

"Now you're getting it."

Jude peers at his friend. "You ever think about what you might do when this is all over?"

"I don't yet have the luxury of thinking beyond tomorrow." Cephas sighs. "You?"

"Start a family."

"You could have done that years ago."

"I won't bring children into this world. Not in the state it's in."

"Let's hope today is the first step in changing all of that. You changing diapers will be quite a sight."

"Hopefully that happens before I'm changing yours." Jude snorts.

"Just keep your eye on The Wall, will ya?"

Jude takes another peek through his binoculars. "There!" he shouts.

A section of The Wall opens. Cephas grabs his binoculars to see for himself. He looks at the section.

"It's Sector 309."

"Wasn't he supposed to open 304?" Jude inquires.

"That was the plan, but since when does anything go according to plan? Maybe that's the only one he could open?"

Jude's teeth clatter. "Maybe it's a trap?"

Cephas stands. "Gather the men and weapons. Let's make our way down."

"Shouldn't we scout it first? To be sure," Jude implores him.

"When was the last time you were sure of anything? We don't have time for reconnaissance or to ponder maybes! This is our one and only chance. Asher could be on the other side, under attack as we speak, needing our assistance. We go. Now."

Jude jumps up. "Reckless as always."

"Ain't that the way of the Dreck," Cephas grunts.

"Some more than others," Jude retorts, gathering weapons and men.

"Buckethead always has to have the last word," Cephas mutters while taking another gander through binoculars.

Within ten minutes Jude has gathered the remnants of The Defiance, along with their cache of Civil War-era weapons. Jude edges up to Cephas.

"Perhaps a word to the men."

"What for?" gripes Cephas.

"You know, like a speech or something? Rally the troops?" Jude quips, knowing Cephas hates speeches.

Cephas concedes and saunters towards his men, who create a circle around him.

"Listen up. You all know that I'm not one for speeches."

"Ain't that the truth!" a Dreck yells, followed by a chorus of cackles.

"Okay, okay, I get it. Listen, I try to lead as best as I know how, but even I know that I wasn't built for this. I am no Asher. I am no Silas. I have made a lot of mistakes in my life, done a lot of stupid things I regret. I hurt a lot of people."

Cephas pulls his tattered Bible from his coat and holds it up high. The wind flutters its frayed vintage pages.

"But it doesn't matter who you are, where you come from, nor what you have done. There is redemption in these here pages. Like many of you, I too was reckless with much of my younger years when we knew a second life was available. You were angry when second-life rights were revoked, and so was I. But how stupid was that? Is the guarantee of a second chance an excuse to waste the first? Then the Good Book showed me a different way. Renatus and his ilk think they have cornered the market on eternal life. But what he doesn't know, and what he has tried to outlaw, is that eternal life can be had for all! It's right in here, plain as day. Doesn't matter if you're rich, poor, Dreck or Lazurite. It's free for the having.

"Who are we to think we know better than the creator of the Earth and the universe? You're probably thinking, 'Why am I telling you this now?' Or 'Does the old man think he's some kinda preacher or something?' I'm just a man, plain and simple, like everyone here. I may die today. You may die today. But this isn't our home. Not permanently anyway. We are mere visitors . . . this is all temporary. Your flesh, your fears, what little that you own. Your hunger. That isn't eternal! Look, I want to live on, I want to see peace, I want a world with no walls. I pray God grants us victory. But if that doesn't come, I would rather die today with all of you, my fellow Drecks, my friends, my family, fighting side by side for what's right, fighting for freedom, than dying years from now a starving slave in hiding!"

His men pump their fists, hoot, and holler.

"Now, I may be just a crusty old man with a rusty old gun. But I'd take a Dreck over ten Lazurite elites any day! Which is good, because I'm guessing those are our odds."

This elicits more cheers along with a bit of laughter.

"Now, let's go show them cell-pirates what gunpowder smells like!"

His men roar even louder.

Jude nods, impressed, "Where did that come from?"

"I wrote it two years ago," Cephas admits.

CHAPTER FIFTEEN

Cephas and his army cautiously march towards Sector 309, the open portion of The Wall. It is eerily silent, almost serene. Jude takes note.

"It's terribly quiet."

"I don't like this," Cephas agrees but marches on.

"At least the drones are gone."

His men wheel a Gatling gun on their left flank. Weapons at the ready. Then, out of nowhere, hundreds of Lazurite soldiers storm the opening in The Wall, heading directly towards them. A dozen helidrones that were hidden on the other side of The Wall ascend into the air and hover above them. Then The Wall closes, shutting them off.

"I knew it was a trap!" Jude growls. "Your nephew's luck has run out!"

"Spread out! And fire up that Gatling! Take out the drones!" Cephas barks.

His men take a knee and fire their Springfield rifles. At first the Lazurites are confused as they see some of their comrades quickly go down, lead penetrating their exoarmor. Then they realize the weaponry The Defiance now wields.

"They've got bloody gunpowder!" a Lazurite screams.

"Our exoarmor is useless!" another bellows.

"Do not retreat," yells the Lazurite commander. "Continue your charge! Any soldier that disengages will be shot!" But the commander stays in the back, letting his men charge forward, now unprotected.

The Lazurites return fire with their plasma rifles taking out a few of Cephas's men. The helidrones rain down pulse-grenades, sending more of The Defiance flying into the air. Two of the men manning the Gatling gun are also taken out. Jude sprints towards it, aims the massive gun up at the helidrones, and operates the rusty hand crank, sending an array of bullets into the sky. Two drones are hit and crash into a platoon of Lazurite elites. This is not the battle the Lazurites were expecting, but even so they outnumber The Defiance in men, weapons, and of course winged annihilators that continue to search and destroy.

Cephas commands his troops, "Take shifts as we practiced! One group fires as another reloads! Cover one another!"

Reloading takes way too long, and the Civil War-era weapons aren't as accurate as those of the Lazurites. Cephas sees this is quickly becoming a rout.

"Retreat and take cover!" Cephas bellows painfully.

As he fires his rifle, the musket jams. "Rusted piece of junk!" Cephas tosses it to the ground and whips out his sidearm and lays down more covering fire as he lumbers towards the trees. The helidrones relentlessly inflict a monsoon of destruction. The ground around their feet is razed and burned.

In shifts, Cephas's men head back towards the forest while the others provide covering fire. Soon, Cephas and his men are huddled on top of a ridge under a canopy of thick trees. They fire back at the Lazurite army with another Gatling gun keeping them at bay for now, but the helidrones prevent their escape. It's now just a matter of time. Either they run out of ammo, or Lazurite reinforcements arrive to finish them off. They can do nothing but wait for Asher and his army and hope he arrives soon.

"Now what?" Jude asks solemnly.

"Pray."

Sarai and I lead my third army near one of Zion's control towers on the other side of The Wall, just miles away from where Cephas and his men are besieged.

"You sure this is it?" I ask Kenan.

"I was assigned to one of these posts before being transferred to your army," Kenan replies. "If we can get inside, I can hack into the system and open a portion of The Wall."

"And the drones?" Sarai adds.

"It's possible I can shut them off."

I take notice that Kenan's stutter is but a fraction of what it was. His timbre now confident.

"How do we get in?"

"That's the rub. The door is just about bloody impenetrable and can only open from the inside."

"Pulse-grenades?" Sarai asks.

"Not enough to breach those doors."

For once, my army outnumbers their guards, but I'm stuck by a stupid door. We need to do something fast. I'm not sure how long I can leave Cephas hanging. I look at Kenan's stripes on his exoarmor. Three of them, for third army. I rip two of them off.

"What's that for?" he asks confused.

"There. Now you're first army."

"I don't get it."

"You think they're gonna let us in just because we are dressed like first army?" Sarai asks astutely.

"If Asher the Traitor is your prisoner, they will," I reply.

"That could work, assuming our luck doesn't run out," she says.

"C'mon, haven't you ever seen *Star Wars*? Han and Luke dressed as storm troopers, Chewbacca pretending to be their prisoner?"

"Let's get some cuffs on the Wookie."

I turn to Kenan. "Approximately how many guards should we expect inside the tower?"

"Ten or twenty. And another ten controllers."

We march up towards the tower with ten of my men donning only one stripe on their exoarmor. Kenan to my left, Sarai to my right. Everyone is wearing helmets except me; we want them to see my face. My cuffs are unlocked.

"I'm Han," Sarai announces as we make our way to the door.

"That fits," Kenan shoots back.

"How so?" Sarai asks with a smile.

"You've got quite the acid tongue," Kenan replies.

Kenan is fitting in nicely. Soon he'll be a Dreck. They wave at the video camera perched above the door and point to me, letting them know of their prize. We wait a minute. Nothing.

"Let's hope we don't end up in a trash compactor," whispers Sarai.

Then, a voice from the intercom. "State your business."

Sarai steps up. "First army patrol with special prisoner drop off."

"We have not been informed. Nor is this on the schedule," the voice booms back.

"We got cut off, our communications were destroyed. Take a close look, we have captured Asher the Traitor."

Moments later the massive steel door slides open. We are greeted by five guards who escort us into the main operations room. The Lazurite guards and technicians manning the computers stare at me in awe. A tall man with squinting green eyes and long silver hair approaches us.

"I'm the facilitator of this outpost."

Sarai responds, "We were on patrol just south of here, found Asher with a small band of The Defiance. This was the closest safe place."

"Excellent," he responds and motions to two guards. "Take him to holding facility eight." He then turns to Sarai and my men. "Thank you chaps, you may be on your way."

"On our way?" Sarai exclaims. "We just brought you Zion's most wanted man, and now we are to leave and let you get all of the credit?"

"You're an astute one. And you would be right. This is my ticket out of the outpost and into Zion West, where I shall receive a most honorable commission," the facilitator shamelessly smiles.

Not going to happen, I'm afraid. As the two guards approach me, I reach into my coat, slip off my cuffs, and pull out my ricochet. Before they know what is going on, I hit the closest guard across the head and then throw it, hitting the other guard. Sarai whips out her scourge, quickly taking out the facilitator. Neither of our plasma weapons does any good since both sides' attire consists of exoarmor. The scene turns chaotic as we resort to stunclubs and hand-to-hand combat. But my men are well trained, and the Lazurite guards posted here are second-rate. The elites don't babysit outposts that are supposedly impregnable. Within minutes we overwhelm this subpar contingent.

"Guess the chap won't be receiving an honorable commission after all?" Sarai chaffs.

"Insult to injury, you are more Dreck than Lazurite," I smile at her.

Kenan stations himself in front of one of the many computer terminals and hacks away. He's a conductor of code. A maestro of zeros and ones.

"I'm in!" Kenan proclaims after a few minutes of typing.

"Open Sector 304," I request.

"Why not open the entire Wall now?" Sarai asks.

"Each outpost only controls a few sectors," Kenan explains as his fingers rap the keyboard. "Only Renatus at headquarters can do that. I have drone footage."

On the massive video screen are live video feeds from the helidrones that beleaguer Cephas and his men.

"Shut them off," I tell him.

"I'm trying."

I watch in horror as the helidrones shed pulse-grenades onto Cephas's army. They are trapped. It is quickly becoming a massacre.

"C'mon Kenan, you can do this!"

"I can't. There's just no . . . no way."

I turn to one of the controllers huddled in the corner. "Maybe they can."

Kenan shakes his head, "Not possible unless you speak Tunica."

"Tunica?"

"It's a rare Native American dialect. Renatus made sure that all of Zion's technology gatekeepers only spoke this language just for this purpose."

I ponder what to do next. With The Wall open, I could lead my army to rescue them as they are just miles away, but I fear by the time we got there, the annihilation would be complete. I point to a door that leads to a massive steel room that looks like a warehouse.

"What's in there?"

"Weapon's cache."

"Bring up the manifest."

Kenan brings it up on the monitor. Among the usual Lazurite weapons is also a helidrone. I point to it.

"Can you operate it from here?"

"No," Kenan says solemnly.

"Is there a manual override?" I ask.

"I suppose if you can find someone crazy enough to pilot the thing."

Sarai touches my shoulder. She spots that look in my eye. The one I get when I'm about to do something reckless.

"What are you doing, Asher? You aren't planning on flying that thing? I mean, you might take out one or two drones, but you'll surely be shot down. There has to be another way."

I point to the manifest. "I won't be the only cargo."

Cephas and his men are still hunkered down in the thickest part of the forest. The helidrones hover above them to the south, systematically dropping pulse-grenades as they take suppressing fire from the Lazurites from the north. Some divine intervention has given them a helping hand as light fog rolls in, enhancing their cover.

One of his men manning a Gatling takes aim at an incoming drone.

"Hold your fire," Cephas tells him, not wanting to give up their exact location.

Jude peers up at the fog, "The Almighty has granted us a gift for now, but once it burns off, we need a plan."

"Patience," Cephas responds calmly.

"How can you be patient at a time like this?"

"It was impatience that got Adam and Eve booted from the Garden."

"Ha! This coming from the most impatient man I know," Jude cackles.

Cephas shakes his head as he has more than enough firepower and guns; he just doesn't have the manpower to utilize all of them at the moment. Then he spies another helidrone coming in low from the west. It swoops down, almost tapping the treetops, cutting through the fog.

"Incoming!" Jude utters.

It is almost directly above them. The guard at the Gatling prepares to fire. He looks to Cephas for permission.

"Not yet."

Then Cephas can't believe his eyes when he spots Asher manning the drone.

"That Asher?" Jude asks, bewildered.

What is that kid doing?

They watch Asher fly the helidrone until it is positioned almost directly in the middle of the ten other drones. Then its payload doors open. A small box attached to a parachute begins to float down.

"What is that?" Jude squints.

Cephas knows right away and grins. "It's a crafty boy I raised is what that is."

The box pulses, sending electrical currents spreading through the air.

"An EMP!" Jude hollers.

The electronics inside the drones buzz, then shut off. They fall from the sky like shot pigeons, as does Asher and the drone he is manning. The Lazurite army looks on, confused as to what just happened. Asher crashes in an open field between Cephas and the Lazurite army. Cephas sees Asher's drone begin to smoke; Asher is having trouble opening the hatch.

"Get him outta there!" Cephas yells.

Jude and a contingent bolt towards Asher's downed drone. They dodge potshots fired by Lazurite soldiers on the ridge. The fog has still provided some cover. Jude is the first one there and sees Asher bang on the glass hatch as his drone fills with smoke.

"Cover your head!" Jude screams as he shatters the glass with his large wooden club.

Shards stick to Asher's arms that were covering his face and scalp. Coughing, he is pulled out of the drone in a plume of black smoke. They race back to the cover of trees, zig-zagging to avoid being hit by the plasma blasts. Asher stumbles a few times, hacking like the Marlboro Man, his lungs still filled with smoke. Cephas gives Asher a once-over to be certain he is okay.

"Nice of you to *drop* in, Buckethead."

"That took stones!" Jude adds.

Asher catches his breath. "More like stupidity. I forgot that it would take out my drone as well."

"Seems life with the Lazurites didn't completely suck the Dreck out of you," Cephas says.

The three of them share a much-needed laugh. But only for a moment, as the Lazurites have begun to march towards them. They spot the Lazurite commander in the back of his infantry, barking commands at them.

"To arms!" Cephas orders.

"No need," Asher tells them, still trying to clear his lungs.

Sector 304 of The Wall suddenly opens. Pouring from it is Asher's third army. They quickly overwhelm the small detachment of Lazurites. Most of them surrender. Cephas slaps his giant mitt against Asher's shoulder.

"Nice work, Son."

"Where'd you learn how to fly a drone?" Jude nudges him.

"On the way here. Wasn't sure how to land it, so I guess it's good that I crashed."

"A Dreck landing if I've ever seen one!" jabbers Jude.

Asher peers over at Jude's Springfield rifle, "How many of those you got?"

Cephas smiles. "Not enough to arm your entire army, but I think we have enough to give us a fighting chance."

"A lot of them look rusted," Asher points to the rifles.

Cephas says, "So are we."

They all three nod in agreement. Rusted Drecks against shiny golden Lazurites.

"Renatus's first army is massive and well-armed. Along with the weapons from the armory, we'll need other unconventional methods of battle if we are to win."

Cephas waves his hand at his dirty but scrappy army. "You want unconventional? You came to the right place, boy."

And for what might be the very first time, all three of them truly believe they just might pull this off.

Asher gazes to the sky. "Still can't believe you found the armory. I thought maybe Boaz had given us a fake. Or that it didn't exist."

Jude cackles. "You should have been there. Cephas threw a rock at me."

After twelve straight hours of marching west, we break for camp. My army has become adept at quickly setting up tents and cooking copious amounts of food, as we have been at this for two weeks. We gather in our makeshift command center composed of three adjoining tents. I unfurl a map across a plastic folding table. Kenan flips open a laptop he had pilfered from the Lazurite outpost where we had opened a section of The Wall.

"I was able to hack into one of their sentinel drones," Kenan informs us.

The grainy image on the laptop is live footage of Renatus's first army marching at a good clip.

"Where are they?" I ask.

"I'm not sure. I can't get a GPS reading."

I take a closer look at the footage. "Does anyone recognize any of these landmarks?"

Sarai points to a dilapidated building with crumbling columns. Birds fly from the many gaps in its roof, probably curious about the drone flying above them. "That's the old capital building, old Sacramento, California."

"And we're currently here," I point to a section on the map that used to be Central Nevada. I ponder for a moment and peer closer at the map. "There, Donner Lake. How long do you think it will take for Renatus's first army to get there?"

Cephas measures the distance on the map and makes some calculations. "Three days. Maybe faster."

"And us?" I ask.

"About the same."

"We need to get there in two," I say.

"Why? What's so special about Donner Lake?" Sarai queries.

"Should be frozen this time of year," is all I say, looking up, seeing if anyone else is tracking with me. Blanks stares. "Napoleon? The battle of Austerlitz? Am I the only one who knows their history?"

"You talking getting them in the middle of the lake, then breaking the ice?" Cephas asks with a smile.

I point to the eastern edge of the lake. "If we can get there before them, make a fake camp here, we should be easily spotted by their drones."

Sarai points to the western side of the lake. "So you'll be bait, and their quickest attack route will be here, right through the middle of the lake."

"From their perspective, we'll be sitting ducks."

Sarai isn't so sure. "My father's first army isn't stupid. What makes you think they'll come straight at us instead of attacking our flanks?"

Smart as always.

Cephas looks to me. "She is right, Nephew. Basic warfare dictates they will come at us from our flanks and possibly from behind."

I reply with mock bravado, "Because we are just stupid Drecks, and they are brash Lazurites. Do you sneak up on an ant to smash it? Or do you walk directly up to it and stomp on it with your foot? I have spent enough time among them to know how they think. Besides, it's the only way for my plan to work. So they must."

"We can have two platoons on both ridges to take out whatever army the lake doesn't, as well as protect our flanks," Cephas adds.

"They won't all fit on the lake, we are still going to be way outnumbered," Sarai reminds me.

I ponder for a moment and think about some of my most cherished memories spent with Sarai, fishing on the lake, and it gives me an idea. "How do you catch a lot of fish at the same time?"

"Nets?" Jude guesses, bewildered.

I look to Cephas. "You said unconventional, right?"

"I'll take one of the ridges," Sarai says.

While I admire her bravery, I want her next to me or in the rear with the second wave where it will be safer, but I know it's a lost cause mentioning it, so I simply nod in agreement. I cannot cage who she is—a warrior, a leader. Cheerleading on the sidelines would never suit her. Besides, if I'm to lead, I cannot play favorites.

"We'll have to march eighteen hours a day if you want to get there in two," Cephas informs me.

"And I'm not carrying you either," Jude snorts.

I dig out one of the remaining grenades from the Fort Worth

Armory stash and hold it up to Kenan. "You think you can rig a remote detonator to these?"

"I'll see what I can do."

"If you can't, our plan doesn't work."

"I'll see what I can do," Kenan repeats himself.

"Not to be a downer, but y'all know what happened to the Donner party, right?" Jude blurts.

Cephas snickers, "Ha! No one is eating you, toothpick!"

"Our ambush against Cephas has failed, my sultan. He has now linked up with Asher and his third army."

The way Omar says *his* third army irks Renatus to no end. *It's not Asher's army, it's mine!*

"Unacceptable!" Renatus pounds his fist against the war-room table. "Where are they now?"

"Heading west, towards us. Drone footage has them in Central Nevada."

"This rampant incompetence must come to a bloody end! Fly me to my first army, I will lead them myself!"

Omar tries to mask his surprise. "Of course, my sultan."

Renatus then raises his plasma rifle at Omar. "And I grow tired of your floundering ineptitude."

Omar raises his hands, "My sultan, I do not understand."

"Did you think your failure to capture Cephas would go unpunished?"

"But sir, it was . . . it was your idea," Omar replies boldly.

Renatus manically waves his hand in the air. "True, but you agreed, didn't you? You always agree, Omar. You only tell me what it is I want to hear. Asher might have been a traitor, but he dauntlessly told me when he thought I was wrong and pointed out my blind spots. You, on the other hand, are a sycophantic feckwit!"

Before Omar can reply, Renatus shoots him with no intention of sending his advisor to The Mountain again for protocol. He casually steps over Omar's body and makes his way to his chambers.

In a closet the size of a small house, attached to his master suite, Renatus slips on his battle gear. Red-and-black exoarmor with a gold sash whipped around his waist. His shoulders are decorated with medals and ranks he did not earn. He removes his Gen2 plasma rifle from its charger and then inexplicably thinks of his son Eleazar. *Maybe things would be different if Eleazar was still here. Maybe I would be different. Maybe there wasn't a need for a wall.* He quickly scoffs at his own thoughts. *Of course there was a need for The Wall. The Middle had become reckless and lawless. A wasteland.*

In the mirror he spots the twinkle of a glimmering evening gown. Behind him is his wife, Joanna. She rests her dainty hand on his shoulder.

"Going to battle?" she asks, surprised.

"Time to finish this palaver once and for all."

"And what of Sarai?" she asks, twirling her blood-red hair with her long, delicate fingers.

"What of her? She is a traitor, Joanna! She is with him now. I can't bear to speak his name." As the anger wells up within him, he is starting to have second thoughts about sparing her life. After all, what were the chances of her bearing a wounded one like his own son?

"Eleazar wasn't the only child that loved you," she tries to convince him.

"She has a strange way of showing it, taking up arms against me, against Zion, our way of life. She has decided to stand with the Traitor of Zion, The Son of Silas. She is not only married to him but also to their bloody cause."

"She is young and in love. She doesn't know what she is doing. Please, Renatus, I beg you, bring her back to me. Bring her home."

Renatus turns with fire in his eyes. "And according to her, just where exactly would that be? She is a Dreck now."

She grabs his shoulders and turns him to face her. "Yes, she is a Dreck, but she is a Dreck carrying our grandchild."

Renatus's mood shifts slightly. "She's pregnant? How do you know?"

"I have been there, I just know."

He grabs both of her hands and grins. "Yes. Yes, Joanna, you are correct. A grandchild is exactly what this family needs."

CHAPTER SIXTEEN

Donner Lake is just over two and a half miles long and a half mile wide. At close to six thousand feet of elevation, the lake has frozen over. Fresh snow has salted its surface. It wasn't easy, but we made it here in two days. Forty-nine hours, to be exact. I shiver for a moment. Is it out of fear? Or maybe because it's six degrees Fahrenheit. My men boil the drinking water that has frozen in our packs. We are exhausted, and the battle has yet to begin. The ice is thirty inches thick, plenty to hold Zion's marching army. Kenan drills holes into the ice and plants Civil War era grenades on the western side of the frozen lake. I only hope the remote detonators he rigged work and that the grenades are powerful enough to crack the ice. He assures me they are. We set up tents and a makeshift camp on the eastern side as we want it to look like this is where we have massed. A drained and bone-weary Cephas slides next to me, almost slipping on the ice. He points to the other side of the lake.

"If they don't come this way, this will be the quickest defeat since the Anglo-Zanzibar war."

I have no idea what war he is talking about. "You forget there were no schools when I was a kid."

"That's right, if it's not an 80's movie, you have no idea what I'm talking about. Thirty-eight minutes. That is how long that war lasted," Cephas informs me somberly.

"If they don't cross the lake, then we'll be lucky to last twenty," I reply. "I pray we are granted God's favor today."

He pulls me close. "You believe, boy? I mean, really believe? Cause if you do, then no matter what happens today, you have His favor. And mine." He scoops up a clump of snow and squeezes it in his hands as if he could absorb its cleanliness, its purity. "Win, lose, or draw, I'm proud of you, Son. And I'm sorry for how I raised you. I did my best for who I was at the time. I wish I could do it over."

I turn to him. "You don't have to apologize anymore. The good things inside me may have come from my father, but I only know how to act on those things because of you."

"I was too hard on you," Cephas whispers, shaking his head.

"Iron sharpens iron."

"Yes, I guess it does."

"How are the legs?" I ask, still amazed he made the trip without a single gripe or squawk. At least not about how long the trek was.

He smiles, then peers over at Sarai, who is overseeing the sowing of the giant nets.

"Don't worry about me, Nephew, better go check on those nets," he says with a wink.

I approach Sarai. "How are you?" is all I manage.

"How are *you*?" she says with more gravity than my question.

A wave of sudden honesty and vulnerability washes over me. "Just want it to be over. I really don't know how I got here. I'm not fit to lead these men, this war. It should be somebody else."

"'God doesn't call the equipped; he equips the called.' Your uncle told me that."

"I hope so. I hate to admit it, but he's right more than he's wrong."

"So, when this is all done, what then?" she asks, almost questioning if our relationship could withstand peace. We have only known war, strife, and separation. Under such conditions the primal emotions are at the forefront, such as love. Is she wondering if it will still be there during times of peace and harmony? When it is just us. No Wall, no Defiance, nothing to fight for.

I assure her it will. "I picture us in a small house in the mountains, near a lake where the fishing is good.

"I want to rebuild the parks so the children can play on swings with new chains and slides that aren't rusted or broken. Where you can walk down the street without smelling the trash of those believed to be above you. Where freedom reigns, not drugs. I want a place where The Middle and Zion are one. An America that is once again united, once again a beacon of light. Where everyone only has one life, and that life is not taken for granted. A place where you would want to bring children into the world. Our children."

Before I could continue, she shut me up with a kiss.

"Now, go win this war!" she snarls.

She kisses me again; then someone near plays an ancient Celtic tune on their harmonica. Sarai pulls me in tight, her feet rocking back and forth to the dulcet tune.

"Dance with me," she pleads.

"You know I don't dance," I reply.

"And I don't marry Lazurite princes, yet here we are."

Realizing this could be our last chance, I finally oblige her. My feet shimmy back and forth. I step on her toes more than once. Some of my men stop what they are doing and watch us awkwardly dance by the fire while our unknown serenader picks up the pace. I didn't know such sounds could emanate from a simple harmonica. I should feel self-conscious, but I don't. The world is so small when I'm with her. Everything else shrinks away, as nothing else can compare.

"Now I see why you don't dance." She kisses me again.

For a surreal moment, we are all alone, just us and the haunting melody. No war, no frozen lake. I can feel the warmth of the sun on my neck even though I know it's obscured by the clouds. I can smell spring, even though I stand on snow. The musky fragrance of wisteria. The sweet and spicy scents of lilac. The fresh, earthy aroma of rain. For just a few seconds the burden of leading these men is lifted. I feel light, so light she has to catch me.

Before I can tell her to be careful up on the ridge, one of my scouts run towards us, yelling, "They're here! Three miles away on the other side of the ridge."

The harmonica abruptly stops.

I'm cold once more.

The end is about to begin.

Renatus's first army finally appears over the hill. They march their way down towards the frozen lake. So far, so good. Sarai and a contingent of our army hide up on the ridge to my left. Jude is on the ridge to my right. Like a never-ending colony of ants, the Lazurite army keeps coming and coming.

"Perhaps we underestimated their numbers?" Cephas huffs.

There are so many of them. Their black exoarmor against the white snow looks like a giant cloud blotted out the sun. They look like a massive tree that won't stop growing. I turn to my army behind me and see a mix of fear and subdued optimism. I feel as if I should say something, but the thought of delivering another speech just has me feeling like a used car salesman. So instead, I simply tell them the truth.

"I wanted to say something, but in all honesty, there are no words that I or anyone can say that you should die for. Just do what's in your heart. Follow what it is you believe. I know many of you well enough to know that you don't need me to tell you what is worth fighting for. Dying for. If you wish not to be here, if you wish not to fight for our cause, you may leave freely now. You can even have a horse and a day's ration."

With that, Cephas and I anxiously wait to see if anyone changes their mind. Not a single soldier moves.

"Wasn't expecting that," Cephas whispers.

"What?"

"That you would give your men a way out, a chance to surrender minutes before battle. Some commander you are," Cephas says, tongue way in cheek.

I don't tell Cephas what he already knows; one soldier fighting for what he believes in is worth more than ten fighting for someone else's cause. As for me, I have come to believe that the reluctant leader is the one that is more pure. They value cause over power. I have seen it in my father, my uncle, and now myself. And if I die today, so it will be with Sarai, a reluctant leader, as we have seen firsthand the pollution of eternal power when wielded by man. For too many, past and present, have yearned for a position in power just for the sake of power.

I peer up to the ridge and watch Sarai prepare the nets. I wonder if we will ever have a chance to dance again. I chastise myself for waiting this long. I wonder how hard it is for her to fight against her own father. I draw inspiration from her strength and courage. She gazes down at me and winks. It isn't until that moment that I realize I'm ready. I peer up at the sky, surprised that it is empty. "No helidrones?"

"I'm sure Renatus has a plan," Cephas replies.

"Maybe we destroyed them all back at The Wall?"

"And maybe I could've been a male model?" Cephas jests.

We share a short-lived laugh as Zion's first army finally finishes their march over the hill and into the valley. Half of them are on the frozen lake. So many, in fact, I wonder if the ice will crack on its own and if we won't need Kenan's explosives after all. I peer through my binoculars when I spot Renatus himself leading this attack. Leading is being generous, as he is in the back, of course. His gold sash whips in the wind. He slips his helmet over his smug face and points his hand forward in a chopping motion. His first army restarts their march toward us as he and his generals hang back on horseback, barking orders.

"Tell . . . tell me when," Kenan states, his stutter bubbling to the surface.

"Not yet."

They march closer.

Cephas nudges me. "They're mighty silent over there; time to break the ice, what say you?"

"Not yet."

"They're almost in plasma range," Cephas hisses.

"Not yet."

Just as they pass the middle of the lake, they raise their plasma rifles and ready to fire.

"Now!" I command.

Kenan presses his remote detonator.

Nothing. We stare at one another. Now what?

"Dreck luck. Seems you are one of us," Cephas tells him.

Kenan's thumb plunges down on the button again, and we wait. Our breath practically freezes in front of us. Then the sound of leaves crunching. But it's not leaves; it's the ice. We are too far away, and the wind too fierce to hear the grenades go off. The cracking is getting louder now.

"It worked!" Kenan shouts.

"But they're still above water," Cephas reminds him that nothing has worked yet.

The Lazurite soldiers freeze in their tracks, confused for a moment as to what is happening. Some may not even realize they are on a lake. The ground below them shakes, and the fracturing of the ice is so loud that it sounds like steel is ripping in half. We hear them yell that the ice is breaking. In a formation nothing less than chaotic, they turn to run off the frozen ice. But it can no longer hold the weight. The entire middle of the lake snaps. Well over a thousand soldiers drop into the freezing waters. We can barely hear their muffled screams, and I can imagine it's too cold to find your breath. Their arms flutter like hummingbirds, creating a thousand tiny whitecaps as they try to swim back up upon the ice. I fell through a frozen lake once when I was nine. It feels like a thousand tiny daggers stabbing you all at once. I do not wish this for them, for anybody. I wish they would just surrender and throw down their arms instead. I wish this could be solved with a pen and a handshake instead of the sword.

But my wishes and reality are two different things.

Such is war.

A quarter of Renatus's army has fallen through the lake. We are still outnumbered, but not by much. Renatus sends his troops around the fractured lake, just underneath where Sarai and Jude lie in wait. It could not be going any more perfectly. I raise a blue flag that alerts them. With that, Sarai, Jude, and their garrisons drop the two-hundred-foot-long nets anchored by boulders tied to the ends. The Lazurite soldier's arms and legs become entangled. As they try to break free from their encumbrance, they aren't firing their weapons. This slows them down just enough for my army to have free, unimpeded shots.

I can only imagine Renatus's surprise when he realizes we have gunpowder weapons. His army is in shock as the lead penetrates their exoarmor. They fall like dominoes, unable to fire back as they struggle to free themselves from the nets. I wonder how Renatus could be so careless? It could be his over confidence, a Zion trait for sure. I think it's more likely he has gone to The Mountain too many times for protocol. Surely that has warped his judgment, his risk-assessment. For Renatus, if things go wrong or he makes a mistake, he is used to having a free pass, another chance. He has mistakenly taken this attitude to war with him. I am not proud of my time with Renatus slurping up Zion's opulence, getting fat from her udder. But now I know why God had me there, to learn the ways of my enemy. For this very moment. My uncle used to quote Sun Tzu's book, *The Art of War*. "Every battle is won before it's ever fought." I hope we have done enough to live up to that axiom today.

"Split!" I scream and wave a green flag in the air.

Half of my army scamper up the ridge towards Jude. The other half, along with myself race to link up with Sarai. We want to keep the high ground. When we reach the top, I find Sarai and her platoon firing their Springfield rifles at the Lazurites below us. I join in.

"So far so good," I say.

"We're getting low on ammo," she responds, reminding me it's way too early to pat myself on the back.

But the truth of the matter is that this is going well, too well, so easy in fact, I feel something isn't quite right. Why aren't they firing back with their plasma rifles? Is it because they know we have exoarmor, and it would be moot? Renatus may be presumptuous and cocky, but he's not dense. Then I look in the distance and see what appears to be a flock of crows approaching. But they aren't birds. They are helidrones—winged annihilators. At least fifty of them. So many they blot out the sun. I knew they were coming but didn't want to admit it.

"Get the Gatling!" I order.

The Lazurites below us form a line and aim their plasma rifles. I spot Renatus casually trotting back and forth behind them as if on an afternoon jaunt. Then he orders them to fire. Then, to my acute horror, my men begin dropping like flies. Their exoarmor does nothing to protect them from whatever this new weapon is that Renatus now wields.

"They have armor-penetrating plasma!" one of my soldiers yells dreadfully.

"And our lead can penetrate theirs!" I shoot back, trying to remain optimistic. But Sarai and I exchange glances, both of us realizing how bad it is. We just lost our one advantage.

Some of my men begin to panic, and I'm not far behind. I now realize my utopian battle plan was just a mirage. It was ludicrous to think I could take out Zion's first army with cracked ice and fishing nets. His commanders have years of battle-planning and experience. His first army war-hardened. We are but rabble in arms. Making this up as we go. I utter the words I had desperately hoped to avoid.

"Retreat!"

We fall back into the woods, its canopy giving us some cover from the helidrones as they indiscriminately drop pulse-grenades. God has also gifted us a heavy fog once more. Cephas and Jude join the retreat. When in view, our Gatling gun takes out a drone here and there. Within minutes the first army has entered the woods, and we now fight a different kind of war. We scatter, hiding up and behind trees, taking shots at the Lazurites, then hiding again. I quickly realize that we can't win this way, just prolong our survival. Sometimes shootings turn into hand-to-hand combat. I spot two Lazurites to my left. To save ammo, I fling my ricochet and take out the first one. When it returns to me, I dive to my left, avoid a plasma blast, and hurl it back at him, taking out the second. A third arrives before I can do anything, Jude takes care of him with his crossbow.

"You're welcome," he grins.

Another helidrone swoops down. Our Gatling gun fills it with holes; it crashes down like a giant brick of smoking Swiss cheese. Three more circle overhead, more pulse-grenades rain down causing the trees to convulse. Pine needles land on my head, jarred loose from the blast.

"We can't fight like this forever!" Cephas growls, blinking sweat and dirt from his eyes.

It's time to set things aflame.

"Scorch the trees!" I scream.

This section of forest is one of our pre-planned evacuation routes. I had my men slather them with oil last night. Drecks begin lighting the trees on fire. The covetous flames spread from tree to tree. We have the same setup on the other ridge. They see our flames and do the same. The lively soot and dark smoke swirl with the lazy fog, adulterating the once pristine crisp mountain air that helps with our retreat. The innocent trees are yet another casualty of this war. I'm hoping that the smoke will also give us extra cover from the helidrones.

"Keep moving back!" I yell to Sarai.

"I'm staying by you!" she barks back.

Then shots come in from my right and then behind me. We have no choice but to scurry deeper into the burning forest. I fall more than once. The smoke is getting thicker. The fire is moving fast, jumping from tree to tree like a squirrel being chased by a dog. For a moment I'm turned around. *Sarai!* I can no longer see her. Through the commotion, smoke, and fog of battle, we are separated.

"Sarai!" I yell, not caring if the enemy hears me. I will not lose her again.

"Sarai!"

No answer, but who could hear me over the thundering tenor of an entire forest on fire.

A drone zips by me overhead. The whiz of a pulse-grenade tumbling through the air. It lands near me. I'm only afforded a couple of steps before it goes off. The percussion from the blast sends me flying through the air. My ears ring, and my eyes sting. My head feels like a horse stepped on it. I peel bark from my forehead; the blast must have sent me into a tree. Blood trickles from my ears.

Then everything goes black.

Sarai and a contingent of third army have gone north down the other side of the mountain. They too are separated and engage in skirmishes. Dense fog and residual smoke from the fires keep the visibility low. The sound of riders on horseback, snow crunching underneath their hooves. When she lost sight of Asher, she ran back for him, with no luck. Under heavy fire, she could do nothing but continue her retreat. In the process, she also lost Cephas and Jude. *Asher must have gone down the other side of the ridge*, she hopes. She can't dwell on that right now. She has to focus; she has to lead. Be what Asher believes her to be.

"They're heading towards us; take cover," Sarai whispers.

Her men hide within the trees, rocks, and bushes. Sarai activates her scourge, holding it in her right hand and a LeMat revolver in her left. Smoke rises behind her, and the sun punches through the fog, illuminating her slate-black hair. From afar, she looks like a radiating warrior princess of Zion. But from close up, that radiance is just sweat glistening from the sun, dirt, and blood on her face; she is a dingy Dreck, a guerrilla warrior. She would have it no other way. She peers down at the handgun and can't help but be somewhat amazed that the last time someone fired this weapon, it was for the cause to unite this country. It will be used for that same purpose once again. The Lazurites on horseback are closer now. She can see their frosty breath. Hear their snorts.

"Now!" she yells.

Like a dirty paintbrush on white canvas, the gunpowder and smoke pollute the crisp, pure air and unadulterated snow. The fog suddenly lights up from plasma blasts, a fantastic light show under any other circumstances. From Sarai's left flank, a horse appears out of thin air like a ghost and almost tramples her. She rolls to her left and whips her scourge. Its electric tentacles wrap around the hind legs of the magnificent animal, sending its passenger flying into a tree.

But they keep coming. She fires the revolver until her ammo runs dry. She tries to retreat but trips over a dead body, one of hers. She looks up and sees the ground littered with the third army and soldiers of The Defiance. She jumps to her feet, and then it hits her. A shock of electricity galvanizes her muscles. A deep, searing burn in her chest where the plasma melts away her exoarmor and penetrates her lungs. She stumbles back against a tree and falls to the ground. She manages short breaths, each one more labored than the last. A rider holding the plasma rifle approaches her and removes his helmet to survey the carnage.

It is Renatus.

He aims his rifle again to finish her off.

She uses her last bit of strength to remove her own helmet. As life drains from her, the only word she manages to say is, "Daddy." More of a reflex than an emotion.

"Sarai!" Renatus yells as he dismounts.

As he approaches her, Jude and a hundred men emerge from the fog. Renatus quickly mounts his horse and takes one last look at his only daughter.

"Sarai, I'm—," but he doesn't say the words.

He turns and disappears into the fog. Jude and his men arrive seconds later. Jude bends and spots the hole in her chest.

"Sarai!" He turns to one of his men. "Wrap it!"

They wrap the wound to stem the bleeding, but she can barely take in oxygen. She looks like a writhing fish out of water gasping for air.

"Stay with me, Sarai!"

She peers up at him with hazy, barren eyes.

"Daddy."

The loss of oxygen is causing her to hallucinate.

"It's me. Jude. Stay with me!"

"I tried to save him, Daddy, I tried. The waters were just too rough."

"Just keep breathing!"

"It should have been me instead."

"Breath Sarai! Deep breaths!"

"Your wounded prince is gone, Daddy, but he is not the only one marred."

Heartbroken.

Her lungs can no longer taste oxygen.

Her eyes close.

I should have told Asher I was pregnant.

She is barefoot on the beach. Eleazar holds her left hand. Asher holds her right. The wind is warm.

She no longer fears the waves.

CHAPTER SEVENTEEN

I am aroused from my unconscious slumber by a gruff voice. A calloused hand shakes me.

"Wake up, Son," Cephas grumbles.

My eyes blink rapidly as I come to. It takes me a minute to distinguish that the cloudiness is from the fog and smoke and not my vision as I shake my head.

"You alright, boy?"

I nod as Cephas lifts me up.

"You're lucky to be alive," Cephas tells me. "Seems fire doesn't like you."

By some miracle, the fire had scorched the earth and trees all around me, but not where I lay.

"That, or someone is watching over you."

Kenan stands behind him with approximately two hundred of my third army, some of The Defiance are scattered here and there.

"Sarai?"

"Haven't seen her," Kenan replies.

"She's probably chasing down some Lazurite elites, like we should be doing," Cephas says somberly.

They help me up, and Kenan hands me my ricochet.

"This was some plan I had, now what?" I ask, uninformed as to what has been happening around me while I was out.

Cephas snorts, "Let's go find a battle before it finds us."

Too late.

Below us a horde of first army emerges from the fog at full charge, plasma blasts incinerating tree branches near our position. They have us outnumbered at least two to one.

"I bet you are all sick of me saying this," I sigh. "Retreat."

We try to escape down the other side of the mountain, but another two hundred Lazurites await us. We have nowhere to go but up the mountain. We pull back in shifts, laying down covering fire for one another. After twenty minutes of this we reach a plateau at the top of the mountain. We may have a tactical advantage from our elevated position, but we are completely exposed, especially to the helidrones. Hiding behind rocks and boulders, we fire down to keep them at bay.

"We won't last much longer like this!" Cephas bellows.

"Drones!" Kenan shouts, further piling on to our misery.

"Any ideas?" I shout.

Then, as if the world stops turning, I can no longer hear the sounds of war. As I watch Cephas, everything seems to move in slow motion. He stands and raises his hands to the sky, his head bowed down. I can hear him praying, probably in tongues, but somehow I understand what he is saying:

"Grant us victory today, my Lord.

Bring us a miracle.

We sit at your right hand and wait for you to make our enemies a footstool for our feet.

May the will be done of the Almighty."

I try to pull him back down, but he rips his arm from my grip. His hands raised even higher now:

"Grant us victory today, my Lord.

Bring us a miracle.

We sit at your right hand and wait for you to make our enemies a footstool for our feet.

May the will be done of the Almighty."

The world again speeds up as plasma whizzes by his head. With all my strength, I can finally pull him back down behind the rocks.

"Are you crazy?" I yell, wide-eyed.

He just laughs and points to the heavens. "It's out of our hands now nephew."

Then I hear the whirl of rotors. Five helidrones are coming in hot. We are completely naked. Nowhere to go. Nowhere to hide. Even the fog is burning off.

"Bring it on!" Cephas whoops.

Now I wonder if he has really lost it. We fire at the drones as pulse-grenades hail down. We are surrounded from all sides, even from above.

"Bring it on!" Cephas cackles once again at the top of his lungs.

I shake my head. We are about to die, and Cephas has gone bonkers. We have lost. Our demise is upon us, and all I can think about is Sarai. Our weeping willow. I did not accomplish what I came here to do, but I did become her husband, and that is enough for me. Fear has been siphoned from me, replaced by an inexplicable peace. I am ready to accept our fate, arms wide open, stretched out to the heavens like my uncle, as I am reminded of this truth:

"If God is for us, who can be against us?"

Then.

I hear a guttural scream that almost sounds nonhuman. A piercing howl. A lion being uncaged. I know that voice. That primal timbre.

It is Legion.

He trounces up the mountain like rolling thunder. He leaps into the air; gravity fears him almost as much as the Lazurite soldiers. He swings a massive club the size of a small redwood tree, knocking down Lazurite elites as if they were bowling pins. Even elites stand in fear and shock as Legion mows them down. He picks up rocks the size of bowling balls and hurls them into the air like they were pebbles, knocking the low-hovering drones out of the sky. Then, behind him is a ragtag group of men armed with spears, clubs, hammers, grenades, and contraband handguns smuggled in through Zion's garbage.

The Sons of Levi.

Somehow Legion must have told them what happened to their leader, Dagger, and convinced them to fight. With my jaw in my lap, I look to Cephas.

"I don't believe it."

"Ye of little faith," he grins.

I stand, raise my ricochet, and turn to my men, "Let's go help the big man down there, what do you say?"

With that, we charge down the mountain, fighting with the spirit of my uncle and the fire of Legion. I watch Legion pick up soldiers and toss them through the air like they are small dogs, and I wonder how I defeated such a man. Then a thought hits me. *Maybe he let me win at the Canonization? Perhaps it was his way of defying Renatus?* Either way, I wouldn't want to face him again, seeing how he fights now that he believes in something.

As we continue to race down the mountain, we scream fierce battle cries of which even Legion would be proud. I fling my ricochet so many times my arm is numb. Cephas limps beside me. He has taken a shot in the leg. Kenan is bleeding from more than one place but is undeterred. We fight with that indomitable spirit that only a Dreck could know. It's not much longer until it's all over, and the Lazurites are overwhelmed. Those remaining throw down their weapons and surrender. They look as shocked as I do. I can see it on their faces as they must be wondering how they were defeated by this starving band of rabble using three-hundred-year-old weapons. Some of them shake and cower at the mere sight of Legion.

"Gather the prisoners in one place," I tell Kenan. "And be sure they are treated well."

Down in the valley, I see a regiment of elites escaping on horseback. I have no doubt Renatus is with them. I approach Legion, whose skin glistens with a crimson sheen of sweat and blood. As I reach him, I'm still awed as to how far he towers over me, how massive his frame is. And his heart. I think he just needed a little grace for the good in him to bubble to the surface. I showed him that at the Canonization. He repaid that kindness in spades today.

"Thank you," I tell him.

He responds with a snort.

"Anything I can do for you?" I ask him.

"You have done it already."

Without looking back, he trudges off. I turn to tell Cephas something, and when I look back towards Legion, he is gone. I am left astounded at what one man can accomplish when righteousness is on his side.

A squadron of men belonging to The Sons of Levi approaches me. "We are with you Son of Silas. We are now The Defiance."

"I thank you for coming to our rescue. Let's hope after today there will no longer be a need for The Defiance."

Cephas lifts me up from behind and engulfs me in a bear hug.

"Now what, my nephew?"

"We go to The Mountain, and we free our brethren."

"To The Mountain!" Cephas bellows with laughter and elation.

But the joy of our victory is short-lived. Marching toward us is Jude. It looks like he is carrying a sack of potatoes in front of him. I take a closer look.

Sarai.

My heart cannot imbibe what my eyes are showing it. I am fractured. I fall to my knees. I cannot find the strength to run to her. Jude lays her down next to me. I cannot even say her name. My tears splash onto her cheeks. Her look is serene. Peaceful.

"How?" I somehow manage to speak.

"Renatus. I'm so sorry, Asher," Jude says softly.

Killed by her own father, again. It was supposed to be me, not her. Why was Legion sent to save me and not her?

"WHY?!" I scream.

Cephas rushes to me. "Nephew."

"I don't understand why God would grant me victory in one moment and take her in the next!"

"I have no words, Son. I cannot explain, for the ways of the Lord are sometimes a mystery."

"This was all for her! This war, the Canonization, me becoming Amos! I have Lazurite blood infecting my veins, and for what?"

Cephas pulls me into a hug, and I realize the last time I was held like this, except by Sarai, was by my father when I was a child.

"I have no answer for you, Son."

Sensing I want to be alone, Cephas and Jude quietly back away.

I hold her in my arms until well past sunset. I start a fire, then delicately dress her in oil and linen cloth. I brush her silky smooth hair, then attempt to braid it how she likes it. She would laugh at how pathetic of a job I did. People will tell you it's better to have loved and lost than not to have loved at all. Those people have not lost their eternity mate.

Cephas slowly approaches and tosses me an apple.

"You haven't eaten since yesterday."

I toss it aside. "You afraid I'm gonna turn out like Jude?"

Cephas clears his throat. "When I lost my wife, I spiraled downhill, as you well know. I became fueled by the tonic and the inferno of my own anger. I was consumed by it. I was controlled by it. Until I found freedom from it, I hurt a lot of people. Mostly myself. She would not have wanted that for me, nor would Sarai want that for you."

"How long did it take you to recover and move on from such a loss?" I ask, realizing for the first time the pain that he went through.

"You never get over it. You just learn to live with it. I still think of her every day."

"And why do you think she was taken and not you?"

"I don't know, Nephew. But there was a reason I was left behind while she ascended to her heavenly Father. And that's why I'm here.

That's why I fight for The Defiance. I know I have purpose."

"I'm angry, Uncle."

"It's okay, Asher. And it's okay to be angry with God. He is a big guy, He can take it."

I stare into the flickering flames with my swollen eyes and realize how exhausted I am. The high of defeating Renatus's first army to the absolute low of losing Sarai. Without her, our victory feels hollow. Below us, my third army and soldiers of The Defiance dance and celebrate around massive bonfires. Even The Sons of Levi have joined in. I should be down there with Sarai, keeping her warm while she teaches me how to dance.

"I can help you bury her; we can do it here if you like, or in Zion, or back at your reservation."

"The ocean," my voice hoarse, my throat dry. "She should be with her brother."

"The ocean," Cephas confirms.

"But first, we go to The Mountain and free my parents. I want them to be there for her funeral," I say with a growing resolve.

"Of course."

"And her Van Halen shirt. Can you find it for me?"

After two days of solemn marching, we reach the base of The Mountain. I barely uttered a word to anybody the entire trip. I now see Cephas in a different light. I understand him a bit more. Shared grief leads to bonding.

A vestige of Renatus's first army guarding the entrance scatters when they see us approach. We snake our way up the mountain, where the fleeing guards did not bother to close the massive steel door. Cephas, Kenan, Jude, and I enter. Their disbelief at seeing their brethren frozen in cryogenic chambers is palpable, as I have forgotten that out of the four of us, I'm the only one who has been here before. I quickly instruct Kenan to go to the control room and start figuring out how to unfreeze our people. We walk in silence and stare at the never-ending array of bodies cemented inside the pink translucent fluid.

How many lives have been stolen? How many families ripped apart? I wonder if they have thoughts and feelings while in this suspended state? *Can they see?* I shiver at the thought. I can't bear to look at the children. But I am confident that Kenan will figure it out. That they will soon be reunited with their mothers and fathers. Cephas and I turn the corner and walk until we find my parents. Cephas approaches the body of his brother, Silas. He places his weary hand on the glass chamber. A tear rides the roller coaster that is the scars on his face. Again, I had only considered my loss.

"Brother."

My parents' last expression is one that describes them best. My father still has the look of a yielding, patient servant-leader. My mother oozes empathy. Both look like they were on the verge of smiling. It is almost as if they purposely set their countenance the moment they were frozen, to let their captors know they could take everything from them except their spirit, their souls. Cephas takes note of this as well.

"I think they knew you'd come."

"What will you do now? Once they are free?" I ask.

"Your father will lead once again. I will do whatever is necessary to help him succeed. I wasn't made to be a leader, you know that. I have done my part. We have gotten this far, but I'm not suited for what is needed to rebuild this country. I wouldn't even know where to start, Nephew. Your father and mother, they will know."

I turn to him. "Give me a minute?"

"Of course," he answers, trudging off.

I step close to them, place a hand on each of their chambers.

"Father, mother."

I wonder what they would say to me in this moment, knowing who I have become and what we have accomplished. I look into their eyes, and it seems they are looking back at me, beaming with pride.

In that moment I know what it is I must do. I tell them.

"Uncle once told me that the point of life is to die empty. I am there now, well, almost there. There is one more thing I need to do," I begin to tear up. "I have done my best to be the son you wanted me to be, you raised me to be. I'm sorry I won't see you when you awake."

I know it's my imagination, but I swear that I see my father's head nod. I know that he would understand. As there is no greater love than this.

"I will see you again, just not in this world."

We load Sarai into one of the sealed chambers. Cephas does not agree with what I'm about to do.

"Are you sure, Son?"

"Yes," I answer plainly.

"What about The Defiance? The New America? You are their leader now. You are the only one loved by both Dreck and Lazurite."

I motion to Sarai. "I'm not the only one."

"What about your parents?" Cephas asks.

"Tell them I died in battle."

"They would not agree with this."

"They would, in fact, they would do the same."

"And me? What if I need you," Cephas says, betraying his vulnerability.

"You have everything you need and you know it. You and Sarai need to rebuild this country, restore the people. Along with my parents, you don't need me."

"Let's make Jude do it instead." Dreck humor never seems to stop.

I point to his pelican tattoo, the symbol of The Defiance, the symbol of sacrifice. "It's time for me to be the pelican."

"And you are a blood match?"

"Yes. We are an everything match."

Kenan approaches. "You will be in this chamber here."

He connects tubes from that chamber to the one Sarai is in.

"You sure you figured this thing out?" I ask him.

"Pretty sure," he smiles.

Kenan is still learning Dreck humor. He is almost there. I grab the back of his neck and tell him, "You are courageous, Kenan; you are meant to be a leader and a peacemaker. Don't let anyone ever tell you different."

"Thanks . . . thanks for everything," Kenan replies. I can see the sadness overtake him as he battled not to stutter.

"And don't worry about that stutter. Let your actions speak for you."

I analyze the chambers, the facility, and for a moment I'm awed at the technology. Like a sin I don't want to shed, I'm tempted not to have Cephas destroy the facility and, with it, the lure of immortality. Man wasn't meant to be omnipotent or eternal, not on Earth anyway.

"After Sarai awakes, destroy The Mountain. Be sure it is never replicated," I tell Cephas.

"We agree on something," Cephas snorts, fighting back tears.

I feel like I should say something more, but the words do not come. Sometimes silence is the best conversation. Despite what I just told Kenan, I have learned words have power, for good and for bad. There is nothing more for me to say. I undress, and naked as the day I was born, I crawl into the chamber. I am face-to-face with Sarai. My only regret is that I won't see her awaken. I almost feel guilty as I know how hard it would be to live without her. Now I am passing that sentence along to her. But she is stronger than I.

Cephas lumbers closer. "Nephew, I am proud of you. Your father would be too."

I swallow my emotions. I don't want the last image of me to be one of sadness. I smile at Cephas. "You were right about me, Uncle."

Kenan waits at the controls. I nod. The chamber hatch closes and fills with the cold pink gel-like substance. Robotic arms painlessly inject me with various tubes and wires. In minutes, nanobots will enter my bloodstream, remove my LifeCell, and deliver it to Sarai.

Life is a series of moments. You are defined by them. Not months, years, or even decades. Not your accomplishments.

But moments.

A helping hand to someone who has fallen.

A kind word to the despondent.

A matchbox car to a child who has nothing.

A homemade meal for a grieving widow.

Dying for a friend.

Moments.

Mine has come.

Within seconds I have lost the ability to move; I know it is happening and it's painless. Both Cephas and Kenan turn away. Neither of them can watch. My eyes close, and when I open them I am warm, the sun against my back. I gently rock back and forth, then I hear her voice.

"Look at the size of this one!" Sarai exclaims, holding up a colossal fish.

We are on our small makeshift boat in the middle of the paltry lake where I proposed. I see my reflection in the crisp, clear water. It is me, but a different version of me. One without pain or sorrow. My scars have been erased. My grays have receded. My heart is replete with peace and forgiveness. It is not Amos's face but my own. Sarai tosses the fish into a bucket of water filled to the rim with ones just like it.

"Bait me?" she asks in a flirtatious tone.

I pin another worm on her hook. She casts her line back in. Her guileless braided hair flutters in the breeze. She peers up at the sun, breathes in that familiar smell of jasmine and lavender. Her smile is like a spring sunset. Her eyes the color of autumn. Her skin warm like summer. Her spirit is as pure as a fresh winter's snow.

"Isn't it a beautiful day?"

Yes.

Yes, it is.

Cephas places his meaty paw against Asher's chamber and wipes the tears from his face with the other. The room instantly seems colder.

"I'll see you again, my nephew."

The computers connected to Sarai's chamber come to life. There are beeps announcing the resurrection of her vitals.

"It'll take a couple of weeks before she is ready to come out," Kenan informs Cephas.

"How long for everyone else?"

"About a week to bring everyone out of cryo-state."

Cephas thinks for a moment. "Have a debriefing plan in place for when they awake, surely they will be confused and disoriented."

"Will do."

"And for the families, awaken the parents first, I do not want the children to see them like this, as they will be terrified enough. I want the first people they see to be their mother and father."

"Of course," Kenan answers.

Asher's actions remind Cephas of one of his favorite Bible verses in John: *"There is no greater love than to lay down one's life for one's friends."* Cephas thinks that it should have been him instead of Asher, that he should have volunteered to sacrifice himself. After all, he got Asher into this mess in the first place. But he knows Asher would not have had any of it, especially for Sarai. It had to be him.

Kenan approaches. "When we are all finished, we can destroy The Mountain and all the data inside the computers. I was thinking of using pulse-grenades and an EMP. What do you think?"

"Yes, of course," Cephas replies, then looks back at Asher's lifeless body, "but not yet."

CHAPTER EIGHTEEN

I am Sarai, former sultana of Zion, widow of a man who has no equal. I am now the reluctant leader of a New America. It has been three months since Asher laid down his life for me. Not a day, hour, or minute goes by that I don't think about him, his sacrifice, his love, his laugh. It's a mystery to me why fate has not allowed us to be together. At first, I was angry at him for leaving me behind, leaving me to live in this world without him. But, as with everything when it comes to Asher, I'm never sullen for too long. I try not to opine over it, for I have work to do.

Most of The Wall has come down. My father has retreated to the Eastern Coast, where he has resurrected his fourth and fifth armies. Zion East is where he is attempting to rebuild his empire. They provide a few skirmishes here and there for control of the eastern section of The Wall yet to be deactivated. I know another war is coming. But not today. As for today, I am tasked with restoring a nation and the people's trust, but I have to start small. Today, we are rebuilding a park. This is part of what I have called The Asher Plan. And a continuation of what his mother and father started so many years ago. In fact, they stroll with me now, each of them holding my hands as if I was their daughter. They are the parents I never had. I place my hand on my belly; at sixteen weeks, I'm just beginning to show. I'm unable to yet even think about being a mother without Asher.

We cover our eyes to block out the brilliant sun as we oversee the construction of the new park. Fresh grass. New swings. A massive spiral slide. A baseball field is in the works. The park's location is no accident. It sits directly between the two majestic weeping willows where we were married. And exactly where The Wall once stood. Where there was once separation, there will be unity. And it starts with the children. The narcdrops have stopped, and the rehab centers are beginning to reopen. I have turned my father's opulent castle into an orphanage. The children can't get enough of the pool. I even convinced Cephas to read them stories while Jude has volunteered to be the lifeguard on Sundays. As for me, I'm not quite ready to return to the ocean, but I think I'm getting close.

I peer into the eyes of the people passing me by, Drecks and Lazurites are starting to assimilate. Mothers, fathers, children. And even though society has a long road ahead, I can still see a tinge of apathy and oppression that was abundant on this side of The Wall. There is still poverty, addiction, and ruin. It takes time for people to learn to be free again. To remember what it is like to not be oppressed.

But I also see a glimmer of something different in their eyes. Something I have not seen in a long time.

Something powerful.

Something necessary.

Hope.

If you enjoyed this novel and are so inclined, any reviews would be greatly appreciated!

If you would like to stay informed on my upcoming novels and other news, feel free to subscribe to my mailing list: https://www.BrianAlanPenn.com

ACKNOWLEDGMENTS

The idea for this novel germinated many years ago. At the time I was writing screenplays and thought The Wall would be my next one. But the more I thought about the story and the themes, I realized this would be better served in novel form. Then, to my dismay, I realized this could and should be a trilogy. I never thought I could pull off one novel much a less trilogy!

But this was something I definitely couldn't do myself. First and foremost, my wife, Erica, has given me unending support for this crazy dream of mine. She lets me talk about ideas and scenes as well as reads my first drafts offering support and feedback. I want to thank my three children; Noah, Madelynn, and Marshall, who serve as my daily inspiration. To my family members who have supported me and offered to be my beta readers. I want to thank Frank Peretti for his invaluable mentorship and advice while writing my first novel. I would also like to thank John at Koehler Books for his feedback and expertise navigating the publishing and marketing arena as well as the entire team at Koehler, from the editing to the cover.

Lastly, I would like to thank God for making this possible, giving me the desire to write, and to help fulfill this dream.

He gets all the credit.

www.ingramcontent.com/pod-product-compliance
Lightning Source LLC
LaVergne TN
LVHW041914070526
838199LV00051BA/2604